I0575943

EMERGING FROM ETNA'S SHADOW:

A Sicilian Family's Story of Faith and Hope

by

JOANNE GIULIETTI

ISBN: 979-8-9926777-1-3

Printed in the United States of America

Cover Image by Paul Bonagura
BrushedOnCanvas.com

In loving memory of my grandmother, Santina, and her children, Orazio, Alfio, Frances, and my mother, Maria. Dedicated with love to my grandchildren and all of Santina's descendants, who will carry her legacy forward. May her example guide you always.

Back Row: Alfio (Alfred), Mario, Orazio (Horace)

Front Row: Maria (Marie), Santina, Francesca (Frances)

Table of Contents

Introduction

"We do not merely study the past: we inherit it."
—Sir Roger Scruton

I've classified this book as historical fiction, but it's really a tapestry of non-fiction, fiction, and those murky family stories we'll never pin down as true or false. The non-fiction is what I could prove: births, deaths, occupations, cities, and other details pulled from old records—though I've changed all the surnames to protect the privacy of their descendants. These facts are the bones of the tale.

The fiction steps in where the records stop, letting me imagine the words they spoke, the reasons behind their choices, and the personalities that brought them to life.

Then there's the murky stuff—stories we heard as kids, maybe true, maybe exaggerated, maybe dreamed up entirely. Unable to verify these tales, I've let them stand as they were told, trusting they hold some kernel of truth.

Here, on these pages, is my family's story—what mattered most to them: their faith and their family. Yet as I stitched it together, I saw it was more than that. It's a thread in the vast fabric of millions who left everything familiar for a chance at something better. Their triumphs and struggles, their quiet faith and fierce loyalty, echo in the lives of so many others who crossed oceans and borders, then and now.

I wrote this to keep their memory alive, but also to offer a window into a past that shaped the world we live in, a reminder of the courage, faith, and grace it took to start anew. Perhaps you'll see your own people in these pages, or maybe you'll just feel the weight of what it means to belong somewhere, to carry a legacy forward. This story is theirs, and mine, and, if you let it, yours too.

Part One

A Cradle Hymn

Hush, my dear, lie still and slumber;
Holy angels guard thy bed!
Heavenly blessings without number
Gently falling on thy head.

Sleep, my babe; thy food and rainment,
House and home, thy friends provide;
All without thy care or payment:
All thy wants are well supplied.

How much better thou'rt attended
Than the Son of God could be,
When from heaven He descended
And became a child like thee!

Isaac Watts

CHAPTER ONE

Birth Day

Thursday, July 18, 1895

The wooden bowl crashed to the ground, peas rolling everywhere as Maria dropped into a chair and groaned. Sweat beaded on her face and her dark hair looked damp. She grimaced. After several agonizing minutes, the labor pains eased enough for her to bark out orders. "Rosa, go get Signora Bonaccorsi and Nonna! Quickly! Domenica, help me into the bedroom." Turning to Concetta, Maria told her, "Take the little ones and go with Grazia to Zia Stella's house." The little house erupted with activity.

Domenica, close to panic, whispered to Rosa, "Be quick. Remember how fast Giuseppe was born? Signora Bonaccorsi didn't even make it here before the birth." Rosa, ten, flew out the door to summon her grandmother and Gioia Bonaccorsi, the village midwife. As Rosa raced toward the midwife's home, she saw smoke rising from Mount Etna in the distance. It seemed thicker than usual. Normally that would worry her, but not today. Concern about Mama and the baby crowded out every other worry.

Her footsteps echoed as she ran down the cobblestone street. Strands of Rosa's dark hair broke free of her hair clasps and flowed behind her like a horse's mane. Rushing past the rows of attached homes on each side, their walls gave the illusion she was running through a canyon. This canyon blocked any breeze that attempted to sneak through, holding tight to the hot air of that midsummer day. Rosa forced her way through the oppressive hot air, refusing to allow it to slow her down.

As she neared Signora Bonaccorsi's home, Rosa whispered a

prayer that the midwife was home and not out somewhere helping deliver another baby. She didn't want Domenica to be all alone for the birth, like last time.

Skidding to a stop in front of the wooden door, Rosa reached up to grasp the knocker and banged it against the door with a sense of urgency. She could hear footsteps inside, and then the door was opened. To her relief, she saw it was the midwife and not her husband.

Gioia Bonaccorsi was a short, stout woman. Streaks of gray made her dark brown hair appear lighter. Signora Bonaccorsi smiled and grabbed a bag that was on a table by the door. Stepping outside, she put an arm around Rosa, giving her a quick hug. "Don't be so worried. I'll head right over. Go get your grandmother."

Rosa ran off toward her grandmother's house as Signora Bonaccorsi walked back along the narrow streets of Via la Rosa to the Primavita home. For someone of her girth and small stature, Gioia walked quickly, her short legs moving faster than what seemed humanly possible.

~ ~ ~

Nine-year-old Concetta marched out into the courtyard where the two younger children were playing with other children from the neighborhood. Grazia followed her outside. "Grazia, hold Agata's hand so she doesn't wander off," Concetta commanded.

Grazia immediately went to three-year-old Agata and held out her hand. Agata glanced at the outstretched hand and turned away, continuing to play. Bending down, Grazia whispered to the little girl, "Don't you want to go see Zia Stella?" Looking up at Grazia, Agata nodded. Once again, Grazia held out her hand. This time, Agata took hold of her older sister.

Giuseppe squatted over the ground, digging in the dirt and lava ash with a stick alongside another little boy, both covered in dust. Concetta picked up her two-year-old brother, who started to cry, tears making tracks on his dirty face. Giuseppe didn't want to stop playing. "It's okay," she told him. "We're going to Zia Stella's. You can play with Rosina and Graziana. Leave the stick here with

Gino." At that, he stopped struggling in her arms and held out the stick to his companion. Carrying him, Concetta walked toward the street with Agata and Grazia following.

Grazia, six, and Concetta walked along Via la Rosa with their youngest siblings toward their aunt's house. Concetta still had Giuseppe in her arms and Agata was tugging on Grazia's hand, attempting to break Grazia's hold. Grazia clasped her younger sister's hand despite the sweat that threatened to allow Agata to slip free. All four siblings had dark brown hair and dark brown eyes. Any stranger seeing them pass knew instantly they were siblings, although there were very few strangers in Pedara.

Zia Stella lived only a short distance away on the same street. The younger children were excited about playing with their cousins, unaware there would be a new baby in the house upon their return.

On the way, they saw their father, Alfio, with their brother, Francesco. Papa and Francesco had traveled to the town of Nicolosi that morning to pick up some olive oil to bring back to a local merchant. The cart was dusty, and the donkey was tired. While Alfio tended to the donkey, Francesco cleaned the cart.

Concetta called out to Alfio as they passed, "Papa! It's time!"

Alfio nodded. "Stay with Zia Stella until Domenica comes to bring you home." Then he went back to work as the children continued on their way.

As they neared their aunt's house, they could see her hanging clothes out the second-story window. Their cousins, Graziana, five and Rosina, three, were by their mother's side, helping her by handing her the wet clothing and clothespins. Soon as the little girls saw their cousins, Zia Stella lost her helpers as they quickly abandoned her to run downstairs, greeting their cousins.

At the sight of the two cousins, Giuseppe wiggled so much to get free that Concetta put him down. Carrying the little boy even a short distance was a struggle in the heat and it was a relief to put him down. Agata finally managed to slide her hand out of Grazia's grasp. Neither of the older girls was concerned as the two younger siblings ran straight to their cousins.

Zia Stella, who followed her daughters downstairs and outside, hugged her nieces and nephew. "Who went for the midwife?" she asked Concetta.

"Rosa went to get Nonna and Signora Bonaccorsi. Domenica stayed with Mama."

"Then my sister is in good hands." Zia Stella smiled to assure them she was unconcerned. "Children!" she said, addressing all of them. "Go play in the courtyard." Turning to Concetta and Grazia, Zia Stella told them, "Make sure they don't get into any mischief. Try to get Giuseppe cleaned up a bit. He can't go near a new baby covered in dirt." The cousins ran off to play.

Zia Stella went back to her task of hanging clothes. As she continued putting out the clothes, she watched the children. Giuseppe found another stick and started digging again. Graziana, Rosina, Agata, and Grazia were playing with an old, battered doll. Concetta attempted to distract Giuseppe from the dirt, but finally gave up the battle and sat near the other children. Zia Stella started saying the Rosary, praying for her sister and the newest child about to arrive.

~ ~ ~

Santa Sambataro was outside her house, sweeping the ash that coated the street when she saw Rosa fly past. Realizing Rosa was heading east, toward the midwife's house rather than toward her aunt or grandmother, Santa knew it was time and made her way to Maria's house. Maria and Santa were both cousins and neighbors, but more than that, they were friends. They often did their wash together in the courtyard as they shared family news and neighborhood gossip.

Santa entered the house. Peas scattered on the floor of the typically spotless kitchen surprised Santa and she tiptoed around them to avoid crushing them. Domenica, the oldest at twelve, knelt on the floor gathering the green orbs. Seeing Santa, she jumped up and hugged her with relief, happy that she wouldn't be entirely on her own until the midwife and her grandmother arrived. The birth of Giuseppe two years ago was still fresh in her mind. At the age of only ten, she was forced to help her mother when the midwife was busy elsewhere and the baby boy wasn't waiting for anyone. Mama had guided her on what to do, but it was a scary experience that she had no desire to repeat.

"Go get some water while I tend to your mother," Santa told her. "Then bring some clean clothes and rags into the bedroom." Domenica grabbed a jug and hurried out to the cistern in the courtyard, while Santa went to Maria. Maria was propped up on the bed, grimacing. Santa took her hand. "Bad this time?"

Maria didn't respond right away, immobilized by pain. After a couple of minutes, she took a deep breath and said, "The pains are in my back this time. It took me by surprise and I dropped a bowl in the kitchen. I haven't had pains like that since Francesco was born."

Santa took a wet rag and put it on Maria's forehead. "It's the worst. I had the back pain with Vito. Twenty years later and I still remember how it felt." Santa shuddered. "The other four children were much easier." At 47, Santa was 14 years older than Maria. She gave birth to five children before losing her husband.

Gioia Bonaccorsi arrived. Moments later, Rosa returned home with her grandmother. The midwife and grandmother took over tending to Maria. This child would be the ninth Maria gave birth to, and they expected her labor would be quick. Santa joined Rosa and Domenica in the kitchen. Remnants of the preparations for the evening meal were scattered about the kitchen. Rosa started cleaning up the remaining peas from the floor while Domenica finished shelling the rest. Santa began preparing supper. With all the excitement of the impending birth, none of the women were hungry, but Alfio, who would likely arrive home at sundown, would expect a meal.

~ ~ ~

Francesco was eight and would often accompany his father when Alfio had short trips into the neighboring towns. Alfio was teaching him the trade of a cart driver. In the winter, they carried wood and charcoal and in the summer, their cargo was typically snow and ice from the caves near Mount Etna. The entire family looked forward to the summer trips, which meant Alfio was bringing back granita - a mixture of snow, fruit juice, and honey.

Francesco especially liked when they traveled into Trecastagni, where Alfio's parents lived. Trecastagni was just two miles east of Pedara. Every trip there included a stop to visit with his grandparents. The trip to the olive oil merchant in Nicolosi was not nearly as much fun. There were no hugs, and no treats given to him in Nicolosi.

Families who had more money could afford a horse to pull their cart, but Alfio was not rich and they just had the donkey. Some cart drivers had elaborately painted carts. To Alfio, that was frivolous and unnecessary. Painting a cart did not make it carry its load any better than an unpainted cart. After the donkey ate and the cart was clean, Alfio asked Francesco, "Would you like to visit Zia Stella?" It was an unnecessary question. All the children loved spending time with their aunt. She was a joyful woman who made each of them feel loved.

Francesco ran off to join his cousins and siblings while Alfio spoke briefly to Zia Stella and Zio Angelo, her husband. "I'll send Domenica for the children after I see the new baby. Hopefully, it won't be more than an hour or so while we still have some daylight left." Alfio and Maria didn't want the younger children home while Maria was in labor. It was impossible to shield the children entirely from childbirth and the potential complications, but they could at least shield them from the process with the accompanying groans of pain and spare them the grief of witnessing a stillborn sibling.

Before going home, Alfio walked in the opposite direction toward the Church of Santa Caterina Alessandrina, the family Church. He walked up the steps and into the Church through a wooden door set into a much taller wooden door, blessing himself with holy water as he entered. The scent of incense lingered as though the lava stone walls absorbed and refused to let it go. Walking up to the side altar where the statues of the three saints stood, he lit a candle. The smell of melting wax intensified and smoke from the candle intertwined with that of the nearby candles as it rose. He knelt down to pray for his wife and their new baby. "Sant' Alfio, Filadelfo, and Cirino, Santa Maria, Santa Caterina, protect Maria and this new life. And, if it is Your will, another boy would be most welcomed. Still, a healthy girl will be celebrated just as well."

Looking at the images of biblical scenes and saints covering every surface of the ceiling, walls, and pillars of the Church, he felt calmer. Crossing himself again, he rose. Turning, he saw Father Pappalardo standing a few feet behind him, watching him. When the priest saw Alfio was finished praying, he approached. "Maria is giving birth today?" Alfio nodded. "I will pray for Maria and the baby, that all will go well. Bring the child here at 10 a.m. tomorrow morning and I will perform the baptism."

"Thank you, Father. We will be here then." As Alfio neared the door, he kissed two fingers and touched the toes of the statue to the right of the doorway, representing 'Faith' on his way out. "I have faith. My wife and my child will be well." He hurried out of the Church.

Alfio walked back down the narrow street toward home. As he walked, he listened for either cries of labor or wails of sorrow, but the only sounds he could hear were those of children playing in the last rays of daylight. He entered the house and saw Rosa and Domenica sitting at the kitchen table with Santa. Neither of his daughters looked up at him. Both of them seemed upset.

He burst into the bedroom, his heart pounding. Maria sat on the bed, propped up, holding a tiny infant with a full head of dark hair. The midwife had already left and Maria's mother, Nonna Rosa sat on the bed next to her daughter. "The baby?" Alfio asked, not finishing the question.

"She is healthy," Nonna Rosa replied.

"Why are Domenica and Rosa sitting inside looking sad?" he asked.

His mother-in-law laughed. "They wanted to see the baby, but I told them the father must be the first. Alfio, you need to go to the Church to arrange for baptism."

He smiled. "I already took care of it. Father said to be there at 10 a.m."

Maria nodded toward Santa, who followed Alfio as far as the doorway of the bedroom, but did not step over the threshold. "Santa will be the godmother," she told them. Tears in her eyes, Santa went to Maria and hugged her.

Gently, Nonna Rosa took her granddaughter from her daughter's arms. "Rest now."

Alfio kissed his wife and followed his mother-in-law and Santa into the kitchen. "Here is your new sister!" he announced.

Domenica and Rosa crowded around the infant in their grandmother's arms while Santa looked over their heads, smiling at the tiny baby. "Domenica, go to Zia Stella's house and bring your sisters and brothers home so they can meet their new sister."

Domenica hurried toward Zia Stella's house while Etna, in the background, seemed to celebrate the birth of this baby by shooting a display of bright red lava and sparks into the sky.

The excitement at having a new baby in the house meant the children were up a little later than usual that night, but everyone was up early the following morning, regardless of the hour they went to sleep. Santa and Nonna Rosa were there early, getting breakfast ready for the family so Maria could rest. As the time neared 9:30 a.m., Nonna Rosa and Santa went into the bedroom to dress the baby for her baptism. Nonna Rosa handed a white cotton garment to Santa. "Maria was baptized in this dress," Nonna Rosa told her.

"And each of my girls, as well," Maria added.

The dress had short sleeves and a v-neck. Embroidered white flowers covered the front, and lace edged the hem. Carefully, Santa put the baby's arms in the sleeves and tied the garment closed.

Alfio entered the room and asked, "What shall we name the baby?"

"Santa," Maria replied. "After her godmother."

Alfio nodded in approval. "Santina. Our little saint." Turning to Santa, he said, "We don't want to be late and cause Father Pappalardo to be angry."

Santa took the baby in her arms and left the bedroom, Nonna Rosa and Alfio following behind her. They walked outside. The day was already hot. Earlier that morning, a rare summer rain fell and steam seemed to rise from the wet cobblestones as the sun baked them. As they passed the Tordaro home, Zia Stella came out and joined her mother, cousin, brother-in-law, and new niece. The Church of Santa Caterina Alessandrina was a short walk from the Primavita home and they arrived early.

All in the group seemed to pause as one in front of the steps of the Church. The building was a simple square Church built of lava stone in the early 1700s after an earthquake destroyed the original Church. Alfio looked up at the square bell tower. He took his mother-in-law's arm and helped her up the steps. At 68, Nonna Rosa's knees had seen better days, and she struggled with climbing steps. Reaching the top step, the women pulled their veils up to cover their heads and Alfio removed his hat. Alfio pulled open the wooden door, holding it for the women to enter ahead of him. They entered the building and found Father Domenico Pappalardo waiting for them in the narthex.

There, between the doors leading outside and those leading into the Church itself, the rite of baptism began. The priest said the prayers in Latin and Santa, as the godmother, gave the responses. Father Pappalardo made the sign of the cross on the infant's head and chest. He then laid his hands on the baby's head, praying. Next, he put a speck of blessed salt on the baby's tongue. The priest led the small group over to the baptistery where the stone baptismal font stood.

There were more prayers, and the priest poured water over Santina's head. The infant opened her eyes briefly and then closed them again. Father Pappalardo anointed her with chrism (blessed oil). During the baptism, the women were attentive, but Alfio felt his mind drift. As his eyes adjusted from the bright sunlight outside to the dim Church, he looked through the open door leading from the narthex into the Church. His eyes focused on the domed ceiling over the main altar. On it was a fresco of St. Catherine kneeling before Christ, who was placing a crown on her head while the Blessed Mother stood behind her. St. Catherine was tortured and beheaded at a young age because of her refusal to denounce her Christian faith. "Lord," Alfio prayed, "Let this child grow to see adulthood; to be a good and holy woman. I know martyrs are held in high esteem for their devotion, but surely there are enough of them in heaven already. Please allow this child to live a long life, to see her children grow up, to see grandchildren."

Before sending the newly baptized baby off with her family, Father Pappalardo blessed what appeared to be a small piece of cloth. He gave the item to Alfio, who saw it was, indeed, a cloth. On it was an image of the three saints, outlined in black on white, rimmed by a gold colored border. "May your namesake, Sant' Alfio and his brothers, watch over this little girl always. In nomine Patris, et Filii, et Spiritus Sancti. Amen."

When they returned from Church they found Zio Angelo and the cousins at the house waiting to meet the infant. Santina's godmother removed packages from a large tote bag. The children watched with great interest as she opened the paper packages revealing the contents inside - cookies and granita. Giuseppe jumped up and down with excitement and Agata clapped her hands. They did not have treats like these very often.

"Today is a very special day," Nonna Rosa told her grandchildren. "God has blessed us with little Santina. Yesterday she joined our family and today she joined Christ's family in baptism." Nonna Rosa helped Santa hand out the treats to children and adults alike. Alfio poured wine for the adults. He then raised his glass and all the adults followed suit.

"In thanksgiving and to the health of this beautiful baby girl! Salute!" Shouts of 'salute' echoed throughout the house. The sound of the infant's cry filled the room, as though Santina wanted to raise her voice with the rest.

As the family gathered around the newly baptized Santina, the joy in the room was palpable. Yet, even in the midst of celebration, Alfio's thoughts wandered to the unpredictable nature of life under Etna's watchful gaze. He remembered the stories his father had told of the mountain's wrath, how it could destroy in a matter of moments.

Alfio's gaze drifted to the window where its occasional puffs of smoke served as a constant reminder of its power. "We live in the shadow of a giant," he murmured to himself, a sentiment that carried more weight than just the physical presence of the volcano.

The laughter of the children brought him back to the present, their innocence a stark contrast to the foreboding he felt. He shook off the unease, forcing himself to focus on the joy of the moment. However, deep within him, a whisper of concern lingered, a premonition that the tranquility they enjoyed now might not last forever.

Several years later, their family had grown to nine children with the birth of Stella. On a blustery January day, that whisper of foreboding would become a shout, as an event unfolded that would alter the course of their lives forever.

CHAPTER TWO

Rage

January 1899

Pinned against the wall, Domenica, now sixteen, struggled to break free from the man holding her there. Moments earlier, Rosa left the shop they both worked in to deliver bread to an inn half a mile away. That left Domenica alone in the store with the baker's son, Bruno. He seized the opportunity to drag her out of the store into the small adjoining storage area. "You think you're too good for me?" he snarled, his face inches from Domenica's face. "Your family has nothing, but you think you can do better than me?"

"I don't know what you're talking about," Domenica whispered. She wiggled under his grasp. The room was small and lined with shelves holding sacks of flour and bowls of dough. There was no room to maneuver. Bruno was a large man and easily overpowered her. He was also blocking the only exit, the door leading back into the store. Clouds of flour billowed from Domenica's apron as he pushed at her, making sure she could not escape. His black hair was greasy, and his body odor was overwhelming; his breath was even worse. Although it was a chilly forty-five degrees on this January day, inside the shop and storage area, it was stifling hot. The ovens were blaring, heating the rooms to mid-summer temperatures. Sweat dripped down both their faces.

Bruno grabbed Domenica's chin, lifting her head, forcing her to look into eyes the color of horse dung. "You never look at me, you do not reply to my greetings, and you completely ignore me! Yesterday you had the nerve to turn your back on me!" As he yelled, Domenica felt his spittle hitting her face. Domenica was shy and avoided interacting with anyone outside of her family any more than necessary. That was why only Rosa dealt with the customers. Domenica helped with the baking and cleaning up the shop.

"I... I never... didn't mean to... I don't know... When... When did... I never spurned..." Domenica was too frightened to complete a sentence. Her stammering explanations only made him more irate. He struck her across the face.

"Don't you lie to me!" His eyes wandered where no decent man should look. A sneer crept onto his face. "I think you need to be taught your place! Now you will have reason to avoid me. You will tremble in fear at the very sight of me. You are nothing!"

~ ~ ~

Maria was startled when Domenica burst into the house. She was about to ask why Domenica was home from work in the middle of the day, but the sight of her daughter's appearance stopped her. Domenica's long brown hair was down and all over the place. There was a reddening bruise on her face. Her dress was ripped in multiple places, and she was sobbing.

Santina, who was now four, didn't know what happened to her sister. She saw Domenica was upset and wanted to comfort her. She ran to Domenica, arms opened to hug her. Domenica held her hand out, stopping her. Maria told the little girl, "Santina, take Stella and go into the other room." Santina took her two-year-old sister by the hand and the girls left the room, a look of concern on the face of the older one. The other children were in school. When they were alone, Maria turned to Domenica, the anger that she suppressed around the younger siblings in full view. "Who did this?"

Domenica's sobs increased, and her entire body trembled. "Sit," Maria told her. Going to the stove, Maria put a pot with water on a burner. She put chamomile flowers into the water and waited for it to boil. Her back was to Domenica, whose crying slowed down. Coming back to the table, she put a cup of tea in front of Domenica. Sitting down opposite her daughter, Maria waited. She didn't press Domenica for answers, as she could guess who did this. There was only one place this could happen. Maria was quite certain it could not be the shop owner himself. The baker, injured in a fire at the shop two decades earlier, did not have the physical strength to attack anyone. His wife died in that same fire when they were both in their early twenties, leaving the baker to raise their young son alone.

No. One of his legs was burned, and he now limped. One shove from Domenica would have stopped the older man. Maria knew the son did this. She reached out and put her hand on top of Domenica's. Domenica pulled her hand away as if a jolt of electricity went through it. Tears welled in Maria's eyes. The two women sat without speaking while Domenica sipped the tea.

Different emotions pulsed through Maria as she bounced back and forth between rage, sorrow, and fear. "It was Bruno," she stated. Domenica looked down at the table, tears flowing again. "We cannot tell your father," Maria continued. Domenica nodded. It would do even further damage to the family if Alfio confronted the son of a prominent businessman. They would be outcasts, unable to find work in the village.

"Get cleaned up. Remove those clothes." Domenica obeyed her mother's command. Maria took the discarded clothing and put them into the fire, stabbing at them with a stick, wishing it were Bruno she was shoving in there instead of clothes. They could ill afford new clothes for Domenica, but Maria did not want these tattered symbols of violation in their home. With all traces of what had happened removed, they could pretend this terrible thing had never occurred.

Maria stood. "I am going to get Rosa. Neither of you will ever set foot in that evil place again. Stay here with Santina and Stella." Maria left the house and walked toward the bakery, going over in her mind what she would say to Bruno. Prudence was required, but she wasn't sure she could control her temper. As she neared the bakery, she saw Rosa leave the shop with an armload of bread, heading in her direction. Raising her eyes up to the sky, Maria said a silent prayer, "Thank you for helping me avoid an occasion of sin because I would have given Bruno a tongue lashing, using such foul language he would never forget!" Maria stopped walking and waited for her daughter to reach her.

"Mama, is something wrong? What happened?" Rosa never saw her mother look enraged, sorrowful, and agitated all at the same time. "Why are you carrying a stick?"

Maria looked down, surprised to find she still clutched the stick she'd used to push Domenica's clothes into the fire. She had no memory of walking out of the house with it. "Did Bruno ever touch you?" she asked her daughter. Maria's knuckles were white as she gripped the stick, awaiting Rosa's response. If the answer was yes, she was prepared to attack that animal.

"Of course not," Rosa said. "He's disgusting. If he ever tried anything with me, I..."

Maria cut her off. "Bruno attacked your sister." Releasing her grip on the stick, it dropped to the ground. "You are not to go into that shop ever again. And do not speak about what you would or would not have done if it happened to you. It's easy to talk about something you never went through."

Maria took the loaves of bread from her daughter and threw them into the street toward the bakery. Children raced rodents to grab the scattered loaves as Rosa watched. Maria put an arm around Rosa, turning her away from the bakery and toward home. "Come back to the house. We will find another place for you and Domenica to work. A business where you both will be safe." Rosa was silent as they walked home, trying to banish the images that were popping up into her head.

Rosa and Domenica found work in a fabric shop. It was the only shop in town run by a woman. Domenica refused to walk into any shop where there were men. Each day, the two oldest girls would go off to work, returning home just before nightfall. Domenica did little else but work and go to Church. Insomnia plagued her. Scenes played over and over in her head as she tossed about in bed. No matter how much she tried to banish those memories, nothing seemed to stop them. Frequent nightmares woke her the few times that she fell asleep. Often Domenica would scream in her sleep, waking herself up as well as her family. Something seemed broken inside her and Maria ached for her daughter.

Several months passed, and the family grew used to this new Domenica. It seemed things were always this way. Maria deluded herself that things were normal. Then something worse shattered that delusion.

~ ~ ~

May 1899

There was no longer any denying the horror of what happened. Domenica was pregnant. Maria could not hide the truth because, in several months, everyone would be able to see it. In a panic, she went to her sister and told her what happened to Domenica. For months, Maria held this secret inside, sharing it with no one. Telling Zia Stella didn't remove the burden, but it was a relief to no longer carry it alone.

Over the past several months, Zia Stella saw for herself how Domenica had changed. The quiet woman had become even more so, but there was something more than that. Although shy, Domenica had been joyful, quick to smile with a sparkle in her dark eyes. Something had extinguished that sparkle and Zia Stella could not remember when she last saw her niece smile. Zia Stella thought it was nothing more serious than a relationship gone bad or adjusting to the new job. Nothing prepared her for the terrible news she just received from her sister.

The two women wept for several minutes and then Zia Stella rose to put a pot of coffee on the stove. Sitting at the table, crying, would accomplish nothing. They needed to figure out how to handle the situation. Zia Stella paced and thought while waiting for the coffee to finish. She knew any of the ideas they came up with were futile because Alfio would make all decisions. Still, she was incapable of idly sitting around while her niece and sister suffered. It was against her nature.

"We can find a husband for Domenica and arrange for a marriage quickly," Zia Stella said. "Domenica is a sweet girl, and she is pretty. This is a common situation, and there are many older men in Pedara with no prospects. They would be lucky to have her and will protect her honor."

"She can barely stand the sight of men right now," Maria told her sister. "Her father and Father Pappalardo are the only men she feels safe around. The nightmares have lessened, but she still wakes up, crying out. How can I send her off to live with a man she doesn't even know?"

"What if you hide her for the rest of the pregnancy and then pretend the child is yours?"

Maria pondered the idea. "That might work if Signora Bonaccorsi is the midwife but if she's unavailable and we end up with that new young gossip..." Her voice trailed off as she realized the flaw in the most hopeful solution they could think of. She tried to think of a way to ensure they did not get Signorina Tulipani. It was possible to give birth without a midwife, but this would be Domenica's first birth. There was no way to predict complications, and Maria did not want to put her daughter's life at risk. She sighed. "No, we can't take any chances. That won't work."

Zia Stella continued to pace, not ready to give up. "Send her away to a convent. The sisters will help you. They can arrange for the baby to be adopted. No one needs to know anything."

Shaking her head, Maria told her no. "I considered that. I even spoke to Domenica about that. She said she can't bear to give up her child."

"You need to tell Alfio. He will take care of this."

"Yes," Maria said. "I will tell him tomorrow after Mass. I will pray for guidance, for the right words."

Zia Stella agreed. "After Mass would be perfect. Mama can take the children home with her so you have some privacy and the children would not find that unusual."

Maria looked at her sister. "I have been praying for Domenica all these months, and then this happens. It feels like God is ignoring my prayers. Everything has become so much worse. I don't know why we are being punished."

"Oh, Maria!" Zia Stella responded. "God is not punishing you or Domenica. It is man's fallen nature that leads to sin and its results. The evil one entered that awful man. Poor Domenica was an innocent victim." As Zia Stella spoke, tears rolled down Maria's face. Zia Stella continued, "Do not despair. That, too, is the influence of the evil one. Keep praying and trust in God. We have no control over other people's actions, but we know God can bring good even out of the worst circumstances. And always remember our ultimate goal is eternal life, not an easy, earthly life."

"Sometimes it is so difficult to have faith," Maria told her. "Thank you for reminding me." With that, Maria left her sister to return home.

~ ~ ~

The following day, Maria arranged a time to talk to Alfio. As the family left Church after Mass, Maria whispered to Nonna Rosa, "I need to talk to Alfio privately about an important matter."

Nonna Rosa did not ask questions. She simply turned to her grandchildren. "Come back with me to my house."

The children, used to obeying their elders without question, went off with their grandmother while Maria and Alfio continued toward their home. Alfio looked at Maria, a question in his eyes. After seventeen years of marriage, Maria could read all of his looks. She knew this quizzical face meant he wanted to know if she was pregnant. "If only it was me instead of Domenica," Maria thought while staring straight ahead, pretending not to notice her husband's expression.

The sky was a deep blue, and the sun shone down on the couple as they made their way along Via Capitano Tomaselli toward Via la Rosa. Flowers were in bloom everywhere as they walked along, their scent pouring out, but the beauty of that day and the wonderful smells went unnoticed.

Once home, Maria delayed the difficult conversation for as long as possible by preparing a pot of coffee and putting the pot on the stove. Getting out cups for the two of them, she placed the cups on the table. She took a rag and wiped at invisible marks on the tabletop. Alfio was losing patience. "Maria, talk to me. What is troubling you?"

Maria turned to Alfio. "Do you remember when Rosa and Domenica left the baker's shop to work in the fabric shop?"

Alfio nodded. At the time, he knew there was more to the story about why they changed employers. He let the women handle their own affairs as long as they contributed to the household, and he never questioned that decision. His brown eyes stared into her moist eyes of the same color. He could not read her expression. Sadness was familiar. Alfio saw it too many times before and it was an expression he knew well. This one was one he had never seen, an odd mixture of both intense anger and deep sorrow. He knew this was something terrible and his heart started pounding in his chest. He put his hand on top of Maria's. "It will be okay. Tell me what is wrong."

"They left because Domenica was attacked."

Alfio pushed himself up from the table, cups clattering with the force, his face red. He was shaking with rage. Maria did not have to go into detail nor tell him who had done this. It was clear what happened and who was responsible. Then he saw the expression on Maria's face worsen and the tears leak out. Silently, in his own head, he screamed, "No, no, no! Don't let her say it!"

Maria squeezed her eyes shut for a minute and took a deep breath. Still, she struggled to get the words out. Nearly inaudible, Maria told him, "She's pregnant."

Alfio slammed his fist into the table, spun around, and rushed out of the house.

Maria followed him out, not in an attempt to stop him, but to go to her sister's house. Maria banged on Zia Stella's door. The door flew open. Angelo stood there, ready to berate whoever was on the other side. Seeing Maria, seeing her tears, he knew something was wrong. He moved aside and Maria went to her sister. "I told Alfio. I'm afraid he will kill Bruno."

"He would never do that," Zia Stella responded. Her daughters were young, the oldest only nine. If someone did that to one of their daughters, she realized it might tempt her own husband to do the same. Zia Stella looked at Angelo, who nodded and left the house.

"Am I an evil woman for wishing that Alfio would succeed in killing Bruno before Angelo arrives to stop him?"

"You are a mother who is furious that this man hurt her daughter. It is the anger speaking. In your heart, you do not want Bruno dead." Zia Stella paused for a moment before continuing. "Angelo will see that nothing like that happens, but there's really nothing we can do about the situation, either. Bruno's father is a man of status. Our family is not. If Alfio hurts Bruno, or worse, the shop owner will take legal action." As Zia Stella told her this, she knew what it meant: she was going to lose her sister. Biting the inside of her cheek to fight back tears, she scolded herself, "This situation is bad enough already. You cannot cry. You are being selfish and thinking only of yourself, so don't you dare cry! Maria doesn't need that burden."

"Yes," Maria said. "There is no choice. The only way to protect our family is to leave Pedara." The dam broke in both women, who embraced each other, sobbing.

~ ~ ~

Alfio opened the door to the baker's shop and walked in without knocking. Since it was Sunday, the shop was closed, empty of customers. Bruno and his father lived in an apartment upstairs with six rooms, a luxury Alfio could only dream of. The idea of this privileged young man, who could have whatever he wanted, daring to violate his daughter infuriated him. He yelled out, "Bruno!"

Minutes passed. Alfio heard only silence. He yelled again, "Bruno, get down here or I will come up for you!" The sound of creaking stairs filled the silence. Bruno was much bigger than Alfio, but Alfio had fury on his side as he launched himself at Bruno, beating him with his fists.

As with most bullies, Bruno was not as brave now. He raised his hands to shield his head from Alfio's blows. Bruno whined, "My father is going to bring you to court. You're going to jail!"

Alfio continued to batter Bruno. He blackened both of Bruno's eyes and Bruno's nose spurted blood. He fell to the ground and Alfio still pounded him. Suddenly someone came from behind Alfio, grasping Alfio's arms. "Enough. You cannot kill the boy."

Alfio twisted around and looked at Angelo. "He deserves to die for what he did. His punishment should be eternal damnation." Alfio attempted to shake off Angelo's hands.

"You are right," Angelo told him. "He does deserve that for what he did to my niece, but that is not for us to decide. God will judge him. Please don't do this. Your family needs you."

In the silence, they could hear shuffling footsteps on the

stairs and realized Bruno's father was approaching. As he limped down the stairs, he yelled out, "What have you done to my son?"

"The question is what did your son do to my daughter?" Alfio shouted back.

"You are peasants! Get out of here! You are going to jail! You will never make a living in this town. I will see to that."

Angelo spoke softly to Alfio, still holding his arms, "Enough. Let's go. You do not want to kill him."

Alfio gave one last kick to Bruno in a place that hurt more than any of Bruno's other injuries and walked out with Angelo. It was midday, and the streets were empty. "At least there are no witnesses," Angelo thought. As the two men walked back home, Angelo said, "You did what needed to be done for your daughter's honor. I would have done the same. But you know there will be consequences for your actions."

Alfio mirrored what his wife said. "Yes. We will need to leave Pedara." The adrenaline was gone now. Suddenly, his body felt like he was dragging it home rather than walking, weighed down by sacks of rocks. The burden of tearing his family from their home, their family, was almost too much to bear. How would he tell them they needed to leave everything behind?

CHAPTER THREE

Leaving Pedara

May 1899

Silence blanketed the couple as they sat at the wooden table in their home. Tears rolled down Maria's face, which surprised her. There couldn't be a drop of liquid left inside. Alfio stared at nothing as he thought, trying to come up with a plan. He knew they would have to leave Pedara quickly, but where would they go? A loud knock on the door made them both jump.

"Don't open the door!" Maria begged. "What if it's the police?"

Alfio pulled out his pocket watch and saw it was only two o'clock, although it felt much closer to evening. "It won't be them. They would not come out until late afternoon." He opened the door while Maria closed her eyes and prayed her husband was right. It was Father Pappalardo.

"Angelo told me what happened."

Alfio looked down at the floor, ashamed that he gave in to his primal instincts by beating Bruno. He still felt it was a well-deserved beating, but now the entire family would suffer because of his actions.

"You need to leave by morning," Father Pappalardo continued. "I will take care of the police so you will be safe until then." Father handed Alfio a piece of paper. "Go to Regalbuto, to the Church of Santa Maria della Croce. Find Father Guglielmo and give him this letter. He will help you."

Alfio took the letter and nodded. "Thank you, Father." This letter was an enormous blessing and Alfio held the letter carefully as though it was made of the most fragile glass. He would guard it with his life.

"It will be a difficult trip, but you will be alright. You are people of faith and the Lord will not abandon you. I will pray for you."

"Father," Alfio said, "Will you hear my confession before you leave?"

"Certainly."

"And mine, as well," Maria added.

Father Pappalardo heard their confessions, each spouse retreating to the bedroom when it was the other's turn. After they all returned to the kitchen, Alfio said with a wry smile, "With your help and with clean souls, we are ready for our journey. I no longer have to worry about being attacked and killed by wild boars and ending up in hell for beating Bruno."

"I haven't heard of anyone being killed by a wild boar in Sicily in a long time, but your souls are safe," Father Pappalardo replied. With that, he blessed Maria and Alfio one final time, and left.

Alfio and Maria rose from the table and left the house. They slowly walked to Nonna Rosa's house to break the news to Maria's mother and the children. Each was lost in thought, looking at the familiar homes and shops along the way. Maria was permanently storing everything in her mind, determined not to lose a single detail of the only town she knew. Every brick, cobblestone, the very cracks in the road and dust from Etna were suddenly precious to her. For centuries, her family walked along these very roads and now all this would be lost to her. She knew she would never return to Pedara.

Alfio didn't let his gaze linger on anything for more than a second. He felt it was better to forget, to erase all of this from his mind. Remembering would be too painful. There was no looking back, only looking forward. They would start a new life in Regalbuto.

They entered Nonna Rosa's house. Maria took Nonna Rosa aside and briefly told her what had happened to Domenica and what Alfio had done to Bruno. Before Maria could get the words out about needing to leave Pedara, Nonna Rosa stopped her. "Alfio has decided you are leaving?" Maria nodded. "It is what's best," Rosa continued. "You must do what your husband says, for his own safety, and to protect Domenica. Do not be afraid. God is with you." That settled the matter in Nonna Rosa's mind, and she approached the situation as she did everything else-calmly and with great faith.

"Mama, I may never see you again," Maria whispered.

Nonna Rosa refused to allow her emotions to surface, shoving them deep down inside. There would be time to mourn the loss of her daughter, son-in-law, and grandchildren later. She turned away from her daughter for a minute and took a deep breath to calm herself.

Turning back, she said, "If it is God's will, we shall. Don't trouble yourself about things we have no control over. Wait here a minute." She disappeared into the bedroom and came out with her Rosary and Bible, which she handed to Maria. "Take these. Then I will be with you always, no matter how far away you are."

Maria hugged her mother, then left with her husband and children to go back home. Once home, Alfio broke the news to the children. "Everyone, pack up your things. We leave in the morning for Regalbuto." No one dared ask him why.

Rosa, Concetta, and Francesco knew what happened to Domenica and assumed they were moving because of that. As they followed their father's orders and directions, Francesco noticed Alfio's bruised hands and discretely pointed them out to his sisters. "Papa found out who did it and beat him. The police will be coming." Realizing there was more at stake than just Domenica's reputation diminished some of their resentment.

~ ~ ~

An hour before dawn, Domenica stood in a corner of the empty kitchen, tears rolling down her cheeks. Rosa, fourteen, scolded her. "Stop standing around crying. It does no good and changes nothing. Go help the little ones finish packing. It is best to keep busy. Yes, it was terrible, but you need to put it in the past and move on." Under her breath, Rosa grumbled, "Just like we're all moving on, literally. To Regalbuto. Where we know no one."

While Domenica's sadness manifested itself in tears, Rosa tended to channel her emotions into anger, which was easier for her to deal with. She knew none of this was Domenica's fault, but that anger needed an outlet and her sister was a convenient target.

Francesco scowled at his sisters. "That's the point, isn't it? To know no one?"

A wave of nausea overcame Domenica and she ran outside. Feeling sick was awful enough without the added burden of knowing the entire family was in upheaval because of her.

Their mother rushed around the kitchen putting their belongings into wooden crates and sacks, which their father and Francesco carried to the cart out front. Concetta followed her mother, grabbing up whatever Maria pointed to. The family didn't own much and they carried everything in the kitchen outside before Domenica made it to the adjoining bedroom.

Agata and Grazia were already in the bedroom. Giuseppe and Santina were copying their older sisters, taking clothes and haphazardly stuffing them into sacks. Stella, who was only two, 'assisted' by removing the clothes from one place and putting them into another. The three youngest children didn't understand why they were leaving nor that they were leaving their home forever. For them, this was an adventure.

Maria entered the room and stood with her hands on her hips, surveying the small house. "Do you have everything?" She could see that they did, but asked, anyway. The children walked around the room, examining every corner and then all nodded. "Alright, then. Go outside."

Excited about their new adventure, they ran outside. In the east, the sun was just beginning to peek over the horizon. Alfio was hitching the donkey to the wagon while Francesco carried the last of the boxes from the house. Regalbuto was nearly 30 miles away. Traveling alone, Alfio could make the trip in a day, but with all the little ones, this trip would take two.

Zia Stella and Zio Angelo arrived to see them off. Zia Stella held back tears, trying not to let her nieces and nephews see how upset she was. She handed Maria a sack filled with fruit and cheese for the journey. Zio Angelo looked solemn as he helped Francesco load the last of the crates and sacks onto the cart.

Santa came outside with a sack that held bread and cookies, which she gave to Maria. Then she slipped a small package into Maria's pocket. She whispered something to Maria before pulling her into a hug.

Tearfully the women and girls all hugged goodbye and the Primavita family started their long journey. In the distance, Etna put on a display, spitting fire, and ash as though it were saying farewell.

They made their way west along the dusty roads. All were on foot as they started out. Maria wanted the youngest girls to ride in the cart, but they were too excited about going on an adventure and Maria knew they would never sit still.

Stella held Giuseppe's hand as they walked; chatting with her older brother about everything they saw. "Look! A yellow butterfly! I see a bunny! Did you see the squirrels playing?"

Santina kept running ahead until Francesco suggested he give her a ride on his shoulders. She agreed and he lifted her up. "Francesco, what are those tracks? Is that from a wolf?"

"No," he told her. "It looks like bear tracks."

"Really? I didn't know there were bears here," Santina replied.

"Oh, yes. Those are special bear tracks from a bear that likes to eat little girls."

Santina giggled. "That's silly, Francesco! Bears don't eat little girls." Then Santina had another thought. "Will they have granita in Regalbuto?" Her voice was full of concern that this new town might not have the summer treat they all loved.

"I'm sure they will," Francesco said. "There are mountains all over Sicily that have snow."

They traveled through the town of Nicolosi, a road well known to Alfio and Francesco because they often had business there. It was only an hour away and as they passed through Nicolosi, Maria was surprised by how many men greeted Alfio as they walked by. No one asked any questions as they saw the entire family with all their belongings. Most assumed they were making their way to Palermo, on their way to America. It seemed odd that Alfio's family traveled alone, but perhaps they thought the family was meeting others along the way.

Once outside of Nicolosi, houses were few and the scenery changed to woods and farmland. By now, they were all getting a little tired and they started taking turns riding in the cart, sitting among their belongings. Alfio had Maria and Domenica ride first.

"This is all my fault," Domenica told her mother as she looked down, avoiding Maria's gaze.

Sternly, Maria responded, "No, it is not! You did nothing wrong. That man allowed evil to enter his heart, his soul." Maria put her hand under her daughter's chin and lifted Domenica's head. For the first time in months, Domenica met her mother's eyes. Maria repeated, "None of this is your fault."

For what seemed like years, Domenica carried the guilt of what happened, blaming herself. She exhaled and her shoulders slumped as she felt some of that guilt slide off.

They did not see another town for nearly three hours, until they reached Ragaina. They came to a stop where everyone sat down to rest and eat. Alfio went off with Francesco to refill their jugs with water. Alfio wanted to make sure the donkey had frequent breaks. This two day trip would push the donkey to his limits. They continued past woods and farms traveling to Biancavilla. Biancavilla was their last stop within the province of Catania, where they were all born, where all their family lived. It was the last town they would pass through that day. They would continue their journey in the morning.

"Are we there?" Giuseppe asked when the town of Biancavilla came into view. He wasn't sure where 'there' was, but this seemed like a good place to be 'there.'

"No," Alfio said. "We still have another day of travel, but we are stopping here for the night."

"Will we stay at an inn?" Agata asked, hopeful that the answer would be 'yes.' None of them had stayed in an inn before and it seemed very exciting.

"No," her father responded.

"Is there no room at the inn, like for the Blessed Mother and San Giuseppe? Will we sleep in a stable?" Agata asked.

"The Blessed Mother and San Giuseppe traveled in December when it was cold. They couldn't sleep outside, but we can. It's a beautiful night," Alfio told her.

They found a grassy clearing a short distance from the road and decided to stop there overnight. After their evening meal, Maria got the youngest four children settled in the cart. Santina and Stella fell asleep almost immediately, but it took Giuseppe and Agata a little longer. Although they were tired from the long journey, they were excited about taking a trip.

Once the youngest were asleep, Alfio took out a bottle of wine that Angelo gave him before they left. He poured some for himself and Maria. The smell of it made Domenica nauseous and she declined having any. Rosa, Concetta, and Francesco had a little. They offered none to Grazia, being only ten.

Soon they were all asleep. All but Maria. Her mind kept spinning, looking back on the life they were leaving behind with sorrow and looking ahead with worry and concern. Different scenarios played out in her mind. What if Alfio hadn't beaten Bruno? Could they have stayed? What if Alfio couldn't find work in Regalbuto? What if they couldn't find a place to live once they arrived in the new town? It seemed the more she tried to force herself not to think about their future, the more intense her imagination became. Finally, hours later, she drifted off.

In the morning, they prepared for their second day of travel. Alfio went into the town with Francesco where they stopped a man on horseback to ask where they could find water. After watching them fill their jugs, the man asked where they were heading.

"Regalbuto," Alfio told him.

"There is nothing but woods and farmland between here and Regalbuto," the man told them. "There are no towns in between. You will need to cross the Simeto River in two places. There are bridges. Ponte dei Saracenti will take you out of your way but it's the best route. Take the road that goes north to get to the first crossing. After you cross the bridge, follow the river south and then west. You will come to the second bridge. Then you have a couple more hours to journey before reaching Regalbuto."

Alfio thanked the man and he and Francesco returned to their waiting family. All but Maria felt refreshed and ready for the second part of their journey. They followed the instructions given them and traveled north. After close to three hours, they arrived at the river and Ponte dei Saracenti. Alfio and Francesco were the only members of the family to see a body of water before, the Mediterranean Sea, during trips to Catania. The rest of the family was fascinated by the river.

"I want to go in the water!" Giuseppe begged.

"Yes! Agata added. "Please, Papa!"

Maria looked at Alfio with a slight smile. She thought it would be nice to splash some water on her face.

"Okay, but it is too steep near the bridge. We need to find a better spot to walk down." He took them a short distance where the river was closer to the bank and not as steep. "Be careful going down the bank. It's very rocky and slippery. I don't want anyone falling and getting hurt." Alfio smiled as he watched them climb down, his older children helping the younger ones.

They all took their shoes and socks off and stepped into the water. Stella and Santina were laughing as Giuseppe splashed water on them. Maria dipped her hands into the water and splashed it on her face. Domenica, Rosa, and Concetta did the same. Grazia and Agata joined the younger children and the sounds of their laughter made Alfio happy. He realized that there would always be joyful moments like these in life. Looking at Maria, he saw she was smiling. Even Francesco, who had been solemn the entire trip, was laughing at his siblings.

Reluctantly, they all left the water's edge and put their shoes back on. It was time to continue their journey. It was close to dusk when they arrived in Regalbuto.

Alfio looked for the Church of Santa Maria della Croce. He could see domes and steeples in different parts of the town, but chose the closest, deciding to try that one first. He told the family to wait rather than taking them around to each Church until he found the right one.

As Alfio made his way to the first Church, he saw a priest walking along the road. "Excuse me, Father. I'm looking for Santa Maria della Croce."

The priest smiled. "I am Father Guglielmo. Santa Maria is my Church." The priest had a round face, warm smile and a twinkle in his eyes. His glasses magnified his crow's feet.

Alfio pulled out the letter from Father Pappalardo and gave it to Father Guglielmo. Father read the letter, then folded it and put it away. "I am so sorry your family is going through this," the priest said. He embraced Alfio, kissing him on both cheeks as though they were old friends. "How is Domenico?" Father asked, referring to Father Pappalardo.

"He is well," Alfio, told him.

"Good! It is good you came here. Father Pappalardo made the right decision to send you to me. My brother lives a short distance from here. His wife died recently and they were unable to have children. He is very lonely. I was just on my way to see him now. Why don't you come with me?"

"But my family…" Alfio started to say.

"They will be fine. We won't be long." Alfio joined the priest as they walked through the winding streets toward via Venti Settembre. "My poor brother," Father Guglielmo continued, "He is all alone now and I can't get over to see him as much as I'd like. My parish keeps me very busy. He has two large rooms upstairs that would be perfect for your family."

"I will need work. In Pedara, I drove a cart. My oldest son helps."

"You will be able to find work as a cart driver, but you will not have as many deliveries as in Pedara. Here, you are just starting out. People don't know you and you don't know the routes. Still, it will suffice."

Father Guglielmo knocked on a door and the man who opened the door had a huge smile on his face. Alfio thought he was seeing double as he looked from one man to the other. Both had thinning hair and the same round face. They both wore glasses and were short. Father did have a few more lines on his face than his brother and the brother had a few more pounds on his frame.

"Alfio, this is my brother, Matteo." Turning to his brother, the priest continued, "Alfio and his family need a place to stay. Father Pappalardo from Pedara sent them to me for help. Do you think we can help them?" Father knew his brother's generous nature and Matteo jumped in immediately with an offer to help.

"Certainly!" Turning to Alfio, he said, "Why don't you stay with me?"

"That is very kind of you, but we are a large family. There are eleven of us. It is an awful lot to ask."

Matteo brushed aside Alfio's objections. "Nonsense. There is enough room here and if you decide it's inadequate, you can always look for a larger place. In the meantime, you need somewhere to stay. Come! Bring your family! It will be wonderful to have children around. Hurry and bring them back before it gets dark."

"Thank you." Alfio left them and went to his family with the news they had a place to stay.

The family returned to Matteo's home where he showed them where they would be staying. Once everyone was settled in, Maria went downstairs to speak to Matteo about the use of his kitchen. There was no kitchen upstairs. "It is yours whenever you need it!" Matteo told her. "If you agree, I will hire you to cook and do household chores for myself. That should help with your expenses and it would be an enormous help to me."

Maria agreed. She went to get the little bit of food that was left from their journey and managed to cook an evening meal that was enough for everyone in the household: her own family and Matteo, as well. Years of skimping had taught her how to use what she had to feed a large family. Matteo praised her cooking saying it was the best he ever tasted. Then the exhausted Primavita family went upstairs to sleep.

CHAPTER FOUR

Regalbuto

June 1899

Alfio stopped on Via Plebiscito and consulted the scrap of paper Father Guglielmo gave him with the name and address of a man who would help him find work. Looking up, he confirmed he was standing in front of the door whose number matched the slip of paper. Searching for a knocker in vain, he banged on the wooden door with his fist. A tall, bald man with a gray beard opened the door. The man scowled at Alfio, waiting for Alfio to speak.

"Good day. I am looking for Signore Santoro," Alfio said.

"You found him," the man replied.

"I'm new to Regalbuto. I am a cart driver by trade and Father Guglielmo suggested I speak to you about finding work." Alfio waited to see if mentioning the priest's name would put him in the good graces of the man in front of him but Signore Santoro's expression didn't change.

"Do you have your own cart and horse?"

"I have a cart, but I have a donkey, not a horse," Alfio replied. The scowl deepened. Signore Santoro stared at the smaller man in front of him. "Please," Alfio continued. "I have a large family and need the work." Alfio felt resentment building toward this man for forcing him to humble himself and beg for work. As the man continued to stare at him in silence, Alfio started to turn away.

"Be here at sunrise tomorrow morning."

Alfio nodded. "Thank you."

The next morning Alfio and Francesco arrived at Via Plebiscito. Signore Santoro was waiting outside his home. Stacked around their new employer were crates. "You will bring these hides to the tanner on Via Sant'Antonio in Catenanuova."

Alfio studied the map Signore Santoro handed him. "It's not far. Looks about 12 kilometers away. We should be back by dusk."

"It will take you two days," Signore Santoro told them. "You cannot take the direct route. There are bandits who hide in the caves, waiting for travelers and tradesmen. You will need to go around them, through the mountain paths. When you get close to the city, you will need to pay the mafie. They will not allow you to pass until you do."

"You pay the mafie?" Alfio asked.

Signore Santoro grew impatient. "You must have dealt with the mafia before this. They are all over Sicilia."

Alfio knew about the mafia and heard stories of how they extorted people, but their presence in Pedara was restricted to the farm owners. Cart drivers didn't carry enough wares to make them worthwhile targets. There were some men he and his friends suspected of being part of the mafia but it was all very secretive and no one knew for certain. It provided good gossip but nothing more.

Alfio and Francesco set off on their first trip from Regalbuto with some apprehension. They were not used to traveling over such rough terrain and rarely concerned themselves about bandits when they lived in Pedara. Each time the road became steep and rocky, Alfio and Francesco got out of the cart and walked the donkey over the difficult sections. Francesco's eyes constantly moved from left to right, scanning the road ahead for potential trouble. He sat closer to his father than usual. Alfio was a little hunched and held the reins tight but after an hour of travel, leaned back and relaxed his grip on the reins. He started singing his usual songs as they traveled. When Francesco didn't join in, Alfio put an arm around him. He could feel his son's tense muscles.

"Relax. Sing with me."

"What if we don't make it to Catenanuova before dark? I don't want to camp out here among thieves and murderers," Francesco told his father.

"Do not be afraid. God is with us."

Francesco remained silent and continued to search the road for thieves.

They neared Catenanuova before nightfall and saw a group of five men on horseback blocking the road. As they drew closer to the men, one got down from his horse and walked over to them. "There is a toll you must pay to go any further," the man told them.

"Of course," Alfio replied. He paid the man and the mafie moved aside, waiting for their next target.

Francesco was finally able to relax once they entered Catenanuova. They found the tanner on Via Sant'Antonio and unloaded the cart. When they were done, they turned their cart around and made camp on the outskirts of town. Francesco built a fire and Alfio cooked them a meal of Pasta alla Carrettiera (Cart Driver's Pasta). All cart drivers had some version of this dish but Francesco knew his father's was the best.

"We will head back to Regalbuto at the first sign of daylight," Alfio told his son. After they ate, they spread blankets in the back of the cart and went to sleep.

~ ~ ~

Maria enjoyed keeping house for Signore Guglielmo. He seemed to appreciate every little thing Maria did, gushing with enthusiasm. Every meal was the best he ever ate. He claimed his clothes never looked so clean. Maria knew that was just his way and he treated everyone like that, but it was still nice to hear.

Rosa and Concetta found work, as well. Everyone in the family worked with a sense of urgency, hoping to earn enough so they could move out of that house before it became clear that Domenica was pregnant. When they arrived in Regalbuto, Domenica was four months pregnant, barely starting to show. Domenica was not thin like Rosa and even a month later, the pregnancy was not apparent. Maria knew that would soon change. It was one matter to hide in one's own home, but to attempt a secret like that under the roof of another was difficult.

One evening Alfio and Maria were sitting outside, pondering the situation. Signore Guglielmo was asleep as were the children, so they could talk freely. They sat in the dark, trying to come up with a plan to protect their daughter.

"No one here really knows us. We can say Domenica is a widow," Alfio suggested.

Maria sighed. "You know I can't lie. For one thing, it's a sin. Also, anyone can look into my eyes and see that I am being dishonest."

It was Alfio's turn to sigh. "You're right. You are a terrible liar." He looked at her and smiled. The smile quickly faded as he once again searched for a solution.

"Why do we need to tell anyone anything?" Maria asked. "I can wear my dresses loose. People will just assume the baby is mine. It's better than lying"

"And when she starts to grow larger? How do we handle that? Won't it be evident she's having a baby?"

Maria was silent as she thought about what Alfio said, searching for an answer. "That may not happen for another month or so, especially since it's her first. She's not a small girl. People will just think she is eating too much. She can wear large dresses to hide her stomach. When the time comes where that is no longer possible, we will keep her at home."

Alfio nodded. "Yes, that would be best. I will start looking for a place for us to live," Alfio replied.

A week later, Alfio came home and announced he found a house on via Stradella. They left Matteo Guglielmo with the promise to visit often.

For the youngest children, life went on nearly the same as always. They missed their family and friends but quickly made new friends to ease their loss. Giuseppe and Agata went to school. Francesco assisted his father, making deliveries to the surrounding towns. Rosa and Concetta found work in a bakery. Grazia took over the care of Matteo's household so Maria could devote herself to taking care of Domenica.

As the pregnancy advanced further along, Domenica went out less often until she finally just stayed indoors all the time. She grew more frightened about giving birth. Maria did her best to reassure her daughter that it wouldn't be as bad as she imagined.

Late one Saturday night in October, Domenica went into labor. Early the following morning, on October 29, she had not yet given birth. Maria sent the worried family to Church while she stayed with Domenica. "Shouldn't one of the girls stay here with you?" Alfio asked.

"It will be okay. We need all of you to pray." Maria put her hand on Alfio's arm. "When you return, send Rosa in alone." He nodded and headed out to the Church, his children following behind. Maria didn't tell Alfio she knew something was wrong. For the past week, there was no movement from Domenica's womb.

After Mass, Alfio took his time returning home and they didn't arrive back at the house until nearly noon. Rosa went inside and almost immediately came out to talk to her father. "Domenica just gave birth a few minutes ago. The baby was stillborn." Rosa turned and handed Francesco a basket with sandwiches. "Mama said to take everyone into the courtyard and give them lunch." Turning to Concetta, Rosa told her, "Mama wants you to fetch the Signora Trovato. We need someone to say they witnessed the birth. Mama already spoke to her a few days ago."

Alfio went into the house where he found both his wife and his daughter crying. Through tears, Maria told her husband that the little girl, Alfia, was named for him. "What do you need me to do?" he asked.

"Talk to Father Guglielmo. Arrangements need to be made." Alfio nodded and left, glad that he had a goal and a reason to leave the house. Prior to this day, he often wondered how he would feel about this grandchild. Now that it was too late, he realized he would love his grandchild regardless of how the child was conceived.

~ ~ ~

Domenica moved through the days that followed with a mechanical precision, her face a mask of indifference. Stella's antics, which once would have drawn laughter, now passed by her unnoticed, her eyes hollow, reflecting a light that had gone out.

Santina's embraces, once a source of warmth, now felt like weights, reminders of the love she could no longer feel.

She found work sewing. Unlike her sisters, she put in long hours, longer than necessary. Her hands now moved with a purpose, sewing with a speed that spoke of desperation rather than efficiency. She worked until her fingers ached, the physical pain a distraction from the deeper ache within.

At night, the bedroom was silent except for the rustle of sheets as she turned, again and again, seeking a position where sleep might find her. The Rosary beads slipped through her fingers, each prayer a plea, not just for sleep, but for oblivion from the memory that haunted her. The image of her stillborn daughter, so vivid in her mind, replayed like a cruel film, each frame a stab of grief.

As the year drew to a close, the community around Domenica began to stir with a different kind of energy. They greeted the new century, celebrating in the square across the street from Santa Maria della Croce with their neighbors. The last year was behind them. 1899 had been full of sorrow and tragedy, not just for Domenica but for many in their small town. Closing the door on that year, they all looked to the new year, the new century with renewed hope. 1900 would bring good things for their family, or so they hoped.

With no extended family in Regalbuto, they turned to their neighbors and fellow parishioners for companionship. As in Pedara, they joined the processions for the feast days. The festivals followed the same pattern as elsewhere in Italy. Men of the parish lifted up statues of the various saints or the Blessed Mother onto a platform. Priests waving incense and altar boys bearing candles led the processions and the people followed, joining in the prayers and the fellowship. It was a familiar ritual, one that Domenica participated in, her presence a silent testament to her struggle to find solace within the community's collective healing.

~ ~ ~

Months drifted by. Life slipped into routine. Work and Church marked the family's days. Towards the end of 1900, Maria was pregnant. As she showed more and more, Domenica found herself avoiding her mother and the reminder of what she lost. One afternoon, Maria walked into the house, her arms full with food from the market. Concetta, Domenica, and Rosa sat at the kitchen table. At the sight of her mother, Domenica jumped up and left the room, running upstairs to the bedroom. Concetta went to help her mother. Rosa, seeing tears glisten in her mother's eyes, pushed her chair back from the table and stomped up the stairs after Domenica, her steps echoing through the house. Following her sister, Rosa confronted her.

"Must you dwell on this forever?" she asked her sister. "It's been over a year. Life goes on whether you will it or not. Can't you see how you are hurting Mama when you avoid her and don't speak to her?"

Through the fog of her own pain, Domenica had not seen her mother's pain. The idea that she caused her mother sorrow added to her own. In tears, she went to Maria.

"Mama, I am sorry. I was so wrapped in my own sorrow that I paid no attention to how I was hurting you."

Maria hugged her daughter. "I know how difficult this is for you."

"I am being punished."

"No, my sweet girl. Of course you're not," Maria responded.

"At first I did not want my child. I did not want to bear the child of that monster. I wondered how I could possibly love a baby conceived in that way. God punished me for having those thoughts."

"No, God does not punish us for thoughts we have no control over. You went through a horrible experience that no woman should go through. That incident left scars on you. And you did not feel like that toward your child as time went on. I could see your attitude toward that tiny life change."

"It did," Domenica agreed. "I grew to love my baby in spite of everything. But I should never have thought those thoughts in the first place. This was my fault. She died because of me."

Maria put her arm around her daughter and held her close. "It is natural to blame yourself when a child is lost. I blamed myself when I lost my little girl less than ten days after she was born. It was the year before Francesco was born. I thought maybe I did something wrong. But I did everything I could to protect little Grazia. No matter what I did differently, she still would die. You cannot take the blame for this."

"It's been over a year. Shouldn't I be over this loss?" Domenica repeated what Rosa said to her.

"The loss of a child is something you never entirely get over. There is no time line for mourning. You can't rush it and you cannot hide from it. I still feel sadness for the little girl I lost and that was many years ago, far longer than your loss. I promise you this - the pain will lessen. With time, it will become bearable."

"How is it possible to have so much love for a baby you never knew?" Domenica asked. "It must have been so difficult for you to lose a daughter only a few days old but you held her, fed her. That loss makes sense to me. But little Alfia - I never knew her. How can it hurt this much? How can I mourn so much for an infant I didn't even nurse?"

"Because you are a mother," Maria answered. "You carried this baby for nine months. You were connected to her. When you are a mother, you love your children. No matter what happens, no matter what they do, you love them. You may not always like them, especially when they do something you disapprove of, but you always love them. The love of a parent is a reflection of God's love for us. Remember that. God forgives you, He loves you, and He is not punishing you for your thoughts."

Domenica reflected on that love between parent and child, between her mother and herself. She knew without the love of her mother throughout this ordeal, that she would be lost.

On April 29, 1901 in the small house on via Stradella, Maria Nunziata was born. At first, every cry from the tiny baby sent jolts of pain through Domenica. When she first held the infant, she was overcome with sadness. Over time, those feelings diminished. This child filled the void inside Domenica left from the loss of Alfia. A deep bond developed between the oldest daughter and the youngest.

~ ~ ~

On August 15, they celebrated the feast of the Assumption.

After Mass, the procession and prayers, there was food and laughter. Everyone gathered in the square across from Santa Maria della Croce. Children ran around, playing and adults stood around talking. Maria stood with a group of women but didn't join in the conversation. She looked at the Church across the way. It was similar to the only other Church she knew, Santa Caterina Alessandrina. There were the same three wooden doors, with a bell tower on the left. These similarities, rather than bringing comfort, brought pain. The Church was a reminder of what she left behind in Pedara, the people whose loss made her heart ache. Forcing herself to push those thoughts aside, she tried to focus on the conversation.

Domenica stood a short distance away from her mother, little Maria in her arms. For the first time in a long time, Domenica smiled as she watched her younger siblings playing with the other children. Some of the women were giving granita out to the children. Santina and Stella seemed to have more of the sweet, icy treat on their faces than in their mouths. Agata and Giuseppe ate the granita much more carefully lest they waste even a single drop.

Grazia, Francesco, Concetta, and Rosa mingled with other children at the festival, the boys and girls keeping a respectful distance from one another.

"Francesco, is that pretty girl one of your sisters?" Marco asked, nodding toward Grazia.

"All of my sisters are pretty," Francesco retorted, protective. "Grazia's only ten. You've got years before you can court her."

Meanwhile, the girls whispered among themselves. "Paolo's more handsome, but Antonio's kinder," Concetta mused, looking over at the twins.

"I think Antonio is the better looking twin," Rosa countered.

Isabella chimed in, "I think Francesco is the handsomest." The girls glanced at Francesco, who was busy glaring at Marco. Then the group of girls went over to get some granita.

Alfio hadn't made many friends yet and stood a little apart from the men although close enough to listen. It was here that Alfio heard the first talk about men traveling to America.

"Angelo left for America two years ago. He earned enough money to send for his family in less than a year. It is easier to find work there. Families own their own houses. Men own two good suits, not just one, tattered and held together with patches," a bearded man told his friend.

Alfio's ears perked up when he heard the men mention 'America' and he turned to the two men, interrupting their conversation. "Do you believe him, this Angelo? Does everyone have a better life in America? How can you know that he isn't worse off than he was when he lived here?"

The bearded man looked at Alfio. "He has enough money that he can send some to his parents who still live here. Do you have extra money that you can send to your parents?" Alfio shook his head.

Alfio was grateful he was able to support his family but knew he would never own his own home. At best, he might manage to save enough to trade the donkey in for a horse. What would it be like to have enough money to own a home and not pay rent to someone? Could living in America be much different than living here where they were already far away from their family? An idea began to take root in his mind as he imagined a better life for himself and his family. He began taking on extra work, saving every coin with the hope of bringing his family to America.

CHAPTER FIVE

Farewell

1903

Matteo Guglielmo shook his head. "No, Alfio, this is a very bad idea." He was sitting outside with Alfio and another man, Guido. They were playing cards and initially Alfio thought Matteo was referring to the card he just placed on the table. "It is too dangerous to put your trust in the padrone," Matteo warned. "You'll end up being a slave and handing over all the money you earn to him."

"Of course that is sometimes true but not all padrone are the same," Guido responded. "It is the easiest way to get work in America." Guido was in the business of helping people travel to America, especially those who had no family there. It proved a very lucrative business and he made America seem like paradise. He had many friends in America who were padroni, men who preyed on immigrants. A padrone would help immigrants find employment but would take a large cut of the immigrant's salary as payment for his services. Guido received a percentage of his padroni's cut in addition to the fee he charged for arranging passage to America.

"Alfio, trust me. My connections in New York will find you a place to stay and you will earn more money than you'll ever need. You can't travel to America unless you have someone already there to vouch for you. My friend will do that."

Alfio looked from one man to the other. He knew Matteo was

right but he also knew something Matteo didn't know: Alfio wasn't as poor and helpless as he let on. "It will be alright. It's a small price to pay for a better future," Alfio told Matteo. Turning to Guido, he said, "Okay. Three of us will be traveling: myself and two of my daughters."

After a bit of haggling over the price of his services, Guido took three tickets out of his pocket along with a slip of paper and placed them on the table. "The ship leaves Naples on July 29th. You will travel to Palermo and then take a boat from there to Naples. You will need to leave soon. That paper has all the information you'll need: the route you will take to Palermo, what information you should give to the authorities, the name of a 'relative' and the address in New York." Alfio paid Guido who then stood and shook hands with both men. "Good luck, Alfio." He left them with a smile on his face, stuffing the money into his pocket.

Once Guido was out of earshot, Alfio said, "Don't worry, Matteo. I have a plan." He smiled. "I will not be indebted to the padrone. I just needed someone with the proper connections to arrange the travel for us and get us the tickets. He thinks he is taking advantage of me but I'm using him."

"Do not use the name on that paper." Matteo pointed to the slip of paper sitting on the table with the tickets. "Even if you manage to find work without the help of the padrone, putting his name down will still mean you owe him something. I have a cousin in New York, Gaetano. Put his name down instead. You are like family now so he is your cousin as well as mine. He lives in the same building on Broome Street."

"Thank you," Alfio responded.

"Have your family come back here to stay with me. It will be safer for them here. I will look out for them. I can teach Francesco how to cut hair. That will be a useful skill for when he travels to America."

"Matteo, that is more than I can ask."

"Nonsense! I miss having your family around. My house is too quiet. The company will be good for me. They will be helping me just as much as I will be helping them."

The two men continued to play cards as they sipped wine. Alfio seemed distracted and Matteo easily won the game. Matteo looked at Alfio. "You're worried."

"Yes. I will be so far away from Maria and the children and I don't know how long we will be separated. They have no family here. All we have is each other and you and that is too great a burden for you."

"The greater burden will be when your family leaves to join you and I am alone again," Matteo responded.

~ ~ ~

A week later, at dusk in late June, the children were sitting outside in the courtyard to escape the stifling heat indoors. Maria and Alfio were alone in the house, sitting at the table sipping coffee. "I have decided," Alfio told his wife, "that our family will move to America. I will not have my sons driving carts for the rest of their lives. My daughters will not live with their husbands and children in a tiny house like this one, making some landlord rich while they struggle."

Maria could see his mind was made up and didn't argue with him. She did, however, have a lot of questions. "How can we afford it? I heard it's a dangerous trip to get to the port for the ship. And the conditions on board…"

"I have been saving up for two years. The trip is already paid for and there is money for you to survive on with help from the children. I will send more once I find work in America. I know the journey will be difficult, but it will be worth the sacrifices. Our children will have better lives. Our grandchildren will not be poor. We are far from our family in Pedara and we can never return there to see them. Regalbuto offers nothing for our family. I will go and then send for you as soon as I can." He paused. "The arrangements are all prepared already. I have the tickets."

"You plan on leaving us behind?"

"I will go with Domenica and Rosa. I will send for the rest of you as soon as I can." Alfio put his hand on hers. "It won't be long. We will earn money more quickly than we ever could if we stay here. This is for the children. We must do this for them. There is no other way unless we want them to live in poverty for the rest of their lives."

Maria nodded and bit her lip. "No!" she silently willed Alfio, "Do not leave us behind!" When she was certain she could keep an even tone, she said out loud, "You know I trust you but…" She couldn't finish as tears welled in her eyes.

"I wish there was a better way." Alfio put his hand over hers. "Not many people in Sicily can all go together. The husbands or an older sibling always go first and then send for the rest of the family. Francesco will remain here to watch over the family," Alfio continued. "I want you to move back to via Venti Settembre to live with Matteo Guglielmo. You will be safer there, especially when the time comes for me to send for Francesco. Matteo made the offer and is thrilled you will be returning. He will take good care of you. He's been lonely since we moved out. It will set my mind at ease knowing you are not alone. I will sell the cart and donkey when we reach Palermo and send the money to you. Francesco will work as a barber with Matteo. He will teach our son the trade and Francesco can use that skill in America to find a job. There are no jobs driving carts in New York."

Alfio sighed and rose from the table. "I want to tell the children right away." He went to the door. "Domenica! Rosa! Come here." The girls immediately obeyed their father, went inside, and joined their parents at the table, sitting on either side of their father. Maria sat opposite her husband. "We are going to America," he announced.

"When do we leave?" Francesco, now sixteen, was not a part of this conversation but stood in the doorway, listening in.

"First I will go with Domenica and Rosa. You need to stay here and take care of the family. We will work and save money and then send for you." Francesco did not contradict his father but he frowned his disapproval of that plan. Domenica looked down at the table in silence. Rosa clenched her teeth lest her thoughts should escape through her mouth.

"It is only for a short time." Maria tried to console them. "Papa needs your help because I will not be there to take care of him. Before you know it, we will all be reunited." Domenica and Rosa knew better than to argue the point but they could not hold back their sorrow. They had just left behind Pedara and everything they knew and loved and now Papa was going to take them thousands of miles away.

"I know you are upset but this is for the best. Do you really want to live the rest of your lives crammed into a two room hut? In America you will live in a mansion with many rooms. You will have nice things. You will see your children grow up with more than you ever dreamed of with more opportunity. It will be okay."

Alfio stood up. "Tomorrow we will go back to via Venti Settembre. Then we will leave for Palermo." He turned and walked out of the house. With their father gone, the three children vented their feelings.

"This is ridiculous!" Francesco fumed. "No one needs me here to watch the family. Signore Guglielmo is capable of taking care of everyone. I should be going to America with Papa. I could earn more money than Domenica and Rosa. They don't even want to go." He punched the wooden door frame, hurting his fist and then stomped around the kitchen.

Domenica and Rosa still sat at the table. Domenica was crying while Rosa glared at her brother. "I wish it were you instead of us," she told him. "I don't want to go to America!"

"You are all being selfish," Maria scolded them. "Your father knows what is best. Francesco, Giuseppe needs you here. All the little ones need you to fill the void when Papa leaves. Matteo can't take the place of two men." Turning to the girls, Maria said, "Both of you are at an age where you will marry very soon. Papa doesn't want you marrying someone from this village and being stuck here for the rest of your lives. And if he leaves you behind, that is exactly what will happen. He wants better for you. He wants you to meet men in America, men who will give you better lives and fewer struggles."

"But Mama...," Rosa started to protest but Maria held up her hand.

"Trust your parents. Don't be afraid. God is with us. Everything will work out for the best. Papa already has the tickets and everything is arranged. There will be no changing his mind so please, all of you, just accept this. I am not happy, either. I will miss my husband and my girls terribly. It is a burden for me to be left behind. But we all must pray a lot and we all must trust."

~ ~ ~

Alfio's children saw a man in charge of his household, a man whose authority was absolute. What they did not see was the grief he felt when he knew his decisions would cause his family pain. Alfio wandered aimlessly and eventually found himself standing outside Santa Maria della Croce. He entered the Church and knelt in prayer. As he rose, he saw Father Guglielmo who greeted him with an embrace.

"Alfio! How good it is to see you!" He paused. "Why are you downcast?"

"My family is not happy with my decision to leave for America. I leave in two days with Rosa and Domenica. The girls don't want to go and Francesco does not want to stay behind, nor does Maria."

Father nodded. He did not respond, waiting for Alfio to continue.

"How can I be sure this is the right decision?"

"Have you prayed for guidance on this?" Father Guglielmo asked.

"Yes."

"Then trust that you were lead to this decision by the Holy Spirit. This may be your family's road to Calvary, but in the end, it will lead to a Resurrection, a new life for you and your family."

"So you think I am doing the right thing?"

"That is not for me to answer. Do you feel this is the best option for your family?"

"I do. It is our only option for a better future."

The priest smiled. "Then you have your answer. Trust in the Lord." Father Guglielmo put his hand on Alfio's arm. "I hear many good things about America. It will be tough at first but you will do well there. You are a strong man. I will miss you, though. God be with you!" Father blessed Alfio and Alfio left the Church to return to his family.

The next morning the family walked through the streets with their belongings, making their way to Matteo Guglielmo's home. The group of twelve looked somber as they neared via Venti

Settembre. Domenica gripped Maria's little hand and held back tears, wondering if the little girl would remember her when they saw each other again.

When they arrived, Matteo greeted them and gave cookies to the younger children. The treats did not lighten the mood and Matteo withdrew, leaving the family alone on their last day together.

Alfio gathered everyone around him. "While I am gone, Francesco will be the man of the house. You will obey him as you would me."

"When Francesco goes to America, will I be in charge?" Giuseppe asked.

"You're only ten," Agata told him. "You're not old enough to be the man of the house."

"Yes, I am!"

Alfio put his arm around Giuseppe. "We shall see. Meantime, I am counting on you to help your brother and take care of your sisters."

The sun seemed to streak across the sky, sinking into the western horizon long before any of them were ready to see the day end. Early the next morning, Alfio prepared to leave with his two oldest children.

"Be good. Obey your mother and brother. We will all be together again soon." Turning to his wife, "I will write often. As soon as I find work, I will send you money."

There were many hugs and many tears. Maria and the children stood on the street watching the departing backs of Alfio, Rosa, and Domenica until they were out of sight.

Over the next week, Francesco learned to cut hair, working alongside Signore Guglielmo while Maria once again tended his house. Each evening, as they gathered for dinner, the children would ask if there was a letter from their father and were disappointed when the answer was no. Then, one day, rather than responding, Maria smiled. The children all started yelling out at once. "Where is it? What did he say? Where are they? Are they in New York yet?"

Maria laughed. "Just a minute. Quiet down and let me read it." Immediately there was silence.

'July 27, 1903

Dearest Maria and children,

We just arrived in Naples. The ship from Palermo to Naples was quite crowded with so many fellow Sicilians seeking passage to America and South America. I met a man who knew a little English. He told us in New York, people change their names to sound American. My name would be Alfred. What a funny sounding name!

Domenica and Rosa are doing well and met some other girls their age who are also traveling to New York. I think they are glad to have the company.

We leave in two days to start our journey to America. Everyone must put down the name and address of a relative they will be staying with when they arrive in New York. You must thank Matteo for me. Matteo's cousin, Gaetano, was very kind to let us use his name on the form. We will be staying in an apartment on Broome Street. Once we arrive, you can write to us there.

They say it will take about two weeks to sail to New York from Naples. Some people get sick from the ship's movements. Let's hope that doesn't happen to us or it will seem to be a much longer trip.

Pray for us. Pray that our journey goes well and that we find work right away. We will pray for you, my family. We miss all of you and cannot wait for the day we are all together again. I will write again as soon as we arrive in New York.

Your loving husband and father,
Alfio'

"Two weeks on a boat?" Giuseppe said. "That sounds like fun!"

"What's fun about being on a boat with a bunch of smelly people?" Grazia replied.

"Why are they smelly?" Santina asked.

"Because it's summer and it's hot," Grazia explained.

"But there's water all around them," Stella reasoned. "Can't they go in the water and get clean?"

"No, they would be eaten by a shark or swallowed by a whale like Jonah!" Giuseppe told his sister. He used his arms to imitate the jaws of a whale and pretended his arms were going to swallow Stella up. Giggling, Stella ran from him and the little group broke up.

In October, Maria discovered she was pregnant again, a mix of joy and apprehension stirring within her. At the same time, news reached them that a group from Regalbuto was journeying to Palermo, en route to New York. It was decided that Concetta would join them, her eyes gleaming with the promise of new beginnings. Francesco, feeling the weight of being left behind, his dreams of America seeming ever more distant, resolved to save enough to make the journey on his own terms.

~ ~ ~

1904

On April 16, 1904, Giovannina was born, her cries a new melody in the family's life. Just days after her arrival, Francesco, with excitement for his new adventure, shared that he had managed to buy a ticket to New York. He journeyed to Naples, the city's bustling energy a stark contrast to his quiet hometown life. There, he found a letter from his father, Alfio, waiting for him. The instructions were clear: wait for Grazia. He lingered in Naples, the anticipation of America mingling with his longing for home. In August, when Grazia finally joined him, they set off together across the ocean, unaware that back home, little Giovannina's life would be tragically brief, ending in October.

A letter arrived for the remaining family members in Regalbuto in late October. Half the family now lived in New York at 526 1/2 Broome Street along with what seemed half the population of Sicily.

'October 28, 1904

Dearest Maria and children,

We were saddened by the news of Giovannina. I wish I could have been there with you but I'm sure our girls were able to offer some comfort. Be assured of our prayers.

Francesco and Grazia arrived safely in New York in September. They already found jobs. Francesco is working as a barber but he seems to have taken an interest in the motor cars driving about the city. One of the men in the apartment next door is teaching him how to drive. That fellow works as a taxi driver. Driving a motor car certainly seems easier than using a cart and donkey!

We are all learning to speak English. Many here seem fine with speaking Italian. We are surrounded by Sicilians - at work, in the shops, in Church. But our family will be American so we must learn to speak English. The children will learn it quickly. You and I, Maria, may need to work a bit harder but we will also learn it.

New York is very different than Sicily. The buildings are very tall. There are so many people everywhere. Our apartment building is very crowded. Outside, the streets are lined with wagons selling all kinds of meat and fish and fruit and vegetables. Everyone crowds around and tries to bargain for a good price. It seems like every step you take, someone is trying to sell you a newspaper or shine your shoes or cut your hair.

Our apartment isn't too far from the water. During the summer heat I used to like walking over to the river because there was a nice breeze off the water but I think everyone else in the household has had their fill of water for a while. Domenica and Rosa turn a little green at the very idea of being near the sea.

I want the rest of you to prepare to come to New York. I will send tickets. Matteo will help you.

Looking forward to when we are reunited.

Your loving husband and father, Alfio'

"We're going to see Papa!" Santina shouted. Stella ran to little Maria and hugged her. The three-year-old didn't know what the fuss was about or who Papa was. The children were all thrilled but their mother was apprehensive about taking such a journey with five young children.

CHAPTER SIX

Palermo Bound

November 1904

At the end of the All Saints' Day Mass, a whisper of excitement rippled through the crowd as the square buzzed with life. Maria, her eyes scanning the throng, felt a tug at her dress. Little Maria, barely three, clung to her, eyes wide with the fear of getting lost in the sea of strangers. Around them, villagers indulged in the feast of fruits and sweets.

Near the Church steps, a short distance away, Agata, Stella, Santina, and Giuseppe stood, their faces animated as they discussed the saints.

"I am named for San Giuseppe, the father of Jesus," Giuseppe declared proudly. "Who could be more important than him?"

"St. Agata was a martyr, patron of Catania, and she stopped the fires of Mount Etna!" Agata countered, her voice filled with reverence.

"St. Agata was brave, but San Giuseppe had the most sacred duty, protecting the Holy Family," Giuseppe retorted, puffing out his chest.

Santina looked at Stella and said, "They're so silly. Each saint has their own miracle, their own glory."

The children's debate was cut short by Father Guglielmo, who approached with a gentle smile. "What lively discourse you are having here on this holy day," he said, his voice carrying a note of amusement.

"What does 'discourse' mean?" Giuseppe asked, his curiosity piqued.

"It means to talk about serious matters, like the saints," Father Guglielmo explained, his eyes twinkling. "You children speak of holy things with such fervor. It warms the heart."

Agata, always eager to learn, asked, "So, when we talk of saints, we're doing what you do in church, Padre?"

"In a way, yes," Father Guglielmo nodded, handing each child a small sweet. "You ponder the mysteries of faith. Keep questioning, for that is how one grows in wisdom."

The children, their minds buzzing with thoughts of saints and miracles, accepted the sweets, their debate momentarily forgotten in the joy of the treat.

As the day faded, most of the people who gathered for the celebration made their way to the cemetery. Tomorrow was All Souls' Day, and they were going to visit the graves of their relatives. The Primavita family had no relatives buried in Regalbuto so they made their way back home. Upon their return, Maria found an envelope sitting on the kitchen table. "That came while you were gone," Matteo told her. He was nursing a cold and had skipped the festivities.

Maria read the letter twice. She looked at the tickets for passage to America. Feeling both anxious and excited at the same time, she summoned Giuseppe and Agata and they went upstairs to talk. "Papa sent tickets. We will be leaving to join him in America."

"How will we get there? Where will we live? How long will it take?"

"Papa says there is a ship leaving from Palermo on January 9th. He said we should leave Regalbuto right after the New Year. There are other people here who plan to make the trip and we will travel with them."

More questions poured from the two children. Maria put her hands up to stop them.

"There will be time for questions later. We need to make arrangements to travel to Palermo. It will be a long journey." She returned downstairs where Matteo was waiting.

"The envelope was quite thick," he said to her. "It's time, isn't it?"

Maria nodded.

"We knew this time would come. I know you miss Alfio terribly." Not wanting to burden Maria with his sorrow, he didn't add how he would miss this family terribly once they left, but a sadness crept into his eyes. Matteo took a deep breath and then continued, "I will do whatever I can to help you prepare for the trip. I know you will not be traveling alone. I've been keeping my ears open and heard there will be other families leaving for Palermo."

"You knew there were others making the trip?" Maria asked.

Matteo smiled. "Several months ago, Alfio asked me to let him know if there were other families going to America. He would not allow you to travel alone. It is too dangerous for a woman with only an eleven-year-old boy to protect her. Not when you have little ones. It is safer to travel in a group." He took a sip from the glass of wine in front of him. "It was not a task I enjoyed," he added. "I was hoping we would have until the spring but that was selfish of me."

"You are a good man. We can never repay you for your kindness."

"One does not repay kindness," he told her. "And you are family now."

"We feel the same," Maria said.

Their last Christmas with the Guglielmo brothers, indeed their last Christmas in Italy, was bittersweet. They exchanged little homemade gifts. Santina and Stella gave Matteo and Father Guglielmo Rosaries they worked on for the past month. Agata gave the men small cloth sacks she made for them to hold their Rosaries.

Matteo handed out dates and almonds to the children. Then he turned to Maria. "I have one final gift for you. The group you are traveling with in a week consists mostly of women. There is one other boy besides Giuseppe, Rosario. He's only thirteen. I hired a man, Vincenzo. He will act as a guide for your group. He has a donkey and a cart. You no longer have Alfio's cart and donkey and it is far too great a distance to walk."

"Matteo, no! You should not pay to help us," Maria protested.

"It is done," he replied. "Please accept my gift."

The days between Christmas and the New Year sped by, with 1904 rolling into 1905. New Year's Day was on a Sunday and Maria cooked a wonderful meal for the family and the Guglielmos. There was a dish with lentils and sausage to bring good luck into the New Year. There was a casserole layered with rice, cheeses, and smothered with tomato sauce. Bowls with nuts and dried fruits sat on the table. For dessert, Maria brought out the panettone she baked. For a while, they were all able to forget what tomorrow would bring and just enjoyed the feast before them, grateful for the unusual abundance of food.

Matteo and Father Guglielmo taught the children how to play a card game called briscola. Father Guglielmo learned the game when he was in Rome and enjoyed playing it with Matteo. They stayed up playing later than wisdom dictated considering the long day that would follow, but they all wanted to stretch this last day as long as possible. Seeing the yawns of the youngest girls, Father Guglielmo pushed his chair back from the table. "It's time you all get some sleep. I will see you in the morning."

They said their good nights to Matteo and Father Guglielmo, and as the children settled into bed, their soft breathing soon filled the room with the rhythm of sleep. Maria lay awake, her mind a whirl of memories and concerns.

She thought of Pedara, the village where her ancestors lived, where she had grown up with the familiar faces of her family. When they left it behind, it felt like uprooting a tree, deep roots tearing from the earth. Yet, life in Regalbuto hadn't been much different, just quieter and emptier since Alfio and the older children had crossed the ocean.

Her heart ached with the loneliness of their absence. Each day had passed much like the one before, but now, the thought of America loomed large, a vast unknown. What would it be like to live among strangers, to speak in a tongue not her own?

She pictured America as a land of towering buildings and endless possibilities, a place where Alfio's letters spoke of opportunity but also of hard work. Would she find a new home there, or would she always feel like a visitor in a foreign land?

As these thoughts swirled, her eyelids grew heavy, and she drifted into a restless sleep, her dreams mingling with the hopes and fears of a new world waiting across the sea.

The family woke up early the following day. It was cold and dark out, but they could hear shouts outside. Members of their procession were already gathering, anxious to start out. The little family dressed, wearing several layers of clothes. This would protect them from the cold as well as give them less stuff to pack.

Maria sent the children downstairs and stood in the middle of the room. Nearly everything they owned was packed into a trunk and a few burlap sacks. Walking over to the bed, she picked up the last of the items: the Rosary and the Bible her mother gave her when she left Pedara. She put the Rosary into her pocket and then clutched the Bible, hugging it to her chest. "Oh, Mama! I miss you so much! Will I ever see you again?" she whispered to the empty room. Wiping her tears, she turned and went down the stairs to join Matteo and the children.

They had a somber last breakfast with Matteo. Then they collected their possessions and went outside, joining the group of travelers, family, and friends that gathered in the street. Matteo introduced them to Vincenzo, their guardian for this journey. The Romano family was there with a second donkey and cart, negotiating with Vincenzo.

"Yes, certainly I can buy your cart and donkey at the end of our trip, but we will only need them as far as Lercara. From there you will take the train to Palermo." Other passengers heard mention of a train and grew concerned about the cost. Vincenzo turned to address the group. "The train is only a short ride and is not expensive. It is the best way to reach Palermo with enough time. This is why we are not taking the train for the entire trip. That would be far too expensive."

Father Guglielmo was with the group. He walked over to Vincenzo and took him aside. He asked Vincenzo how much the tickets for the train in Lercara were and handed him some coins. "If anyone cannot afford a ticket, use this. When you return to Regalbuto, you will donate whatever is left over to the sisters in the convent of Sant' Agostino." Then the priest went to his brother, embracing him. "It will all be well," he whispered to Matteo. He then blessed the migrants.

"Your family will ride in this cart," Vincenzo told Maria. "The rest of the travelers will use the Romano's cart." Vincenzo lifted three-year-old Maria and sat her in the cart. He then helped Stella and Santina climb up into the cart. The others placed their bundles in the cart, climbing up after their belongings were safely piled. After tearful goodbyes, the fourteen travelers set out. Despite the bumpy ride with its jolts and jerks, the three youngest children were asleep within fifteen minutes of setting out, the long day and late night catching up with them.

Their four day journey from Regalbuto to Lercara wove through the landscapes of Sicily. As the sun dipped toward the horizon on some evenings, their path would lead them into a small town. Here, the cobblestone streets echoed with the clatter of their donkey carts, and they would seek refuge in a modest inn.

On other days, as twilight painted the sky with hues of purple and orange, they found themselves amidst open fields or nestled in the crook of gentle hills. Here, the group would set up camp.

Meals during this journey were simple, prepared over crackling fires that danced in the night, casting long shadows and filling the air with the comforting scent of wood smoke. They cooked whatever they had brought or foraged along the way—perhaps a stew of vegetables, a piece of cured meat, or bread baked in the embers.

To ward off the boredom of travel, they filled their days with song, their voices rising in traditional Sicilian melodies that echoed through the valleys. Games were played, some requiring nothing more than a stick and a stone, others involving riddles and wit. And as the stars began to twinkle above, they turned to prayer, reciting the Rosary in unison, their voices a soft murmur against the night, seeking protection and guidance for their journey.

However, their journey wasn't without its trials. On the second day, as they traversed a particularly rough patch of road, one of the cart's wheels cracked with a sharp snap that halted their progress. The group gathered around, inspecting the damage. The wheel had split near the rim, a common but inconvenient failure.

Quick thinking was needed. One of the travelers, familiar with such mishaps, suggested a temporary fix. They found a sturdy branch and, using a knife, shaved it down to fit the crack. With rope from their supplies, they bound the wood tightly to the wheel, wrapping it several times to secure the makeshift repair, hoping it would hold until they reached a village with a wheelwright.

As they entered Lercara, Vincenzo announced, "We are taking a train to Palermo. We will be there by this afternoon." All traces of fatigue left the group. No one from Regalbuto was ever on a train and the excitement energized them. As they walked through the narrow streets to the train station, animated conversations and laughter filled the air.

Maria stood at the train station with the five children who were all talking at once as they looked down the track, expecting the train to come barreling down at any minute. Vincenzo walked over to them. "The station manager said the train isn't expected for another two hours. You need to go into the office to buy tickets."

"Thank you," Maria replied. She turned to Giuseppe, handing him some coins. "Go into the office and buy six train tickets. Tell the man we are traveling to Palermo." Giuseppe ran off to do as his mother instructed. The two hours passed slowly. Then they heard the steam engine chugging into the station, gray steam billowing from its smokestack.

"Mama, look!" Santina shouted, pointing to the train, "There is smoke coming out of it, just like Mount Etna!"

"Is it going to explode?" Stella asked, with some concern.

Giuseppe scoffed at his sisters. "Of course not! It's not a volcano."

"How do you know?" Stella asked. "You were never on a train before."

Squatting down, Giuseppe smiled. "The train moves using a steam engine. The steam is just escaping through the smokestack. It won't explode. And wait until you see how fast the train goes! It will feel like you're flying. I read all about trains in a book."

The young girls, reassured by their brother, helped carry some of the sacks as they walked to the train with their family. Vincenzo made sure all thirteen people were safely on the train with their belongings. "When the train arrives in Palermo, ask for directions to the port. The ship for America will leave Palermo tomorrow. There are inns close to the port where you can stay overnight." Vincenzo paid the Romano family for their cart and donkey, then said goodbye and turned around, leading the two donkeys and carts.

The travelers found seats on the train, juggling their luggage on their laps. Everyone was startled when the train jerked to a start and a few sacks tumbled into the aisle, owners rushing to pick them up. The train pulled out of the station, gathering speed. All eyes were turned to the windows as everyone watched the scenery rush by.

Two hours later, as the train approached Palermo, they saw a large, three story building filled with arched windows and doorways. Trolleys made their way along the tracks near the building. A fellow passenger told them the building was Palermo Centrale, the railway station. After disembarking, the group asked for directions to the port and they went off in the direction indicated, looking out for an inn. Their progress was slow as the younger members of their group repeatedly stopped mid-step to gape at the large buildings. In Pedara and Regalbuto, none of the buildings were more than two stories. Here, they were five or six stories high. The buildings in their former villages seemed like tiny bungalows compared to the buildings in Palermo. Even the adults found themselves looking up in amazement.

As they passed one building Santina asked, "Mama, is that a castle?"

"I don't know. It certainly looks like one," Maria answered.

"I bet a king lives there," Stella said.

Agata and Giuseppe exchanged glances. "Keep an eye out for knights," Agata told her younger sisters. "The knights protect the king. Sometimes they just come charging out of the castle on horseback. They have these big long spears. You need to be careful not to get trampled on by the horses or stuck by a spear."

"Yes," Giuseppe added. "There may even be dragons."

"Stop," Maria said. "That's enough teasing." They continued in the direction of the port, the cobblestones clicking under their feet. Large structures with balconies, arches, and carved figures surrounded them as they walked. They all made the sign of the cross as they passed a Church. Soon afterward, they came to an inn and made arrangements to stay the night.

The following morning everyone again gathered up their belongings as they made their way to the port. The vastness of the sea took them by surprise. Their limited experience with lakes and rivers had not prepared them for the sight before them. The color was a beautiful deep blue and they could see no land in any direction. Even the smell of the air was different from anything they ever experienced.

In the water were boats of every kind: barges and passenger ships, large ones with masts stretching to the sky, and small boats. Wooden crates were piled on the docks alongside the boats. Everyone seemed to be rushing around carrying things on or off the ships, tying the ships to the dock, or helping them push off from the pier. The flurry of activity was very different from the slower paced life in Regalbuto.

The family made their way to the steerage office in a worn stone building across from the dock. Maria showed their tickets and the man pinned a tag to each of their coats. Then they carried their possessions onto the ship. Once on board, the family stood in a long line as men asked all the passengers questions and filled out forms. As they waited in line, they felt the ship move. The crew was anxious to start out. Processing the crush of immigrants who boarded the ship was taking longer than planned and they wanted to arrive in Naples before dark.

It was several hours before it was their turn to answer the questions. The man at the desk filled out the form with their names, ages, where they were going, and other assorted questions. They went to another line where a doctor looked them over. When the doctor got to seven-year-old Stella, he grunted. "Her eyes are red. She has an eye disease."

"It's just a minor illness," Maria responded. "Her sister had it and now she's better."

The doctor looked down at the list of passengers in front of him and started crossing their names off the manifest. "You will get off the ship at Naples. You cannot travel to New York."

"Stella does not have an eye disease," Maria protested. "My husband is waiting for us! We must go!"

"If you arrive in New York, they will send you back immediately. There are rooms in Naples where they take in boarders. You can stay there until the next ship from Naples to Palermo arrives and then you can return home to Regalbuto."

The crew forced the family to disembark in Naples. Ominous storm clouds hovered overhead, casting gray shadows and the wind kicked up large swells in the sea. Maria stood on the dock, surrounded by all their earthly possessions and five children who were all in tears. She wanted to sit down on the ground and weep along with them. In the distance, she saw the steeple of a Church. Taking a deep breath, she picked up some of the sacks and instructed the children to do the same. They started walking in the direction of the Church when a bolt of lightning lit the sky, followed by an earth-shaking clap of thunder. Large drops of rain began pelting them, and, for Maria, that seemed to be the final straw. Tears flowed down her face as she walked, mixing with the rain that drenched them.

CHAPTER SEVEN

Stranded

January 1905

Naples was similar to Palermo with its endless view of the sea and large buildings stretching into the sky, but seemed to have twice the amount of people. Mount Vesuvius lurked to the southeast, even closer to them than Mount Etna was when they lived in Pedara.

Maria and the children found a boarding house close to the port. They were stuffed into a small room but consoled themselves with the knowledge this was only temporary. Sitting on the edge of the one bed in the room, Maria gathered the children around her.

"We don't know how long we will be here in Naples. Papa left us some money but it will quickly run out if we're here for a while. We will need to work so we can pay the rent. You all must be brave. Trust in God and trust in Papa. Soon we will all be together."

Stella started crying. "It is my fault that we couldn't go to America."

"It is not your fault. It is no one's fault. You did not ask to get sick."

"But it is all because of me. They are angry at me." She indicated her siblings.

Santina put her arms around her sister. "No! We do not blame you."

"No one is angry with you," Giuseppe added. "With fate, perhaps, but not with you."

Agata nodded in agreement and little Maria hugged her big sister whose tears were slowly stopping.

"Now that that is settled, we have important things to do. We are not going to sit around feeling sorry for ourselves. Papa needs to know what happened. I need to find work for us, and Stella needs to get better." Maria looked around at her children. Giuseppe sat up straight, his mouth set in a firm line, and a determined look in his eyes. Stella's prior crying had worsened her red eyes. She was quieter than usual and had a slight pout. Santina sat, holding little Maria on her lap, her attention divided between her mother and her youngest sister. Agata had a slight frown on her face as she tapped her foot against the bed. Standing, Maria put her hands behind her and stretched her back, holding in a sigh. "It's only for a little while," she told herself. "Soon we'll be in America with Alfio."

Maria sent a letter to Alfio telling him how they were forced off the ship in Naples and they waited for instructions from Alfio on what to do next. Each letter took two weeks to travel to America and another two weeks for a reply, so they tried to settle in and make the best of their situation.

Maria found work sewing. Each day, she'd collect clothes from a seamstress down the block, bring them back to their cramped room, and work on buttonholes. Agata and Santina helped by sewing buttons onto the clothes. Every evening, Maria returned the day's work, ready to repeat the process the next morning.

Giuseppe walked down to the bustling port where cargo and fishing boats bobbed in the sea. He was hired at the docks to load and unload cargo. He was up early and returned home late, exhausted and smelling of fish and salt water.

In February, a letter arrived from Alfio. That evening the family gathered around Maria while she read it.

'February 3, 1905

Dearest Maria and children,

We were so concerned when we found that you were not on the ship when it arrived. It was several hours before we were able to learn what happened. It grieves my heart that we must be parted longer than planned.

I am sending money for you to buy new tickets. Wait until all traces of red are gone from Stella's eyes. They are very strict about what they view to be diseases of the eye and any hint of red will cause them to deny you entry to America. Once the red is completely gone, go down to the docks and find the agent who works for the steamship called Prinz Oscar. He will sell you tickets and will tell you when the next ship heading for New York will arrive in Naples.

Now I have some good news - Domenica is getting married in September! The man's name is Domenico Bracetti. He lives in the same building as us on Broome Street. He is a very nice young man. I know you will all like him. I know it will be difficult for you to delay your trip to New York but just think - we will all be reunited in time for this joyous wedding!

Know of our continued prayers for all of you.

Your loving husband and father,
Alfio'

The children all started talking at once. "Hooray! A wedding!" Giuseppe shouted.

Laughing, Santina threw her arms around Agata. Stella clapped her hands, "Oh, I can't wait to see Domenica as a bride!"

Their spirits uplifted, the following day each worked with newfound hope.

Days flowed into weeks and months. Each morning Maria checked the children's eyes. Stella's conjunctivitis took several weeks to clear up, and as soon as it did, another child caught it. Each setback was discouraging but Maria did not allow them to wallow in self-pity. She found things to lighten the mood: little treats she bought the children or festivals at one of the Churches. Finally, in June, there was no trace of pink eye in any of the children. Maria used the last of their money to purchase tickets for travel on *Prinz Oscar*, which was leaving for New York in July. She wrote to Alfio to let him know.

A letter from Alfio arrived in July with enough money to last them until their departure. Domenica's wedding was two months away. They were all excited about arriving in New York in time for a wedding. After seven months in exile, they were finally going to their new home.

On July 25th they stood on the pier with their belongings. They approached the inspector filling out the ship manifests. Again, they gave their information and were sent to the doctor. The doctor paused at the youngest, four-year-old Maria.

"She has an eye disease. You all need to leave the ship."

Maria tried to argue, but it was no use. The family returned to the boarding house to wait. She would miss her oldest daughter's wedding. The reunion would again be delayed. The money Alfio sent was running out. Maria wondered if she should just return to Pedara.

~ ~ ~

On October 1st, the feast day of St. Therese, there was a loud knock on the door of their room at the boarding house. Maria sighed as she went to the door. Even on a feast day there was no escape from the landlady. Stella and Santina exchanged looks, bracing for yet another yelling match between Mama and the landlady. When Maria opened the door, they all saw it was not a woman but a man.

"Papa!" Giuseppe yelled. Santina and Stella ran to Alfio, smothering him with hugs.

"When did my girls get so big? You're both nearly as tall as I am!"

Stella giggled. "No, we're not!"

Alfio went over to little Maria, who was hiding behind her mother. "Where's my little baby? You were only two when I left." The youngest child wanted nothing to do with the man she considered a stranger. He hugged his wife, whispering, "It is so good to see you. I have missed you so much!"

"How did you know we needed you?" Agata asked.

"When the ship came into port without you a second time, I knew I had to come and bring you back to America myself."

"I knew Papa would help us," Giuseppe told his sisters.

Alfio told them all about Domenica's wedding and showed them photos of the bride and groom. The children commented on how beautiful Domenica looked, how short their new brother-in-law was, and the size of his mustache.

"Never mind all that. Where is he from?" She didn't say more but Alfio understood what Maria really wanted to know. Was he from Sicily? She wouldn't shun her son-in-law if he was from the dreaded northern part of Italy but everyone knew what her preference was. Alfio smiled.

"Can anyone guess?" he asked.

"Not Pedara," Agata said. "No one by that name lived in Pedara."

"No, not Pedara. Try a bit more recent."

Giuseppe frowned. "Naples?"

"No, not Naples. I see no one can guess. He was born in Regalbuto."

First breathing a sigh of relief, Maria's brow then furrowed. "I don't recall ever meeting anyone with that last name while we were in Regalbuto."

"The surname would not sound familiar. He needed to change his last name after arriving in America. There was some trouble back in Sicily. It's all rather vague. He doesn't talk about it because doing so will reveal too much and he doesn't want the people involved to be able to find him."

"Is my daughter in danger?" Maria asked.

"No, none. They will be fine. Domenico is a very careful man. There is no need for concern," Alfio told her. That statement eased the worried mother's mind a bit but not entirely.

Alfio went down to the dock and bought tickets for them from the steamship agent. A ship was leaving in late October. During the weeks in between his arrival in Naples and the family's departure, he made several trips to the dock. One day he came back with a trunk.

"What's in the trunk?" Giuseppe asked his father.

"Just a few things I realized we would need once we're back in New York," Alfio replied. "Things one can only buy here in Italy."

The next weeks were a blur of packing, farewells to the few friends they'd made, and the constant buzz of anticipation.

On the morning of October 22, 1905, the family stood on the pier, their belongings at their feet, watching as the *Prinz Oscar* loomed against the horizon. As they stepped aboard, the ship's horn blasted, a sound that seemed to echo their excitement. The transition from the bustling streets of Naples to the deck of the ship felt natural, as though the city itself urged them onward. The family found their place among the other hopefuls, ready to cross the ocean, their past in Naples now just a memory, with America's promise just within reach.

Everything seemed so much easier now that Alfio was with them. "I couldn't pay for first class tickets for the seven of us. We'll be in steerage like everyone else," Alfio apologized to Maria. "You'll want to try to stay outside as much as possible to breathe in the fresh air. The conditions can get a little…" He trailed off.

Maria put her hand on his arm. "We will manage," she assured him. "All that matters is our family will be together again."

Everyone crowded onto the upper deck. No one was sure where they were supposed to go. Men herded them down the narrow stairs into the lower deck. There were bunk beds lined up on both sides of the deck. In the center were long rows of wooden tables and benches. Everything was clean but Alfio knew it wouldn't remain that way for long. Mist from the water already created a film on the open portholes.

There were over 300 passengers with them. The crew separated the mob, sending single men to one section, single women to another and families to yet a different section. Alfio led the family to a set of beds. They had straw mattresses and blankets on them, provided by the steamship company. The family dumped their bundles of belongings on and around the beds.

No longer burdened with carrying their possessions, Alfio led the family back to the upper deck. They watched as the crew prepared to start their journey. All the crew members moved about with fluid coordination, each knowing where to step and what to do next. When they moved the gangplank away from the ship, a hush spread though the crowded deck. Everyone seemed to be holding their breath, lest something unforeseen prevented them from leaving. The ropes that tied the ship to the dock were untied and tossed up to the crew members who quickly coiled them on the deck. Finally the giant ship began to move and a cheer rose from the crowd. None cheered louder than the little family, at last on their way to America.

The English lessons began before the port was out of sight. Alfio wanted all of his children speaking some English by the time they arrived. "When we arrive in America, you will use American names," he told them. "Agata will be called Agatha, Giuseppe will be Joseph, and little Maria will be called Mary."

"What about us, Papa?" Santina asked.

He turned to her and Stella. "Santina, you will be called Sarah. For you, Stella, there are no English names." None of the children complained about having to change their name but Santina made a face. With the question of names taken care of, he started teaching them some basic phrases. The children were smart and in the two weeks aboard the ship, they quickly mastered the basics.

Maria tried to follow the lessons along with her children but for most of the voyage, she felt too ill. The motion sickness was bad enough but the odor below deck was overwhelming. During good weather the portholes were opened but there was not enough fresh air in the world to compete with the odors of dozens of sick people. The lessons made the time pass quickly for the children but for Maria, the two weeks felt like two years and often she found herself wishing for death to release her from this misery.

Meals were served at the long tables. In the mornings they had coffee with bread and butter. Sometimes, on Sunday, they were treated to cake for breakfast. Dinner was often stews made with boiled meat or fish. Most of the adults didn't eat much because they were seasick and half the food was wasted, thrown overboard into the ocean.

At night, when the children were asleep, Alfio sat with some of the men. They would talk about their plans once in America. The men had many questions for Alfio. "You have been there two years now. Will it be difficult to find work?"

"No," Alfio replied. "There are many jobs. Not like in Sicily. You will work hard but your efforts will be rewarded."

"What is it like to live in New York?"

"I will tell you the truth. At first it will be difficult. You will live in crowded buildings but it will not be for long. In America you can move up in the world. It will not be long before you have saved enough for a house. A big house with more than three tiny rooms.

After only two years I have already saved up half of what we will need to move into a mansion." The men knew Alfio was exaggerating but they didn't mind because they all dreamed of owning their own home even if it wasn't a mansion.

"The buildings are so high, you can touch the clouds if you go to the top. " Alfio continued with his stories of New York. "There are trains and trolleys to travel about the city. Of course there are also horses and carts but there are also motor cars.

One night, as they sat around, Alfio told them about a strange game he had seen. "The boys play a game called stick ball. It's like another game that men play called baseball."

"Baseball?" The men looked at each other, puzzled.

"It's very popular in America," Alfio explained. "My son, Francesco, likes baseball. He took me to see a game once. A bunch of grown men trying to hit a ball with a stick they call a bat, running around bags on the ground called bases…" He shrugged, then tried to mimic the swing of a bat. "We may all have to like baseball if we want to be real Americans."

The men chuckled, trying to imagine such a game. "And do you like this baseball, Alfio?" one asked.

Alfio grinned. "Well, I don't understand it fully, but there's something about the excitement of the crowd, the way they cheer when someone hits the ball far, or when a player slides into one of those bases. It's like a festival, but with rules I can't quite grasp. Maybe one day, I'll get it, or maybe I'll just enjoy watching my son enjoy it.

"The Church in New York near where I live has priests from Italy. We celebrate all the feasts, just like in Sicily. They do not have large piazzas in which to gather, but they process down the streets."

"My brother in New York said to be careful about the Irish. That they beat up the Italians for no reason," one of the men, Antonino said.

"It used to be pretty bad," Alfio agreed. "There were street fights all the time. The Irish don't like us because they say we are taking their jobs. They don't trust us because they can't understand what we're saying when we don't speak in English. It's better than it was when I first arrived, though."

"Were you ever in a fight with one?" Antonino asked. Alfio rolled up his sleeve to show a scar on his arm. "One of them did that to you?"

Alfio smiled. "I never fight with anyone. One day I was walking on a street called Mulberry. I was heading toward another street called Bleecker to meet a friend. A man was crossing the street. He was looking in one direction, waiting for a trolley car to pass by. Still looking at the trolley, he ran across. He didn't see a horse drawn carriage coming in the opposite direction. I ran out, grabbed him, and pulled him out of harm's way. The back of the carriage brushed against me, cutting my arm. It turns out the man was an young Irish fellow named Ian. He was quite appreciative at being saved and now we're friends."

During the trip, Alfio told the men many other stories about his adventures in New York, some of which were true. Alfio kept some stories to himself, stories about what they would face on Ellis Island. There was no sense in causing anyone anxiety. It was better if they didn't walk in knowing what to expect, especially the medical examination they all would be subjected to.

On the morning of Saturday, November 4, the family woke up to bright light streaming in through the portholes. There was excited chatter as everyone ate breakfast. This was the day they were scheduled to arrive in New York. As soon as the family finished eating, Alfio had them gather up their belongings. "Hurry! We are here!" Maria and the children followed him to the upper deck. Everyone else on board was doing the same and people crushed them on all sides as they made their way up the stairs. Joseph wrapped one arm around Santina and the other around Stella, trying to shield his sisters from the pressing crowd. Alfio carried Mary in one arm and his trunk in the other while Maria held his elbow. He whispered to his wife, "Your suffering will soon be over. You will feel better once we are on land."

They all reached the upper deck together and stood in amazement as the steamship made its way into the harbor. There she was! The lady, a towering figure in green, greeting and welcoming them to their new life.

"She's wearing a crown," Santina said. "Is she a princess?"

"I think she might be," Alfio told her. Softly, in accented

English, Alfio said, "Give me your tired, your poor, your huddled masses yearning to breathe free."

The family stood in silence, amid all the commotion around them. Joseph looked at his father. "What did you say? What does that mean?"

Alfio smiled. In Italian, he told his family, "It means we are all at last together and today we begin our new lives."

CHAPTER EIGHT

America

November 4, 1905

The young children learned new lessons in patience as they waited their turn to step aboard the barge that would take them from the steamship to Ellis Island. On the island was a huge building. The center section of the building had large arched windows and domed towers on each corner. That section rose above the smaller sections that stretched on either side.

For the first time in twelve days, the family stepped onto solid ground. Agatha took a couple of steps and then seemed to trip. Alfio caught her by the elbow, steadying her. "Papa, the ground is moving," she told him.

"It's not really moving. Your body just needs some time to adjust. You're used to the rocking of the ship for so many days."

Maria looked at her husband, holding her stomach. "I thought once we were off the ship, I would feel better. How long will this last?"

"Soon it will stop," Alfio told her. "I promise you will feel like yourself before long."

They entered the building and went up the stairs to the second floor. Unknown to the immigrants, their medical inspection was already underway. Inspectors stood watching the people as they ascended the stairs, looking for signs of people who seemed out of breath or suffering from chest pains. On the second floor there were metal grates where everyone stood waiting their turn in front of the medical inspectors.

The crowded room buzzed with conversation making it necessary for Alfio to yell to Maria to be heard above the din. "Stay close to me. I will hold Mary." He scooped up the little girl and they inched their way toward the front of the line. As they drew closer, the loud talking no longer masked the sounds of howls from young children who were being examined. Alfio's children clung to each other, their panic growing with each step. Maria turned to Alfio, a look of concern on her face. "It's the eye exam," he told her. "That is the worst part. After that, everything else will be easy." His words did not offer her any comfort.

When they reached the front of the line, Alfio spoke to his children. "You endured many hardships to arrive in America with such bravery. I am very proud of you all. I need you to be brave one last time. The doctor is going to check your eyes for disease. It will hurt a little bit but I will be right there with each of you. I will hold your hand. I know it sounds scary but it will be over quickly."

Each child went up in turn. As promised, Alfio held their hands and whispered to them. His hand felt like a wrung-out towel by the time the doctor finished with the last child and he flexed his fingers trying to get feeling back into his hand. The children all cried during the exam but only Mary howled and kicked. Her siblings were glad to see a blow land on the doctor's shin. It seemed fair retribution for their suffering.

Once they were done, they were given small cards and went into another room. There was more waiting before they were seen by an immigration official. The information on the cards was checked against the ship records and the inspector asked them the same questions that appeared on the manifest: their age, occupation, where they came from, and who they were staying with.

Three hours later, they left Ellis Island and took a ferry to Manhattan. "Wait here," Alfio told them after they made their way off the ferry. Still carrying his trunk, Alfio approached a man sitting on a bench. Maria saw Alfio take a sack out of the trunk and hand it to the man who then gave Alfio money. Alfio rejoined his family and led them to Sullivan Street, two miles away. Progress was slow as the children stared at all the sights. The streets were crowded with people and various types of vehicles, the buildings were enormous, and the sounds of the city were loud.

They walked along Broadway, alongside what seemed to be a strange steel bridge. Suddenly they heard an unfamiliar, loud rumble from above. The children froze, looking up. Mary began to cry and clung to Maria. Agatha and Santina threw their hands up over their heads and ducked down in anticipation of something falling from above while Joseph and Stella stared up in fascination. Alfio reassured them that everything was okay. "It's just a train. They go all over the city. That's how most people travel from one part to another."

They arrived at the tenement on Sullivan Street and walked up four flights of stairs. "See that door with the number five on it? Go knock on that door," Alfio told Stella. Stella ran to the door with Santina right behind her. Both girls banged on the door. They heard a man's voice.

"Who is there?"

"Francesco, is that you?" Santina asked.

"There's no one here named Francesco," came the reply. "Are you looking for Frank? And maybe someone named Grace and Rose?"

"Yes!" yelled the girls. "Let us in!"

He opened the door and his sisters nearly knocked him over as they threw themselves at him. The rest of the family followed them into the small apartment. There was a joyful reunion as the family greeted each other with hugs and kisses. Domenica immediately went to Mary. Grace commented on how grown up Joseph looked. Maria kept going from Rose to Concetta to Grace to Frank to Domenica, hugging them repeatedly. The separation of over two years was at times unbearable and she was overwhelmed with emotion.

The apartment had two rooms: a main room that served as a kitchen and living area, and one bedroom. A table surrounded by chairs, along with two beds, filled most of the kitchen. A cast iron stove and a basin with a knob were also there. The bedroom had one large bed and two sets of bunk beds.

Agatha pointed to the basin, "What is that?"

"It's a sink," Grace explained.

"A sink?"

Grace turned on the faucet, and the children were amazed at the water flowing out.

"There's water in the house?" Santina asked. "We don't have to go outside to the cistern?"

"It's great, isn't it?" Rose said. "All the water we want, right here in the kitchen. And guess what? There's a water closet in the hall. We don't have to go outside for that, either."

"I like it here in America!" Joseph said.

"Domenica, where is Domenico?" Maria asked.

"He's in our apartment. He thought it best for the family to be alone at first. We will walk over so everyone can meet him," Domenica told her mother. "He calls me Mamie. Everyone here does."

Maria nodded. "So Francesco is Frank, Grazia is Grace, Rosa is Rose, and you are Mamie. What about Concetta?"

"I'm called Connie," Concetta replied. "Even Papa goes by an American name. The Irish call him Alfred."

"These American names... They are not as beautiful as the Italian," Maria said.

"No, they are not," Alfio agreed. "But we are American now."

"I want to meet Domenico," Santina said.

"I have an idea," Alfio replied. He put his hand in his pocket and took out some money which he handed to Mamie. "Rose, go out with Mamie and buy something for dinner. We need to celebrate our reunion. Domenico will come here and we will have a wonderful meal together."

"I want to go, too," Agatha said.

"Okay," Alfio replied. "Connie and Grace will stay here with Mary. Frank and Joseph—you will go to get Domenico and bring him here. The rest of us will go for a walk with Rose and Mamie to shop for groceries."

Stella, Santina, and Agatha followed their older sisters as they walked over to Broome Street. Wagons lined both sides of the street, overflowing with fruits and vegetables, meat and fish. Men called out as they passed, trying to sell their wares. Rose and Mamie stopped at several carts buying meat from one, vegetables from another, and dried fruit from a third.

"There is so much food here!" Stella said. Stella was looking at a cart loaded with sweets and was not watching where she was going. A dirty boy in ragged clothing, clutching a loaf of bread, barreled into her as he ran past, causing her to fall onto the sidewalk. As Santina and Agatha helped her up, a man ran past them, yelling at the boy.

"Stop! Get back here, you thief!"

"There is an abundance of food for people who have money," Mamie told her sisters, "but not everyone has money."

Santina said. "Imagine being so hungry that you are forced to steal. I hope the man doesn't catch him."

A few yards behind, Alfio and Maria followed the girls, Alfio pointing out different sights along the way. Maria enjoyed walking on ground that wasn't moving under her feet and was starting to get her appetite back after two weeks on the ocean. She linked her arm with Alfio's, pulling him close to her. "What was in the sack you took from your trunk?" Maria asked him. "Why did that man give you money?"

Alfio smiled. "Italians who come to America miss certain items: black coffee, their Italian cheeses. I ask people who are making the trip to America to bring these items with them. I reimburse them for their expenses. Then I sell the items here. It's my little import business. Thanks to what I was able to pick up in Naples, we will be having a nice feast tonight."

"Everyone here is speaking Italian," Maria observed.

"Yes, they call this section of Manhattan Little Italy. If you walk that way," Alfio pointed south, "That section is called Chinatown. This is a foreign country with a foreign language. New people like to live with others who come from the same country. It makes everything…" Alfio searched for the right word. "Less scary. Everyone is far away from their home, their family. They are excited about starting a new life, but it's good to have some things that are familiar."

The sky was darkening as they walked back to Sullivan Street and the setting sun reflected onto the windows of the tenements making them glow orange. They entered the building and climbed the stairs to their apartment.

Mary was in the bedroom, playing with an improvised doll Connie and Grace had made for her. Maria sent the younger girls into the bedroom to watch Mary, relieving Connie and Grace, who then joined Rose and Mamie in preparing dinner.

Frank and Joseph were sitting at the table with a man Maria assumed was Domenico. Domenico rose from his seat as Maria entered the apartment and the brothers did the same. They remained standing while Maria set her daughters to their tasks. Alfio and Maria walked over to the table. "Mama, this is Domenico," Frank said. Domenico put out his hand to shake Maria's. She looked at his outstretched hand.

"Is this the way men greet their mothers-in-law in America?" she asked him. "With a handshake?"

Domenico pulled his hand back to his side, looking from Maria to Alfio. "I'm sorry," he mumbled. "I didn't mean to insult you. I've never had a mother-in-law before."

Maria grabbed her new son-in-law by the shoulders and pulled him toward her, kissing him on both cheeks. Alfio was trying not to laugh. He didn't succeed. "We are family now," Maria told Domenico. "You don't shake hands with family." Maria sat down and the men did the same. "How old are you?"

"Thirty-three."

"You are quite a bit older than Domenica," Maria told him.

"Mamie," her oldest daughter whispered from where she stood by the stove.

"Yes, Mamie. It will take some time getting used to all these new names," Maria said. She then returned to her questions. "Do you have any other family here?"

"My younger brother, Angelo is here in New York. He is twenty."

"What do you do for a living?"

"I am a grocer."

Now Maria came to the most important question. "Do you go to Church?"

"Of course!" came the response.

Maria nodded. "Tomorrow you and your brother will come with us to Church. We will all go together." It was clear this was a statement and not a request. Domenico agreed.

"Dinner is ready," Connie announced. Domenico smiled in relief. Once they were all eating, the questions would stop.

Once all the dishes were placed on the table, brimming with food, everyone looked at Alfio. He made the sign of the cross and everyone else did the same. "Father, we thank you for keeping us safe on our journey and for bringing us all back together. Thank you for the meal we are about to eat. Please bless us and this bounty of food. We thank you for all you have given us, especially the gift of family. Amen."

Everyone helped themselves to meat, fish, bread and vegetables. Alfio poured wine for everyone over the age of ten. Santina looked at her father. "Don't I get wine?"

"Do you want some, Sarah?" Alfio asked Santina, trying out an American version of her name, as he held the wine bottle over her glass.

Santina made a face. "I don't want to drink it. I just wanted to be treated like an adult. And I don't like that name."

Agatha nodded. "And I don't want to be called Agatha."

"It's not much different than Agata. It's practically the same," Santina said.

"I want a more American sounding name. Joseph and Frank are both so American."

"What do you want to be called?" Santina asked.

"I don't know yet. I need to think about it." Agatha turned her attention back to the food in front of her.

Maria looked around the table at her children and husband, a smile on her face. The two years spent apart vanished. She had dreamed every day of the time they would be reunited and now here they were, all together, having their first meal as a family in America. Every once in a while, she found herself brushing away tears.

"Mama, why are you crying," Stella asked. "Are you sad?"

"No, my sweet girl. They are tears of joy because I am so happy." Stella frowned at the odd notion of crying because you were happy. She looked at Santina who shrugged. Maria caught the exchange and laughed. Then she turned to her oldest children. "I want to hear about your time here in New York, your jobs, your adventures."

Frank laughed. "It was quite an adventure getting stuck in the snow in January. There was a blizzard."

"What's a blizzard?" Agatha asked.

"It's when the snow comes down so fast and the wind blows so hard that you can't see anything. All you see is white," Frank said, his eyes widening. "The wind was so bad, people were knocked down. There was snow in piles higher than even the tallest man. The trolley tracks were frozen. You couldn't see the street. Everything was slippery and covered in ice."

"How did you get stuck?" Stella asked, leaning in.

"I learned to drive a car when I first arrived in New York. I work as a cab driver for Mr. Smithe. He asked me to drive a man to Times Square. I told him it would be dangerous with the snow. His car just has a little roof—it's pretty useless against a blizzard. But Mr. Smithe is stubborn, even more than Papa." His siblings laughed, looking at Alfio who chuckled.

"So I get the car out of the garage. The man I have to pick up is on the other side of the block. I have to drive around. The wheels are spinning, unable to grip the road. Finally, I get onto what I think is the street. Everything's covered in snow, looking the same. The car's bumping and sliding when suddenly—BAM! I hit something. I don't know what, maybe a cart someone abandoned. After hitting it, the car spins around in the snow and ends up in a drift. I'm covered in snow, so cold. I had to walk to where the man was waiting to tell him what happened. Then I had to dig the car out and get it back into the garage. I thought Mr. Smithe was going to fire me, but he was just glad the car wasn't damaged."

"That sounds so scary," Stella said.

"No, it doesn't," Joseph replied. "It sounds like a fun adventure. Imagine that much snow! We can make a lot of granita with all that snow."

Alfio laughed. "Trust me, Joseph. When it is that cold out, you will not want to eat granita."

Joseph looked unconvinced. "I could eat granita every single day for breakfast, lunch, and dinner."

"If you had it all the time, it would not be special," Maria said. Turning to the oldest girls, she asked, "And what about you? Were you involved in any adventures?"

"No," Rose said. "We try to avoid adventures." Grace, Mamie, and Connie nodded in agreement. "We had enough adventures getting to America. For now I am content with going to the factory each day to make dresses and coming home each evening."

Dinner was over and the family lingered at the table eating dried fruit and nuts. Alfio rose from the table and came back with a paper sack. He opened it, removing its contents, putting them on a plate. Mary stared at the cookies her father placed there. "Mama, is today a holiday?"

"It is not a holiday but for us, it is a special day. We are a family again," Maria told her as she handed out the cookies.

Agatha looked around the small room and spotted a small pamphlet. "What is that?" she asked.

Frank turned to see what she was pointing at. "Oh, that's a Playbill. It's from one of the Broadway shows. I picked up a passenger from there and he gave me the Playbill to read so I can improve my English."

Agatha leafed through it. She couldn't read English yet. Turning to a random page, she asked Frank, "What does this say?"

"That's a list of the cast in the show, the people who perform." He started reading a couple of the names when Agatha stopped him.

"What was that word you just said? Was that a name?"

"Which one? John?"

"No."

"Katie?"

"Yes!" Agatha said. "Is that a name for a woman?"

"Yes, it is. It's usually short for Catherine, like St. Catherine of Alexandria."

"I like that name," Agatha said. She repeated the name to herself, growing more and more fond of it.

The day was a long one and Maria was getting tired, but did not want to send the family to bed just yet. She couldn't bear to part from any of her children, but when Mary fell asleep sitting at the table, she realized it was time for bed. Domenico and Mamie left for their apartment on Thompson Street, a block away. Francesco had his own apartment in the same building on Sullivan Street. The four youngest girls slept on the two beds in the kitchen and the rest of the family went to sleep in the bedroom.

The children all fell asleep quickly. Maria was certain she would lie awake, her mind replaying every event of this momentous day, but exhaustion overtook her. As she drifted to sleep, she felt Alfio's hand find hers under the covers, squeezing gently. In that simple touch, she found reassurance that despite, the vast ocean they had crossed and the strange new world they now inhabited, some things remained unchanged. Their family, though stretched and reshaped by distance and time, was whole again.

Outside, the city's ceaseless noise continued, a constant reminder of the bustling life that awaited them. But within the walls of their small apartment, for this one night, peace reigned. Maria's last thought before sleep claimed her was a silent prayer of gratitude, her heart full, knowing that tomorrow would be the beginning of a new chapter, not just for her, but for all of them.

Back Row: Agata (Katie), Concetta (Connie), Francesco (Frank), Rosa (Rose), Domenica (Mamie), Grazie (Grace)
Front Row: Santina, Maria, Maria (Mary), Alfio, Giuseppe (Joe), Stella (sitting on the floor) Circa 1906

CHAPTER NINE

Fever

February 1907

Santina, Stella, and Mary were walking home from school with several other girls who all lived on Thompson Street. Behind them, a group of about seven boys followed, keeping their distance from the girls. The boys talked loud enough to make sure the girls knew they were there, joking and teasing one another. "Hey, Ralph, I hear you failed your math test again," one boy yelled.

The boy whose name seemed to be Ralph shouted back, "That's not true! It was Louie."

The first voice called out, "Hey, Peter! Catch!" Peter missed the ball that was thrown at him and it hit Mary who picked it up and threw it into the street. The boys yelled in protest and one dodged wagons and cars to retrieve it.

"Why must boys be so troublesome?" Mary muttered.

"They're just looking for attention," Stella remarked.

"Well I don't want their attention."

One of the girls, Pauline, laughed. "You're only in first grade. I'm pretty sure it's Santina and Stella's attention they want."

Mary didn't reply but her footsteps became louder as she stomped along the sidewalk.

"What's wrong, Mary?" Santina asked.

"Nothing."

Another girl, Laura, joined the conversation. "Mary's best

friend had to leave school early."

"Liz?" Stella asked. "Why? What happened?"

"She's sick," Mary told her sisters. An outbreak of scarlet fever recently hit two of the nearby schools. Mary overheard the adults discussing that and she was worried about her friend.

"It's probably just a bad cold," Santina said. "Don't worry. I bet she's back in school by the end of the week." The girls continued their walk home, their chatter slowly fading as they each retreated into their thoughts. Mary couldn't shake the worry about Liz, while Santina was already planning how she'd tackle her homework.

They arrived home, where they were greeted by Maria. "Sit down and get started on your homework." Mamie, who was five months pregnant, was there as well. Their father and the rest of their siblings were out at work. The three girls sat at the table with Mamie and opened their books. Mary and Santina started their work right away but Stella was telling her mom and sister all about her day at school.

"Pauline got in trouble again for talking. I got all of my math equations right. Two of the older boys got into a fight in the schoolyard and were sent to the principal's office. There's going to be a spelling bee tomorrow. Lizzie was sent home because she's sick. Rocco said the fifth grade is getting a new teacher."

"Okay," Maria said, laughing, "That's enough talking. Get to work, Stella."

Mamie left for her own apartment and the three girls continued their schoolwork until dinner time.

That night, Mary tossed and turned, her sleep restless. By morning, she felt like her throat was on fire. Stella ran to her mother who sat at the kitchen drinking coffee. "Mary is sick!"

Maria went into the room to find Mary buried under blankets, shivering.

"Mama, my throat hurts," Mary whispered.

Maria put a hand on Mary's forehead, her own breath catching at the heat radiating from her daughter. Walking into the kitchen, Maria took a small basin and filled it with a mixture of cool water and rubbing alcohol. Taking a small rag, she stepped back into the bedroom. Pulling a chair next to the bed, Maria soaked the rag in the cold mixture, and put the rag on Mary's head, trying to cool her fever. All day, Maria moved between the stove, stirring a pot of soup, to Mary's bedside, coaxing spoonfuls of broth past her lips, then back to the basin to refresh the cold cloths on Mary's forehead.

The following morning, both Stella and Santina had sore throats with a fever, and Mary had a red rash. The older children were gone already, but Alfio still lingered over coffee, his mind drifting to his daughter, Grace, who had suffered from a fever that brought swelling and pain in the joints years ago. The memory made his heart heavy with worry.

"Go for the doctor. The girls are sick," Maria urged, her voice tinged with the same fear that had haunted them during Grace's illness. Alfio hurried out the door and came back with the doctor.

The doctor told Maria and Alfio to wait in the kitchen while he went into the bedroom to examine the girls. After he was done with the girls, he returned to the kitchen looking concerned and sat at the table with Maria and Alfio. "The youngest has a fever with a bright red rash. The other two may come down with it, as well. Do you have other children?"

"Yes," Maria told him, her eyes darting to Alfio with shared concern. "There are five more."

"The girls need to be isolated. Find somewhere to send the others. Only their mother should stay here." Alfio and Maria nodded, the weight of their past experience with illness making this directive all the more ominous. "I am leaving you some fever powder for them," the doctor said, placing some packets onto the table. "Continue to use the cold rags to help bring down the fever." He rose from the table. "This apartment will be under quarantine. You need to leave with me," the doctor told Alfio. He picked up his black bag and waited for Alfio to follow him out of the apartment.

"What are the arrangements for the others?" Alfio asked Maria.

"Connie, Rose, Grace, and Katie can stay with Mamie," Maria told Alfio, using Agatha's new preferred name now that she'd convinced the family to call her Katie.

"I will visit the dress factory on my way to work and tell them to go to Mamie's apartment," Alfio said. "What about Joseph?"

"Send him to stay with Frank. You should also stay there."

Alfio nodded and followed the doctor out. The doctor put a quarantine sign on the door and walked away. With his hand on the doorknob, Alfio caught Maria's eye. "Do not be afraid. God is with us." Softly he closed the door.

Maria watched the door close with a click. The specter of the fever, which made Grace so ill, now loomed over their family once more.

Three weeks later, all three girls seemed fully recovered. The doctor came to examine them and declared they were no longer contagious. The doctor told Maria to disinfect the entire apartment, especially their clothing, before allowing the rest of the family to return.

They were all together in time for Palm Sunday. Everyone was excited about the upcoming Easter celebration. Easter would be especially sweet this year after their long Lent, filled with illness and fear. Laughter and relieved sighs filled the room as each girl, now healthy, joined the others, their faces bright with the joy of recovery. Alfio was certain the girls were better because of his wife's excellent caretaking.

Easter morning came, bright and summer-like. The week before, Alfio bought all the children new outfits and everyone was getting ready for Mass, dressing in their new clothing. Maria looked around the kitchen. "Where is Santina?"

"I guess she's still getting ready," Grace said.

Maria went into the bedroom. Santina was in bed. "Mama, I don't feel good." She grimaced in pain.

"Where does it hurt?" Maria asked.

"My knees, my arms. Even my chest hurts."

Maria pulled back the sheet. Santina's knees looked swollen and red. Her elbows and wrists were also red but not nearly as swollen. Worried, Maria put a hand to Santina's forehead which was hot. Maria returned to the kitchen. "Take the children and go to Church but send for the doctor on your way."

"What's wrong?" Alfio asked. Maria just shook her head without responding and her panic spread to Alfio. "Come," he ordered his other children. "We must leave right away." With that he walked out the door, the rest of them scrambling to follow. Maria closed the door behind the last of them and leaned on it for a minute, her head sagging. Then she went back into the bedroom and sat on the bed next to Santina waiting for the doctor to arrive.

The doctor arrived at last, examined Santina, and then led Maria into the kitchen. "She has a fever that brings swelling and pain in the joints. You don't need to worry about anyone else because it won't spread but you need to keep a close eye on her. It's concerning that she has chest pains, but I listened to her heart and everything sounded normal." He started pulling items from his bag. "This is a salicylate. You will give this to her six times a day. That will help with the fever and the pain. Afterward, make sure she drinks milk. You will also give her sodium bicarbonate once a day. Both should help her avoid stomach irritation. Make sure she drinks a lot of water throughout the day."

He placed a bottle of ointment on the table. "Use this on her joints and then wrap them in cotton." He held up another item. "This is fly-blister. Place these on her chest. Let her rest as much as possible. Once she starts to feel better, she is to remain in bed for another three weeks."

"How long will she be sick?" Maria asked.

The doctor sighed. "There's no way to know. I've seen cases that resolve in a few weeks. I've seen others where it lasted several months."

"Is she in danger of dying?"

"There is no immediate danger. This is a serious illness, but she is young and she is strong," came the response. It was not what Maria wanted to hear. She wanted reassurance, for him to say there was no danger at all.

The doctor left and Maria returned to Santina's side. "Mama, I've ruined Easter."

Maria brushed strands of hair away from her daughter's face. "No, you did not. The doctor left some medicine for you. You'll be better quickly." After Santina took the medication and drank the glass of milk her mother handed her, Maria started applying ointment to her joints, wrapping them as the doctor instructed her. When she was done, she sat there holding her daughter's hand until the girl feel asleep. Then she took out her Rosary and started praying.

That afternoon the family gathered in the kitchen for their

Easter meal. Alfio went into the bedroom to see Santina. "Do you feel well enough to sit with the family?"

"Papa, I am so tired. And it hurts to walk."

"I can carry you inside."

Santina shook her head. "I don't think I can sit up."

Dinner was subdued. Family members took turns going into the bedroom to talk to Santina and to try to coax her to eat. She refused the macaroni, the bread, and the meat. Only Katie managed to persuade her to take a couple of bites of the Easter cake. Joseph tried to make her laugh by telling her she looked like a mummy all wrapped up in bandages but all she could manage was a weak smile.

As weeks slipped into months, the view out the bedroom window gave no indication of the changing seasons, only of light or darkness, rain or sunshine. Santina slept a lot and waited impatiently for this illness to leave her. Each morning and evening the family gathered around Santina's bed to pray. In the afternoons, when everyone was either at work or school, Maria sat with Santina and said the Rosary. On the weekdays, Mary and Stella came home with schoolwork for Santina so she wouldn't fall behind in her lessons. Either Katie or Joseph would sit with her and help her with any new material that she was unfamiliar with.

As May brought warmer weather, Santina's strength slowly returned. On one of his monthly visits, the doctor told Maria to have Santina sit out on the fire escape for some fresh air. "But only on warm, sunny days," he said. On warm afternoons, Alfio would carry Santina out the window where she would sit on the steel platform. Clothes hung from every section of the fire escapes, their own and each neighboring building. Peering through the tangle of hanging clothing, she looked down into the street. Children ran on the sidewalk, playing games. Women went from wagon to wagon, baskets dangling from their arms as they shopped. Men hurried along the crowded sidewalks on their way to or from work. Horse-drawn wagons and motor cars rolled along the cobblestone. Further down, Santina could see trolley cars and hear the rumble of trains making their way overhead.

Her parents only allowed her to sit outside for an hour and that hour seemed to pass faster as the days grew longer. Each day as Alfio carried her back inside, she begged to stay just a little longer and the reply was the same. "Not this time. I don't want you to catch a chill." Santina wondered if she would ever feel well enough to run again and play with her friends.

It was the first week in June when Santina started to feel better. Her joints no longer ached and she was eating more. The doctor came to check on her and was pleased with her progress. "You need to eat so you regain your strength. I want you to start walking a bit, but no stairs or anything strenuous."

Maria was standing on the other side of the bed, opposite the doctor. Smiling, she told her daughter, "I will make all of your favorite dishes. You will be strong again in no time!"

The doctor pulled out his stethoscope and listened to Santina's heart. The doctor paused, his fingers tightening slightly around the stethoscope. His eyes, previously scanning the room casually, now fixed intently on Santina's chest. He moved the stethoscope back to the same spot, listened again, then shifted it slightly. A flicker of something, concern, perhaps, passed over the doctor's face, but it was gone as quickly as it came, replaced by his usual composed demeanor.

Maria's smile faded. "What's wrong?"

He cleared his throat. "We'll need to be very careful with her activity. Rest is crucial now," he said, not quite meeting Maria's eyes. He turned to look at Santina. "You will want to go out and play with your friends. I know you are tired of being in bed, but you must have a little more patience. I want you to stay inside for three more weeks. Your heart needs to rest even if you feel like running. This is very important. You do everything your mother tells you to do. Do you understand?"

Stating the obvious was not necessary. Santina always did what her mother told her to do. It would never occur to her to disobey, but she nodded. "Yes."

That evening, Santina insisted on sitting at the table for dinner with the rest of the family. Joseph helped her slowly walk to the table. Stella and Katie started clapping with Mary quickly joining in. Santina put a hand to her chest and said, "Oh, I feel just like a movie star!" Everyone laughed, then silence fell as Alfio said grace. Immediately following the prayer, chatter and laughter filled the room. Even though it was a weekday, the evening had the feeling of a holiday with even Mamie and Domenico joining them.

Mamie, with her growing belly, took a seat carefully, her movements a bit more deliberate than usual. Domenico, ever attentive, pushed her chair in gently, his hand lingering on her shoulder with a protective touch.

"Frank is courting a new girl," Rose told the family.

Connie rolled her eyes. "He always has girls going after him. I can't believe how forward the girls are in New York."

"I hope none of my daughters are ill mannered like that!" Alfio said. His daughters all assured him they were raised to behave like ladies.

"Anyway," Rose continued, "This time he pursued her. She's pretty and she seems nice. Her name is Jennie."

"And what about that boy who keeps staring at you?" Grace said to Rose.

"What boy?" Rose replied, her face turning red.

"Giacomo," Connie said. "We all noticed how he looks at you. He's supposed to be working downstairs with the tailor but always finds an excuse to come upstairs where we're working."

"No he doesn't," Rose replied.

"Yes he does, Rose. There's no sense in pretending he doesn't," Katie said. "I wish someone would look at me like that."

"Oh, Katie. You're only fifteen. You'll have boys swooning over you before you know it." Grace attempted to comfort her sister.

"No I won't," Katie replied. "I'm not beautiful like you."

Of the five oldest girls, Grace was the most beautiful. Boys were giving her unwanted attention from the time she was young but she was only interested in one man. She had a crush on Domenico's brother, Angelo, from the first time she met him. Grace was fascinated by the tattoos Angelo had on his arms. She had never known anyone with tattoos before. He was short, only a little over five feet, but she was just as short so that didn't concern her. What did concern her was how shy he seemed. She was worried he would never get around to courting her but she was prepared to wait for as long as it took him.

Halfway through the meal, Mamie shifted uncomfortably in her seat, her hand resting on her belly. "This little one is quite active tonight," she remarked, smiling at Santina who watched with a mix of curiosity and anticipation.

Santina, noticing Mamie's discomfort, asked, "Is it always like that?"

"More and more these days," Mamie replied, her face lighting up with maternal pride.

The conversation around the table continued, but Santina grew quiet, no longer joining the conversations around her. Her eating had slowed. Glancing over at her, Maria said, "This was too much excitement for you. We should not have allowed you out of bed."

"No, Mama. It was wonderful. I'm just getting tired."

"Joseph, help your sister back to bed," Alfio said.

"But Papa, I want to stay here. It is so good to be out of the bedroom and sitting with you all," Santina protested as Joseph rose from the table.

"You need to rest. You were very ill. I'll move the bed closer to the door so you will be close to us," Alfio told her. He got up and adjusted the bed. Then he and Joseph helped Santina back to bed where they propped her up with pillows and blankets. "There," her father said, "You are not far away. And with each day, you will get stronger and spend more time sitting up."

Mamie came into the bedroom and sat on the bed next to Santina. "The baby wants to say hello to Aunt Sarah," Mamie told her sister. "Look at how he's moving around!"

"I don't want to be called Sarah. And you don't know if the baby's a boy," Santina said as she watched the bump on Mamie's stomach move from one side to the other.

"I think Sarah is a nice name," Domenica said. "And of course we don't know if the baby is a boy. I'm just guessing because the baby moves around so much." Mamie took Santina's hand and placed it on her belly.

"You're right! I can't wait to hold her."

"Or him," Domenico added from where he stood in the doorway, a huge grin on his face.

Mamie went to stand up but sunk back into the bed. She attempted a second time. She looked over at Domenico who was laughing. Waving her arm in the air, she scolded him, "Come help me get up!" He walked over, still laughing, and helped her to her feet.

Looking down at her sister, Mamie said, "Rest now. We are so glad you're finally feeling better! Soon this baby will be born and you will be well enough to celebrate with us."

Santina smiled. "It's so exciting!" Domenico and Mamie left the room. Santina thought to herself, "I'll just close my eyes for a minute and rest." A few minutes later, Maria went into the room to see if Santina wanted coffee but Santina was asleep.

CHAPTER TEN

Brooklyn

1916

"I have an important announcement!" It was a late Friday night in early June, hours after everyone had arrived home from work and had dinner. The family was getting ready for bed. Everyone looked at Alfio who had a huge grin on his face. Joseph, Santina, Stella, and Mary looked from their father to their mother. Maria was also smiling. "I've bought a house. We are moving to Brooklyn!"

"Our own house?" Joseph asked.

"Yes," Maria said. "With three bedrooms and two other apartments to rent!"

"Mama," Santina said, "How did you keep such a secret from us? Surely you've known for months!"

Maria smiled. "It was difficult but I gave Papa my word. He wished to surprise you all."

"But you're not one for secrets," Stella remarked to her mother.

"Indeed," Maria agreed. "But this was different. None of you ever asked about living anywhere but this tenement. Brooklyn or a house never came up in conversation."

Joseph chuckled. "If only I had known the right questions to ask!"

"We will go out there tomorrow so you can all see the new house," Alfio informed them.

Sleep did not come easily to any of them that night. The teenagers and young adults were too excited, talking about their new house until well after midnight. Their parents didn't bother trying to silence their children. Instead, they held hands, smiling in the dark as they listened to the conversations around them. Eventually weariness overtook them all and the apartment was silent.

The following morning, Alfio and Maria traveled to the house on 70th Street in Brooklyn with Joseph, Santina, Stella, and Mary. Grace, who was married to Domenico's brother, Angelo, already lived in Brooklyn and met the family at the new house. Rose and Connie, along with their husbands, Giacomo and Sal, made the trip to Brooklyn, as well.

They all gathered on the sidewalk, staring at the three-story house in front of them. The house was smaller than the ones on either side but it seemed like a mansion to the family. The first story was brick. There was a covered porch running the entire length of the front of the house. Three windows faced the street on the second floor and one arched window faced the street on the top floor.

A stone wall about three feet high stood like a miniature fort in front of the property with a metal gate in the center. Alfio walked over to the gate and opened it. He took Maria's hand and led her up the walkway and up the porch steps to the front door. The rest of the family followed behind. None of them spoke, fearful that any sound might wake them from this dream.

As they entered the house, they saw a stairway on the right leading to the upstairs apartment. To the left was a hallway. The first room on the left was the living room. It faced the front of the house and was larger than their combination living room/dining room in the tenement. The living room opened into a large dining room. Then they followed Maria and Alfio into the kitchen. Maria walked into the center of the kitchen and froze in stunned amazement. Then she turned to Alfio. "It's beautiful! Imagine the feasts we'll have!"

In the kitchen was another door that led to stairs going up to the other apartments and down to the basement, as well as a door that led outside. After they were done exploring the kitchen, they went toward the back of the house where the bedrooms were. There were three bedrooms and a bathroom in between the first bedroom and the rear two bedrooms.

"No more sharing a bathroom with everyone on the floor!" Joseph said.

Stella laughed. "Well, you'll still have to share with Mama, Papa, and the three of us."

"Look how big the bedrooms are!" Mary said.

They all went upstairs where there was a similar layout with three bedrooms, kitchen, living room, and dining room. The attic had a small apartment with a large bedroom, kitchen, living room, and bathroom.

"When do we move in?" Joseph asked.

"At the end of the month," Alfio told them. "I have ordered furniture that will arrive next week. Then everything will be ready."

Maria hugged him. "I can't wait. It is perfect."

"We will be so happy here!" Santina said.

The sun was making its way west, signaling it was time to leave. They parted, each traveling back to their homes. As Alfio and Maria walked up to their third-floor tenement apartment, Maria said, "I will not miss all these stairs!"

A month later, Maria closed the door behind the priest who had just blessed their new home. She returned to the living room and sat on her new chair. Stretching out her hand, she caressed the leather cover of the Bible on the table beside her, a link not only to her faith but to her family, her mother.

Alfio sat in his new chair, next to hers. Their house was full. All of their children and their spouses were there. Maria held the newest grandchild, Frank and Jennie's daughter. Across from her, sitting on the couch, Santina and Stella each held one of their nieces. Around them, the other six grandchildren explored the new house. Connie and Sal's son, Joseph, led his cousins upstairs to where he lived with his parents. He was anxious to show them his new bedroom. Their footsteps pounded on the stairs as they ran, Connie on their heels to make sure they behaved.

Maria was overcome with a joy she did not know was possible. Turning to Alfio, she said, "You were right."

"About what?"

"Coming to America. Our grandchildren have a future here, possibilities they never could have in Pedara or Regalbuto."

Alfio looked around at his children and grandchildren and smiled. "Yes," he agreed. "Our grandchildren will have a good life here."

~ ~ ~

The year that followed was a blur of family gatherings and holidays in their new home. The following year, on a Sunday afternoon in July, the family sat around the dining room table in Maria and Alfio's home for dinner. Maria looked around the table as her family helped themselves to macaroni and meatballs. Seeing the smile on her face, Alfio said, "It's hard to believe we've been here for a year already, isn't it?"

"Yes." She watched Mamie breaking a meatball into small pieces for little Mimi. Connie cradled three-month-old Tina in one arm while eating with her free hand. Rose chatted with Stella and Mary as her husband, Giacomo debated politics with Joe, while Santina listened to them, a smile on her face. Maria looked back at Alfio. "God has blessed us."

As they were finishing their meal, Mamie turned to Domenico and smiled. He nodded to her, his smile matching hers. "Mama, we have something to tell you. We're expecting again."

While congratulations burst from most of the family members, Santina glanced at Rose with a mix of empathy and concern. Rose's mind raced, each congratulatory word like a dagger, "It's not fair!" she thought. "They already have four children. All I want is a child of my own. Why am I being punished?" Rose's hands, clenched into tight fists on the table, trembled slightly. Her eyes glistened and her face, which had momentarily drained of color, now flushed a deep red, spreading from her cheeks down her neck. Suddenly, she pushed her chair back from the table with such force that it screeched against the floor, and she ran from the room. Giacomo, his face etched with worry, jumped up and ran after her. The back door slammed behind them, echoing through the now silent room as the remaining family members awkwardly glanced at one another.

Tension hung over the room as the women started clearing off the table and washing dishes. Giacomo returned to the dining room. "I'm sorry," he told his in-laws. "I'm going to take Rose home."

Maria rose and went to him. "I know how hard this is on you and Rose—to see everyone else having children while you struggle in vain," she whispered. "I know how badly my Rose longs to be a mother. I pray for this every day."

Giacomo didn't respond. He simply hugged his mother-in-law and quietly left the house. Maria stared at his back, tears in her eyes. Brushing the tears from her face, she turned around and went into the kitchen to help clean up.

Late that night, Alfio woke to find himself alone in bed. Getting up, he quietly walked down the hallway and into the kitchen where he saw Maria sitting at the table, her hands cradled around a cup of tea, her eyes red. "You're worried about Rose." Alfio said it as a statement of fact.

Maria looked up and nodded. "Rose is in so much anguish. I can't bear to see her in so much pain. She is desperate for a child of her own. Mamie already has four. Rose and Giacomo will be good parents and will be able to provide for a child."

"You're right. And Mamie and Domenico really can't afford another child right now."

Maria stared into her cup of tea, her mind racing as she tried to find a solution. A thought came to her, an idea that both shocked her for even thinking of it and yet one she was sure would solve everything. Barely above a whisper, she began saying, "Do you think we can ask Mamie to…" She couldn't complete the sentence. "How can I even think that?" she thought. "To exchange one daughter's pain for another? But surely Mamie can find comfort in the children she already has. And she can always have more." She shook her head, afraid to give voice to her thoughts. Alfio, however, seemed to read her mind.

"Mamie and Domenico can give the baby to Rose."

Maria's eyes widened in shock at hearing her thoughts expressed out loud. "That would bring such joy to Rose but how can we ask Mamie to give up her child?"

"They've been married for nine years now. It's apparent this is their only hope. If the child is a girl, they will give the baby to Rose and Giacomo. It would be best this way. That is my decision. Come back to bed now." He held his hand out to Maria.

"I'll be there shortly. Go. Don't let me keep you awake." Alfio returned to bed but Maria sat there in the kitchen, now with a new worry on her mind.

The following evening, Domenico and Mamie, Rose and Giacomo all sat in their parents' living room wondering why they were summoned there on a weekday. Maria had sent Santina, Stella, and Mary to babysit Domenico and Mamie's other children, and the house was empty except for the two couples.

Maria cleared her throat, her hands nervously twisting in her lap as her eyes darted around the room, avoiding Mamie and Domenico. "There's something important we need to discuss."

Alfio spoke, his voice steady but carrying the weight of his decision. "Yesterday, your mother and I had a long talk about family and what it means to support each other. We all know Rose and Giacomo have been waiting in vain for a child for years."

Rose's eyes welled up, but she nodded, squeezing Giacomo's hand.

"Mamie, Domenico," Alfio turned to face them directly, "You have been blessed with children, and while every child is a blessing, we understand that resources are stretched thin for you."

Mamie's eyes widened, her hands instinctively moving to her still flat stomach, a protective gesture. Domenico looked between Alfio and Maria, his face a mask of growing realization and concern.

"I have decided that, if the child is a girl," Alfio continued, "You will give the baby to Rose and Giacomo to raise."

Rose gasped, a mix of hope and sadness crossing her features. Giacomo looked at the floor, his jaw clenched. Mamie's eyes filled with tears, her hand covering her mouth.

"How can we do such a thing?" Domenico's voice was low, strained with emotion.

Maria reached out, her voice breaking, "I know, I know how this sounds. But think of Rose's pain, think of all our pain. It could be a solution where everyone gains something."

The room felt charged with a sudden stillness, the kind where every breath seems loud.

~ ~ ~

As the months went by and Mamie grew larger, Rose hid herself, refusing to leave her house. Even the family gatherings for the holidays were not exempt from her self-imposed exile. If the child Mamie carried was a boy, Rose didn't think she could handle yet another disappointment.

In late February 1918, Mamie went into labor. Santina and Stella brought the news to Rose, who slumped onto the couch. She put her hands over her face and her sisters could see tears leaking between her fingers. Santina looked at Stella. "We can't leave Rose to sit here alone. We should stay." Stella nodded and they sat down on either side of their sister, waiting for further news.

"What if the child is a boy?" Rose's voice cracked. Stella hugged her sister but remained silent.

Santina took a Rosary from her purse. "Why don't we pray while we wait?" The three women began praying, their voices barely above a whisper.

Maria was with Mamie for the birth. Domenico and Alfio waited outside, both pacing along the sidewalk in front of the house. Rose's husband, Giacomo, sat on the curb nearby, his head in his hands. This baby's birth would either destroy his wife or fulfill her dream of motherhood. He prayed he wouldn't need to break news to her that would crush her.

When the midwife approached the house, Alfio stopped her. "The women inside, they do not speak English. Come out here to me after the birth and I will write down the information for you: the names of the parents, their ages, whatever other information is necessary."

Several hours later, the midwife approached Alfio. "The baby was born, a girl." Upon hearing this, Giacomo leapt to his feet and joined Alfio while Domenico ran inside to his wife. "What are the parents' names?" the midwife asked.

"The mother is Rose Primavita and the father is Giacomo Savoni," Alfio told her. He gave the midwife their ages and answered her questions. Then the midwife asked for the name of the little girl.

"Vincenza," Giacomo told her.

The midwife looked from Alfio to Giacomo and back to Alfio.

"Yes," Alfio told her. "The baby's name is Vincenza."

Alfio went into the house. Giacomo didn't follow him. He couldn't bear to face Mamie and Domenico. Maria sat in the living room, holding the baby. Domenico was in the bedroom with his wife, trying to console her. Alfio could hear her crying and did not enter the bedroom. He walked over to Maria. "Giacomo is waiting outside. Take the baby and go with him to Rose."

She wrapped the baby in blankets and went outside to Giacomo. Together they went to bring the infant to Rose. The two of them made a solemn little procession. Maria was happy for Rose and Giacomo but that happiness was tempered by her sorrow for Mamie's loss. Giacomo was relieved to have good news for his wife and overjoyed at having a child of his own, but there was an underlying guilt because he was responsible for Domenico and Mamie's grief. He tried to shove those thoughts of their pain from his mind.

Rose and Giacomo called the baby Zina, and the couple felt like their family was at last complete. There was still an awkwardness whenever the family was together for dinner at Alfio and Maria's house but everyone pretended things was perfectly normal. At first, Mamie and Domenico didn't attend family dinners because it was too painful for them to see little Zina. After several months of Maria begging them to come, they relented and joined the rest of their family. On each occasion that Mamie was with Zina, she doted on the little girl the entire time; each evening after they had parted, she cried herself to sleep.

~ ~ ~

One Sunday afternoon in October, the family gathered at the Primavita house. Dinner was over and the women were making coffee and putting dessert on the table.

"Papa, have you seen the newspapers today?" Frank asked.

"About the war?" Alfio asked.

"No," Frank replied. "The influenza. The newspapers are saying it's spreading."

Alfio shrugged. "We have no control over illness. Our family is strong, though. Look at how Santina recovered from that terrible fever that caused her joints to swell. She's fine now. We will all be fine."

Santina glanced at her father and then quickly looked away. She never told anyone about the shortness of breath she sometimes suffered from or the exhaustion from simple tasks. Her mother taught her to offer up her sufferings as penance and so she bore them all in silence.

The newspapers reported on the Spanish flu daily but continued to insist it was not a pandemic in spite of the growing number of cases. In September, the five oldest grandchildren returned to school. The following Sunday the family gathered in Maria and Alfio's house for dinner after Mass.

Maria, Rose, and Mamie were in the kitchen, preparing dinner. Mamie stood at the stove, stirring the gravy. The children were sitting at the kitchen table, talking and sneaking pieces of Italian bread as their grandmother cut the loaves. When the cousins began discussing their classmates who were ill, Mamie put the spoon down, suddenly feeling nauseous. Mamie left the kitchen and sat down next to Domenico at the dining room table. "There were many children absent from school yesterday," she told her husband.

"They may not be sick," he replied. "Maybe their parents kept them home from school because they are afraid. In other states they shut the schools down, but the health commissioner in New York said that's not necessary. I'm sure the officials know what's best."

The following Friday, Freddy woke up with a fever. Mamie called her oldest daughter to her. "I want you to pack up a few things and go with Vito and Mimi to Nonna's house." Two-year-old Mimi was heading toward Freddy with a piece of bread. Mamie scooped her up and held the squirming child. "You can't bother Freddy right now. He needs to rest. You're going with Vito and Josie to Nonna's house."

Vito, Josie, and Mimi arrived at their grandparents' house.

"Freddy's sick. Mama thinks it's from school," Vito reported.

"I'm sure he'll recover soon," Maria soothed. "It's wise your mother sent you here. We'll stay in the attic to keep distance from everyone." She ushered them upstairs.

Josie, the eldest, realized the intent. "I'd hate to bring the Spanish flu to our aunts," she noted as they climbed.

"Pray you don't fall ill," Maria encouraged. "We'll make soup and have fun up here, just us." Her tone was light, hiding her worry.

Alfio appeared at the attic door. "What's happening?" he asked.

"Mamie believes Freddy has the flu. She sent the kids here for safety," Maria explained. "I'll stay with them until we're sure they're not sick. I'm also concerned about Grace's Josephine; she's in Freddy's class."

"I will walk over to their house and check on her," Alfio told Maria. Alfio returned home with the news that Grace's daughter was sick, as well.

"They won't be able to leave the house," Santina said. "How can we help them?"

"We will bring them groceries," Stella said. "We can leave them outside the door so we won't be near them."

Her sisters agreed with the plan. Each day Mary, Stella, and Santina went out, first to Mamie's house and then to Grace's, leaving groceries outside their homes. They knocked and took several steps back when the door opened. They brought news to each of their sisters about how the rest of the family was. Mamie was grateful that none of her other children were sick.

Five days later, when Grace came to the door, it was apparent that she was ill.

Mary walked closer and put a hand to Grace's forehead. "You have a fever. You need to get to bed," she ordered her older sister. Turning to Stella and Santina, Mary continued, "I will stay here and take care of Grace and Josephine."

"We will stay, too," Santina said, starting to approach.

Mary held up her hand to stop her sister. "No! Do you think I haven't noticed how easily you tire? You never fully recovered from that terrible fever. And Stella, you need to be at home in case anyone else comes down with this. Mama will need your help."

Stella and Santina tried to argue with their strong-willed younger sister but were unsuccessful. Mary closed the door and her sisters left for home.

A week after first catching the Spanish flu, Vito's fever broke, and the following day, Josephine's did as well. Grace didn't recover as quickly. The days dragged on and Grace started coughing. "You need to take her to the hospital," Mary told Angelo.

"No. We can take care of her here," Angelo insisted. "People go to the hospital to die. Grace will recover."

"She can't breathe. We can't help her here at home. Grace needs to go to the hospital," Mary insisted.

Angelo took her to the hospital where he wasn't permitted to enter. He said goodbye to his wife and watched as she disappeared into the building. Angelo turned to leave, his jaw clenched so hard he wondered if his teeth would crack. He dragged himself along the sidewalk toward his home, head bowed and shoulders slumped. Three days later, his greatest fear turned to reality when the hospital told him Grace died.

~ ~ ~

Through tears that blurred her vision, Maria took one last look at her daughter's grave. As everyone started out of the cemetery, Maria put her hand on Alfio's arm, holding him back. She waited for the others to walk out of earshot and said to Alfio, "Josephine is only eight. Angelo will need help. We can't leave the two of them on their own."

"Yes," Alfio agreed. "They will come to live with us." That was exactly what Maria hoped her husband would say.

Following the burial, the family gathered at Maria's house. They sat at the table staring at the food their friends and neighbors had prepared. No one had any appetite. The women sat weeping. The men nibbled, pushing the food around on their plates, and avoided eye contact with the women and each other. As night fell, one by one each family left to go home. Connie and Sal were the last to leave. Connie hugged Angelo and Josephine, tears streaming down her face. Then the couple, along with their two children, left, going upstairs to their apartment. Only Angelo and Josephine were left.

"You will move in here with us and take the apartment in the attic," Alfio stated. Angelo nodded.

"Stay here tonight," Maria told him. "Tomorrow we will go with you over to your apartment to gather up your belongings."

Angelo nodded again. "Thank you," he said. "I don't think I can…" He broke off in mid-sentence. To continue would mean he would lose control and cry. He didn't want his daughter or his father-in-law to see him break down.

Part Two

Wedding Homily

You are about to enter upon a union which is most sacred and most serious. It is most sacred, because it was established by God himself. By it, he gave to man a share in the greatest work of creation, the work of the continuation of the human race. And in this way he sanctified human love and enabled man and woman to help each other live as children of God, by sharing a common life under his fatherly care.

Because God himself is thus its author, marriage is of its very nature a holy institution, requiring of those who enter into it a complete and unreserved giving of self. But Christ our Lord added to the holiness of marriage an even deeper meaning and a higher beauty. He referred to the love of marriage to describe his own love for his Church.

May, then, this love with which you join your hands and hearts today never fail, but grow deeper and stronger as the years go on. And if true love and the unselfish spirit of perfect sacrifice guide your every action, you can expect the greatest measure of earthly happiness that may be allotted to man in this vale of tears. The rest is in the hands of God.

Excerpts from the **Tridentine Roman Ritual**

CHAPTER ELEVEN

Mario

March 1923

Arm in arm, the two sisters carefully made their way down the brick steps of their house and walked along the slushy Brooklyn sidewalk. Near the corner, the usual little group of men stood around outside a building, smoking and waiting for exactly 8 a.m. before stepping inside. The sisters exchanged a quick glance, their decision unspoken but clear. They crossed the street, a routine maneuver to steer clear of the men's attention, as they did every weekday morning. As they passed, one of the men yelled across to them, just as he did each morning. "Buongiorno!"

Every once in a while another voice would rise, hushing the first one. "They are not interested in you. They cross to avoid you. Leave them alone."

Mary glared at the men. Santina looked down, avoiding any eye contact with them, tugging on Mary's arm to hurry her along. Slipping in the slush, Mary turned her glare toward Santina as both of them caught their balance and avoided falling.

"That would have made a nice scene for them if we both landed on the sidewalk," Mary said.

"Lucky we're so agile!" Santina replied with a slight smile, disarming her sister's annoyance. They continued their journey to the clothing factory where they both worked. As the building came into sight, Santina remembered her father's stern face as he asked the foreman about fire escapes, his mind haunted by the Triangle Factory Fire they had all witnessed. Twelve years ago, in 1911, when the family still lived in Manhattan, they were horrified by the tragic fire at the Triangle Shirtwaist Company factory. Nearly 150 souls perished in that fire because they were unable to get out of the factory when the fire started. The family lived on Thompson Street at the time, just five blocks away.

The short walk to the factory commenced without further mishap and the women took their places among the rows of machines, joining the other Italian immigrants. Here they sat, working and talking with the other women, five days a week.

The following Sunday, Santina and Mary walked along 14th Avenue toward St. Rosalia's Church. Maria and Alfio were about a block behind them, walking at a slower pace than the girls. It was barely above freezing and windy. The combination of temperature and wind made their eyes tear as Santina and Mary crossed 64th Street. They clutched their veils, which were around their necks like scarves, to keep them from blowing away.

As they stepped onto the curb at the other side, a man's hat, blown by a gust of wind, crashed into Santina's knees and landed at her feet. Bending to pick it up, she didn't see the hat's owner until she straightened up and found herself staring through round glasses into a pair of gray eyes. Santina noticed his square face framed by a small mustache, and his dark hair brushed straight back. The man smiled.

"I was on my way to Church when all of a sudden, a pigeon swooped down and grabbed my hat right off my head. Can you believe that? Of course the hat was too heavy and the bird dropped it, but it seems like he chose to drop it right in front of you just so we could meet!"

Mary rolled her eyes at the obvious tall tale but Santina smiled and handed the hat back to the man. Something about the man seemed vaguely familiar, but Santina was certain she had never met him before. Perhaps she had just seen him here at Church another time.

At that moment, Maria and Alfio joined them. Realizing they were the parents, the man turned to them. "Good morning! I am Mario Patrizio. Your daughter just saved my hat from certain disaster by rescuing it before it could be crushed beneath the wheels of a truck. I am forever in her debt." Mario then turned to an older woman standing a few feet away with a young couple, an infant and another young woman. Walking over to the older woman, he took her by the arm, gently leading her to the Primavita family and introduced her. "This is my mother, Francesca Patrizio."

"A pleasure to meet you. I am Alfio Primavita," Alfio said, addressing Francesca. He didn't quite know what to make of the exuberant man, so he chose to speak to Francesca. "This is my wife, Maria, and my daughters, Sarah and Mary."

"Santina," Maria whispered, a quiet reminder that their daughter didn't want to be called Sarah.

"Mary and Santina," Alfio corrected himself. "Now if you will excuse us, we were just on our way to Church."

"Likewise!" Mario said. "I hope we shall run into each other on the way out."

"You may want to hold onto your hat next time," Mary told him.

"I'm pretty sure I do not want to do that. I much prefer retrieving it from a beautiful woman." Mario smiled at Santina. Then he took his mother's arm and joined the rest of his family as they entered the Church.

Santina looked at Mary and said, "He's an interesting man." Mary shrugged in response. They put their veils on and climbed the steps into the Church. They genuflected and sat in their usual pew on the right-hand side, five pews back from the altar, toward the middle aisle. The familiar scent of wax and the rhythmic clicking of Rosary beads washed over Santina, bringing a sense of calm.

During the Mass, Santina found herself distracted by Mary who was sitting next to her. Mary seemed annoyed about something, huffing in exasperation throughout the Mass. When they exited the Church, Santina turned to her sister. "Are you okay? Is something wrong?"

"He is what's wrong." Mary nodded her head toward Mario who was helping his mother down the steps of the Church. "He was staring at us throughout the entire Mass instead of paying attention."

Santina laughed. "Had you been paying attention yourself, you wouldn't have noticed him. I'm sure you just imagined it."

Mary scowled. "I did not imagine it and he's heading our way now."

Mario approached with a huge smile on his face. "Will you be attending the feast for St. Joseph tomorrow?"

"Of course," Santina replied.

"She will probably be up at dawn baking bread for the tables," Mary added.

"Wonderful! I will be sure to arrive early before all of your bread is snatched up. I am certain it will be better than anyone else's."

Mary turned to Santina after Mario left. "He's too old for you and he's trying just a little too hard."

"We have no idea how old he is and trying hard is not a bad quality. Besides, he may be interested in you over me and is just trying to get on my good side before throwing himself at you." Of the three youngest daughters, men usually gave all their attention to Stella and Santina, tending to ignore Mary. Now that Stella was married, that left Santina as the one their attention was focused on. To her credit, Mary was not jealous of her older sisters and tended to be overly critical of all men, not just her sisters' suitors.

~ ~ ~

The following day the Primavita family returned to Church, carrying baskets filled with freshly baked bread. The usual outdoor procession for St. Joseph's Day was canceled due to the relentless rain, so they descended into the church basement, where the air was cooler and slightly musty. Inside, a bustling scene met their eyes: men were setting up a majestic three-tiered table, adorned with white linens, for the feast. Santina and Mary carefully arranged their loaves among the offerings.

The heavy door at the top of the stairs opened, and Mario appeared, his shoulders squared under the weight of the St. Joseph statue, alongside other men. They navigated the narrow steps with care, the statue's ornate frame catching the dim light. Everyone naturally parted, creating a path to the table. With a collective heave, they positioned St. Joseph at the summit of the third tier, his serene gaze overlooking the feast. Father Appo, following closely behind, his robes swishing softly, said prayers of blessing over the food, his voice mingling with the scent of fresh bread and sweet desserts.

After the blessing, the crowd surged forward, plates in hand, selecting from the bounty of bread, ripe fruit, sharp cheeses, and sweet desserts. In one corner, an elderly man, his face weathered but joyful, settled into a wooden chair with his accordion. As he began to play, the familiar strains of Italian folk tunes filled the room, rising above the clatter of dishes and the laughter of children. Conversations quickly escalated in volume, with everyone speaking in Italian, the words flowing rich with the accents of their homeland.

The basement was initially cold, but the crowd soon warmed it up so much that some people started taking off their heavy coats. People gathered in groups of five or six people, some drifting from group to group, others only leaving their friends to take food from the table. Santina and Mary gathered with their own friends close to the food. Alfio and Maria stood with their friends toward the back of the room, talking and eating. A man broke off from talking to Alfio, walking toward them, and Santina realized it was Mario.

"Good afternoon, Santina! May I ask which bread is yours? Anything touched by your hands will be far sweeter than anything else on the table. I ask only for my sister, Marietta. She deserves the best."

Santina could not contain a smile and it broke free, lighting up her face. In response, Mario broke into a wide grin. Mary, however, was the one who responded. "Ah, so you are selfless and only looking to tend to your sister?"

"I cannot lie. Yes, my sister will be first but I want the bread myself, as well."

"I noticed you were talking to our parents," Mary said.

"Of course. I wouldn't dare speak to a beautiful woman without permission from her parents."

"That didn't seem to stop you yesterday," Mary told him.

"Ah, yes, but that was a hat emergency. Common courtesy required me to thank the woman who rescued my hat."

"So you've asked permission to court my sister?" Mary

demanded.

Mario looked at Santina. "I did ask your parents, but I would not proceed unless I had Santina's permission, as well."

"That's something in his favor, anyway," Mary told Santina.

Santina nodded and spoke for the first time. "Ultimately the decision is not mine, but let us get to know one another." She noticed her parents talking with Mario's mother and a young couple, the woman cradling an infant in her arms. Mario followed her gaze.

"That is my sister, Marietta, her husband, and my new niece. I'm certain they are telling your parents all about what an honorable, religious, hard-working, and trustworthy man I am. They will say anything just to get me out of the house as they need the room for all the children they will have."

As they looked at their parents, they could see Mario's mother becoming increasingly agitated. They could hear her call out, "Dov'è Giuseppe?" At first Santina thought the distraught woman was praying to St. Joseph and looking for the statue, but with repeated cries, it became clear she was looking for someone named Giuseppe. Mario's face completely transformed from cheerful to sorrow as he hurried to Francesca's side, putting his arm around her.

"Mama, Giuseppe is not here. He is in heaven with Papa."

"No!" Francesca became angry. "He is not dead! He is here!" She threw off Mario's arm. Marietta and her husband, Victor, were also trying to calm Francesca down with no success. Their youngest sister, Adeline, reached the group.

"Mama, come with me. We will see if we can find Giuseppe." Her mother calmed down immediately and took Adeline's arm. Together they started walking around the room.

"I am so sorry for the disruption," Mario told Alfio and Maria.

"No need for apologies," Maria told him. "We understand."

"Our brother, Giuseppe, was in the army and was killed in 1917," Mario explained. "We lost our father, Orazio, seven years earlier. Then, when Giuseppe died, Mama was never the same."

Santina said in a whisper, her voice unable to speak normally, "We lost my sister, Grace, to the Spanish flu. We know what it is like to lose a brother or sister when they are so young."

Mario longed to put his arm around her to comfort her but knew such a gesture of familiarity, especially this early in the courtship, would put him in the bad graces of Santina's family so he simply said, "I am sorry." It seemed such an unhelpful phrase.

"No family was left untouched by that scourge," Alfio said. "So many loved ones were taken way too early." The celebration had taken a sober turn. Then the infant, Geraldine, started to cry. "Our mood is affecting the little one. We must put aside our pain and be happy because God has blessed us all. We are here to celebrate St. Joseph so let us be happy."

The two families separated and Santina stood talking to Mary and Maria. Mary was talking, but no words registered as Santina watched the Patrizio family. Little Geraldine was still crying. Mario took her from Marietta and began making silly faces at the girl. After a few minutes, Geraldine stopped crying and began to giggle. "Santina!" Hearing her sister's raised voice, she turned to see her mother and Mary staring at her. "You're not listening to me," Mary said. "I asked you what you thought of Natalie's cake."

Santina looked down at her plate at the untouched piece of sponge cake. She smiled and tasted the cake. "Not as good as yours."

Dusk enveloped Brooklyn as the Primavita family said their goodbyes and started walking home. Alfio walked ahead with Mary but Maria put her hand on Santina's arm, motioning to let her husband and other daughter get further ahead. When the two were out of earshot, Maria asked Santina, "How do you feel about this man, Mario?"

"I'm not sure," Santina answered. "He is funny and seems kind. It is obvious he loves his family and is attentive to them, especially to his mother."

Maria nodded. "I tried speaking to his mother, Francesca, but she drifts a bit in and out of reality. It is so sad. His sisters seem to think very highly of him. They told us he worked as an electrician in a factory when they lived in the Bronx. Now he is a mechanic, fixing sewing machines. He works right down the block from us."

"That's why he seemed familiar right from the start!" Santina exclaimed. "I have heard his voice before. He is the man who sometimes tries to get the other one to leave us alone when we pass by in the mornings."

"He spoke to your father and asked for permission to court you so the two of you can get to know one another." Maria paused. "That was unexpected. I thought he would immediately ask to marry you. He seems to respect your wishes and wants your approval for marriage."

Santina smiled. "That's a good thing, isn't it?"

"He's a likable man," Maria said. "Mario is very loyal to his family and his faith seems very important to him. Otherwise he wouldn't have taken a workday off to attend today's feast. Your father thinks he is suitable. I do have some reservations because of his age. He's 40, twelve years older than you."

"I'm 28 myself, I'm not a young girl anymore. In an ideal world, perhaps someone closer to my age would be preferable, but we know the world is not ideal. Perhaps this is the perfect man for me in spite of our age difference. It's not as if he's Papa's age."

Maria laughed. "No, he's not old like your parents. We will get together with his family and all get to know each other. We have invited them to join us for dinner next week on Palm Sunday."

~ ~ ~

Two weeks later, the Patrizio family joined the Primavitas for dinner. Mario came with his mother, two of his sisters, brother-in-law and little niece. Maria didn't want to overwhelm their company with a large crowd so there were only those still living at home besides herself and Alfio: Santina, Mary, and Joseph.

Joseph squinted at his sister's suitor, his lips pressed together as he shook Mario's hand. Mario smiled. "I looked at Victor the same way when he was courting my sister," he said, indicating the couple with the baby. "No one was good enough for Marietta, but Victor proved himself worthy and I will, as well."

"We will see," Joe replied.

"You work down the block," Mary said. "Santina and I see you in the mornings."

"Yes," Mario replied.

"I don't remember seeing you there until recently. I don't recall seeing you in Church before, either. My sister cannot marry someone who doesn't attend Church every Sunday." Mary sat back in her chair, arms crossed while she waited for a response.

"I am at Mass every single Sunday and, if time permits, during the week, as well. We just moved to Brooklyn from the Bronx two weeks ago. I found a job here a few months ago while we looked for a suitable house. The search took a while." He tried to read Mary's expression to see if his explanation was acceptable but her face revealed nothing other than mild hostility.

"Our family is very protective of one another," Maria told Mario.

"Good!" Francesca said. "That means this is a good family, just like ours. We also take care of our family." Francesca was having a good day and seemed to enjoy the company. She joined in the conversation, asking about Santina's birthplace, background, and various other questions to make sure this woman was suitable for her oldest son.

"Did Santina cook this meal?" Francesca asked as she helped herself to more macaroni.

"Yes," Maria said. "She made everything here."

"Good! My son is used to having excellent food." Francesca helped herself to a hunk of pork that fell apart as she attempted to spear it with a fork. Switching to a spoon, she scooped it into her dish along with a generous helping of gravy.

"She likes your gravy," Mario's sister, Marietta, whispered to Santina. "That's a good sign!"

Mario overheard the comment. "Of course she does! Everything Santina made is delicious."

"I will teach you how to cook macaroni with sardines and prawns." Francesca shook her head sadly. "People who grow up far from the ocean just don't know how to cook fish properly." She looked at Santina. "It's not your fault. I will teach you!"

After ascertaining that her son would be well fed if he married this woman, Francesca turned to Marietta. "Let me hold Geraldine," she said, holding out her arms for the infant. She had no further questions for Santina and her parents. It was now Alfio's turn.

"You are 40 years old. Why did you never marry?" he asked Mario.

"I worked long hours when we lived in Italy. I didn't have time to court anyone."

"He took care of our father when Papa became ill. Mama couldn't handle it alone. When Papa died, Mario supported the rest of us. He worked as a mechanic. He can fix any machine," Marietta added.

"Your English is not very good," Alfio said. "How long have you lived in NY?"

"We arrived only four years ago," Mario replied. "My sister, Jennie, arrived in America first, along with her husband, Peter. Then we sent our younger brothers. I was the last one to arrive along with Mama, Marietta, and Adeline. I haven't been here long enough to speak it well but I am learning more English every day. This is my country now and I plan to apply for citizenship."

"My grandchildren are all American. They will all speak English."

"Of course they will," Mario agreed.

Alfio nodded. There were more questions from both families over dessert. As the Patrizio family parted, Mario and Alfio solemnly shook hands. "We will have dinner again," Alfio told Mario.

When they were alone, Maria turned to Santina. "They will find no fault with my little saint," she told her daughter. "He is getting the better end of this deal. Do you want to marry this man?"

"He seems nice," Santina said. "I'd like to get to know him better. Has he asked permission to marry me yet?"

"He has not asked, but I think he will soon. Papa is inclined to give his approval." Santina was silent. Maria put a hand to Santina's cheek. She lifted her eyes to look into her mother's. "He would only give his blessing if it is what you want, as well."

Santina smiled and nodded in agreement. "I'm not in love with him but I know in my heart he would make a good husband and father."

"Give it time. I thought I was in love with Papa when we first were married but I learned over the years that there was much to learn about love. Our love grew over the years and when I look back on our courtship, I realize I knew nothing about love. It is so much more than a feeling in here." Maria placed her hand over her heart. "Pray and give it time. You will know if Mario is the right man."

~ ~ ~

Over the next several weeks, the two families often had dinner together. The questions between the families decreased as the number of shared meals increased. One Sunday dinner included Stella and her family. Stella and Mario took turns trying to top each other with wildly exaggerated stories that had the rest of the family members laughing to the point of tears. Santina pushed herself from the table, wiping away tears and gasping for breath. "I'll be right back."

Stella followed her sister as Santina stepped out onto the front porch. "I just need to catch my breath. I'm not sure which of you is the better storyteller," Santina said.

"I am, of course!" Taking a step back, Stella grew serious and studied her sister. "You're in love with him."

"I never could keep anything from you. It's funny. A few weeks ago, Mama asked me if I was in love with Mario. I told her no. Then suddenly that changed. I wasn't even aware of when it happened. The more time I spent with Mario, the more I began looking forward to seeing him."

Feigning a stern look, Stella asked, "Is he good enough for my sister?"

Santina smiled. "He is kind and respectful. And he makes me laugh. Yes, he will be a good husband."

Stella threw her arms around Santina. "I'm so happy for you!"

In early May, Santina came home from work and was greeted by Maria when she walked into the kitchen. "You received a letter in the mail," Maria told her. Reaching into her apron pocket, she pulled out an envelope and handed it to her daughter.

Santina took the letter from her mother, glancing at the return address before opening it. It was from Mario. She frowned as she sat down at the table. "Why did he send me a letter?" she wondered to herself. "What could he not bear to say in person? It must be bad news." Her hands trembled a little as she opened the envelope.

Then a slight smile appeared on her face when she realized it was a poem.

Brave is my heart, yet it suffers.
Because you are not always near.
And my soul offers itself to you,
Oh my Santuzza, divine fairy.

Santuzza, I cry and love you more.
Why are you still far from me?
I hope with all my heart
that soon you will be close to me, my destiny.

Santuzza, your innocent gaze
Tells me always one sweet word.
I hope, I love, I adore incessantly
Even from afar, my thoughts are with you alone.

After reading Mario's heartfelt poem, Santina found herself pondering his words daily. When Pentecost Sunday arrived, it seemed only natural that Mario would approach her parents to ask their permission to marry Santina, his poem a preamble to this moment. With their blessing secured, Mario approached Santina. Kneeling before her, with tears in his eyes, he said, "Santuzza, would you make me the happiest man in the world by consenting to marry me?"

Brama il mio cuore, e ne soffre
Perché non t'ho sempre vicina
E l'anima mia che a te si offre
O Santuzza mia fata d'arina

Santuzza io piango, e più t'amo
Perché ancora mi sei lontana?
Io spero o mio amore, lo bramo
Che fra breve sarai vicina o mia fortuna

Santuzzo, il tuo sguardo innocente
mi dice sempre una dolce parola,
Spera, ama, adoro incessantemente
Se lontana io sono, il pensiero a te volo

CHAPTER TWELVE

Wedding

June 24, 1923

"Mario, there's a spot on those shoes. You can't stand at the altar like that!" Francesca scolded her son. Mario looked down at his shoes. They were so shiny he could see his reflection in them, but he obediently buffed at the invisible mark seen only by his mother. He presented them to her for inspection. "Much better!" she announced before changing topics. "You are receiving a sacrament today. Did you go to confession?" Bart, sitting opposite his mother, smirked at his older brother.

"Of course, Mama," Mario replied. "I went yesterday." He paused, then added, "So did Santina."

"Of course she went," Francesca said. "You're the one I have to keep an eye on. Men..." She shook her head and then held up her Rosary to show him. "I pray every day for my boys."

Mario's youngest and oldest sisters, Adeline and Jennie, sat at the kitchen table on either side of their mother. "What about us?" Adeline teased.

Francesca waved her hand at her daughter, "Don't be silly. You know I pray for all of you." Her daughters smiled. Their mother was more lucid this morning than usual. It was as if they had their mother of years ago back with them. Francesca turned her attention back to the groom. "I hope you will have many children. Make sure they know all our traditions from Sicilia, our heritage."

"Of course, Mama."

"I will pray for you both every day. Remember, the Madonna watches over marriages. Keep her close to your heart. A strong faith will see you through any troubles that come to you in life."

Mario smiled. "Yes, Mama."

The newspaper was spread out in front of Adeline. "It's going to be hotter today than it was yesterday," she announced.

"It's already hot out!" her brother, Diego, came into the kitchen with Jennie's husband, following behind him. Both men had beads of sweat covering their foreheads.

"Did you pick up the flowers?" Jennie asked them.

"We did," Diego said as he dragged a handkerchief across his brow to mop up the sweat. "Marietta told us to put them down in the cellar because it's cooler there."

Jennie nodded her approval.

Footsteps pounded on the stairs from Marietta's second floor apartment and the door to the kitchen burst open. Mario's nieces and nephews stomped into the kitchen, the older girls failing in their attempts to keep the younger boys quiet.

"Shush!" the oldest niece, Frances scolded them. "The baby is napping. You're going to wake her up."

The last to come down the stairs and enter the kitchen was twelve-year-old Mona, Jennie's daughter. An only child, she found the noise and commotion of so many children a little overwhelming. She stood in a corner of the kitchen, listening to the boisterous conversations around her.

"Do we need to get ready for the wedding yet?"

Adeline said, "No, it's early. There is plenty of time before we need to be at the Church."

"It's a good thing it's not raining out today," Mario said.

"I thought rain on your wedding day meant good luck," Frances told her uncle.

"Ah, but I'm already lucky because a beautiful woman agreed to marry me. I don't need any rain to bring me more luck. If it was raining, there may be lightning and thunder. Did you ever hear the story of Uncle Vincenzo?"

"No," the children all replied.

"One Sunday Uncle Vincenzo was in Church for Mass. It was a

very hot day, just like today. The windows were opened in the Church so that a breeze could get in. The priest didn't want people fainting from the heat. Suddenly a terrible storm rolled into the area. Lightning was flashing and loud thunder shook the Church. Lightning came in through the open window and it circled Uncle Vincenzo's feet, going around and around. He was so scared, he died of a heart attack right there in Church."

"How terrible," Frances gasped.

"He was not a very nice man," Mario told her. "I think he was being punished for living a bad life." He turned to the boys. "That's why I always try to be nice, especially during a thunder storm."

"If it's not going to rain today, can we go play outside," the boys asked, bored with the company of adults and girls.

Diego waved his hand at the door. "Go on, but don't get dirty." The boys ran outside and the room grew quieter.

The adults passed the next few hours sipping coffee and talking, the sounds of children shouting outside came in through the open window. Adeline glanced at the clock and saw it was nearing two. She folded the newspaper as Jennie cleared away the coffee cups that still sat on the table. Francesca, who sat dozing in her chair, suddenly woke with a start. "It's time to get ready!" she announced. Looking at her son, she added, "You can't be late for your own wedding."

Mona left the kitchen and walked down the hallway toward her grandmother's bedroom with Frances following behind her. They were both in the bridal party and their dresses were laid out on Francesca's bed. "Are you nervous about the wedding?" Mona asked, her voice barely rising above a whisper as she tucked a strand of hair behind her ear.

"A little," Frances replied. "Everyone will be staring at us when we walk down the aisle."

"Don't look at the people while you're walking," Mona advised, her words slow and careful. "Just look straight ahead at the altar. If you concentrate on that, you won't even notice everyone. Besides, it's just family." She said this while fiddling with a button on her dress. When Mona complained to her mother about her discomfort with being in the bridal party, her mother explained what an honor this was. The words Mona told her cousin were what Jennie told her daughter.

"It's not just our family. The other family will be there too. They're strangers." Frances was unconvinced.

"Aunt Santina was here with all of us yesterday. She's so nice. I bet her sisters are nice, too," Mona said. Jennie entered the bedroom and put an arm around each girl.

"It's time to get ready. Let's take these dresses and go upstairs." Suddenly the Patrizio household went from a relaxed atmosphere to frenzied activity as everyone went off in different directions: the girls, carrying their dresses, went upstairs, the men gathered around Mario. The house was filled with the sounds of footsteps dashing about, the swishing of dresses, and the rattle of belts being buckled.

Mario felt a knot tighten in his stomach, not just from nerves but from the weight of knowing he would be responsible for another person. Self-doubt surged as he wondered if he was good enough for her. He picked up his hairbrush which slipped from his hand, falling onto the floor.

"Feeling a little nervous?" Diego asked.

"No," Mario lied, as he wiped his sweaty hands on his pants.

Bart laughed and clapped Mario's shoulder. "Don't worry. As best man, it's my job to make sure everything goes smoothly. Everything will be fine."

"How can I feel nervous on the happiest day of my life," Mario mused to himself. "Is this just a dream? Will I wake up in my bed, alone, and discover that Santina doesn't exist?" He tried to clear his mind but his thoughts started spinning out of control. "What if Santina wakes up this morning and realizes she is marrying an old man? What if she leaves me standing at the altar?" Inhaling deeply, Mario closed his eyes for a moment to calm himself as he prayed to St. Michael for deliverance from the unbidden thoughts. Then he turned to his brother. "Okay, let's finish getting ready. I have a wedding to get to!"

~ ~ ~

Young children ran about both floors of the house on 70th Street, yelling and laughing. All were dressed in their Sunday clothes except for the girls chosen for the bridal party, who wore white dresses made especially for this occasion. Five-year-old Vincenza, who was called Zina, sat at the kitchen table where her mother had placed her.

"Mommy, I want to play," she complained.

Rose bent down so she was at eye level with the little girl. "Zina, you have a very important job today. You and Nan are part of the bridal party for Aunt Santina. You will have lots of time to play after the wedding. We have to make sure your dress stays clean and doesn't get wrinkled."

Concetta, who the family called Nan, nodded. "Don't worry, Zina. They won't have as much fun without us. And wait until they see us walking down the aisle in Church! All the girls will wish they were in the bridal party, too."

Nan's mother, Connie, tended to an enormous pot of gravy on the stove. Both kitchens in the house were a flurry of activity as the sisters prepared for the reception that was to follow the wedding ceremony. Connie and her husband, along with their three children lived in the upstairs apartment where Connie and Rose were now busy at work. Rose browned meatballs and sausage, gently placing them into the pot of gravy.

Mamie and Katie were downstairs, in Maria's kitchen preparing the vegetables, chicken and antipasto. Joseph poked his head into the kitchen. "It sure smells good in here! My sisters are the best cooks in all of America."

"If you're trying to sweet talk us into giving you a taste, you're wasting your time," Katie told her brother. Mamie waved a wooden spoon at Joseph with a menacing look on her face. Joseph backed up.

"Okay, okay. You can't blame a guy for trying." He walked backwards into the living room, keeping an eye on the wooden spoon as he departed. Suddenly he felt a crash as he walked into Mamie's son, Alfred. Joseph spun around. "Are you okay?" he asked his nephew as Alfred picked himself up from the floor.

Alfred laughed. "I'm fine. You got in trouble with Mama, didn't you?"

Joseph pretended to be insulted. "I am on my best behavior today!"

Joseph's fiancée, Rosie, looked up at Joseph. "Why don't I believe you?" she asked, laughing.

Rosie and Stella were watching the youngest children, keeping them out of the way of the cooks. As it neared 4 p.m., Stella went upstairs and walked into the kitchen, four-month-old Joseph in her arms. "Look at the two of you!" she said to her nieces. "Those dresses are beautiful!" Turning to Rose, Stella said, "Would you mind holding Joseph? I want to check on Santina."

Rose eagerly held out her arms, a smile on her face. "Give me that precious boy!"

Stella walked down the hallway and peeked into each of the three bedrooms. Santina was nowhere to be found. Retracing her steps, Stella walked back through the kitchen and into the dining room and then the living room. Still not finding Santina, Stella turned to Alfio who sat in the living room. "Have you seen Santina?"

"I think she's sitting outside."

Stella went out and saw her sister sitting in a chair on the front porch. "Are you having second thoughts?" Stella teased her sister.

Santina smiled. "I tried to help Mama but I've been banished from the kitchen. Mama forbids me to do any work today."

Sitting next to her sister, Stella nodded in agreement. "There will be enough work for you once you're married and start having lots of babies. You should enjoy your last day of leisure." From inside, they could hear Mary calling for Stella. "I guess there's no leisure time for me. Let me go help your maid of honor and then we'll help you get ready." Springing up, Stella departed, leaving Santina alone with her thoughts.

A smile on her face, Santina thought about her new life, just hours away. "I cannot wait to hold our baby in my arms," she thought. She imagined a house full of children, her husband coming home from work, their family seated around the kitchen table for meals. Her thoughts were interrupted by calls from her sisters and mother saying it was time for the bride to get dressed. She went into the house, still smiling.

An hour later, the house was suddenly quiet as most of the family left for St. Rosalia. The only ones remaining behind were Alfio, Maria, Joseph, and Mary.

Santina stood in her bedroom, wearing her wedding dress. Maria worked on ensuring the hat and veil were securely in place. Satisfied, Maria stepped back and exclaimed, "Mia bella bambina!"

"English, Mama," Santina said, pretending not to understand.

Maria hugged her daughter. "My beautiful baby!" she repeated in English. They walked into the living room where the rest of the family awaited.

"Your brother has a surprise for you," Alfio told Santina.

"What is it?"

"Look outside."

She looked out the window and saw Frank. He stood by the curb dressed in his best suit. Next to him, parked at the curb, was his boss' car. Turning to Alfio, Santina said, "What is he doing with the car?"

"His boss told him to borrow it for the day. You will not walk to Church today!"

Santina moved away from the window, back to her father. "I have something for you," Alfio told her. He took out a small piece of cloth. It was the cloth with the three saints. "Father Pappalardo gave this to me on the day you were baptized." He took her right hand and placed the cloth there. Taking her other hand, he closed the cloth between both of her hands with her hands between his, the four hands in a gesture of prayer. Alfio closed his eyes for a few moments. Then he opened them and released Santina's hands. With his right hand, he traced the sign of the cross on Santina's forehead, blessing his daughter.

"What did you pray for, Papa?"

He smiled. "What any father would pray on his daughter's wedding day—that you give me many grandchildren."

It was Maria's turn and she motioned for Santina to come to her. Tears were in Maria's eyes. Silently taking a small, wrapped package, she held it out to Santina. Maria took a moment to gain control over her emotions before she was able to speak. "This is from your godmother, Santa. She gave it to me the day we left Pedara and asked that I give it to you on your wedding day."

Santina took the package. "What is it?"

"I don't know. Open it."

Santina opened the package. Inside was a Rosary with carved

wooden beads. There was also a note, yellow and brittle from the passing years. Carefully Santina unfolded it and read it.

"My dearest Goddaughter, remember that a good marriage is made of three, not two. Keep Christ at the heart of your marriage and it will be strong and joyful, able to withstand any hardships. Turn to our Blessed Mother, the most perfect wife and mother and she will guide you in your new role as wife and, hopefully soon to follow, as mother. You are and will always be in my prayers every day.
  Santa"

Looking at her mother, Santina said, "I wish I could remember her."

"Santa was a good, holy woman. That is why you were named for her," Maria said.

Alfio looked at his watch. "It is 4:45!" Alfio announced. "We don't want to be late. It is time to leave."

Joseph walked over to his sister and gave her his arm. "Your chariot awaits!" They made their way out of the house and down the steps. Mary held the wedding dress up to keep it from touching the ground while Maria followed behind, holding Santina's bouquet. Frank held the car door open while Joseph helped Santina into the car. Mary carefully tucked the train of the dress into the car. Mary and Maria sat on either side of Santina in the back of the car while Alfio sat in front next to Frank. Joseph leaned into the car. "See you at Church!" He closed the door and started walking down 70th Street.

Frank pulled away from the curb and slowly drove down the street, honking the car horn as he went. Neighbors waved as they passed by. At 14th Avenue, Frank turned right and drove the seven blocks to St. Rosalia's Church. Joseph arrived moments later and helped his sisters out of the car.

The little group made their way up the Church steps and crowded into the small vestibule. Joseph and Frank left their parents and sisters, making their way into the Church. Zina and Nan stood with their Aunt Mary, the maid of honor. Bart, Mario's brother and the best man, had his nieces, Frances and Mona by his side.

Maria whispered to Santina, "Are you nervous?"

"No," Santina replied. "I'm excited about starting this new chapter in life." They could hear the organ begin to play music. Maria kissed her daughter and then took her husband's arm as he escorted her to her seat in the Church. Alfio returned to Santina and they stood toward the rear of the vestibule.

Joseph and Frank held the vestibule doors open. Mary instructed Zina and Nan to begin walking down the aisle. The cousins held hands, a basket of flowers in the other, and nervously entered the Church. They were followed by Mario's nieces, Mona and Frances. Bringing up the rear of the bridal party were the best man and maid of honor as Mary took Bart's arm. Frank and Joseph let the doors swing shut, and for a moment Alfio and Santina were alone.

Alfio smiled at his daughter. "You are beautiful."

Santina returned the smile. "Thank you."

Alfio nodded. "You will be happy," he stated.

Then they heard the organ music change and the doors opened. Gazing down the aisle, Santina could see Mario standing near the altar waiting for her, his brother by his side. Her heart began to beat just a little bit faster as she walked down the aisle on the arm of her father. The veil over her face softened her view of the Church, giving everything a dreamlike quality as they approached the altar.

Mario stood just outside the altar rail. Alfio hugged Santina when they reached him. Then Alfio placed Santina's hand into Mario's. She grasped his hand and together they went up the two steps and stood before the altar. The priest began the marriage rite.

CHAPTER THIRTEEN

Fragile Hope

1924

It was a Friday night in late April. Mario and Santina walked through the drizzle to Stella and Jack's house on 74th Street. The front door of the two-family, two-story brick home was ajar and they entered the house. Alfio and Maria were there as well. Thunder rumbled in the distance. As Santina hung up their damp coats, Joe and Rosie arrived. "Okay, I'm here! The party can start!" Joe announced.

"Oh, we started the party without you," Stella called out from the kitchen. Joe and Mario walked through the kitchen and stomped down the stairs into the basement where Jack was cutting the men's hair. Cigarette smoke drifted up the basement stairs, seeping into the kitchen.

Santina and Rosie walked into the dining room where Maria was putting cookies on a plate. Santina placed a cake on the table. Maria went to Santina and Rosie, placing a hand on each of their stomachs. "Soon I will have two more grandchildren to hold! I cannot wait to meet these babies!" Each woman was expecting her first child and both smiled at the excitement shown by Maria.

"That will make it an even twenty," Rosie said. "And we still haven't married Mary off yet."

Suddenly the room lit up as lightning cracked the sky outside, swiftly followed by a rumble of thunder that shook the house and made everyone jump. The house grew darker and the sound of rain pelted the windows. Rosie looked at Santina. "We got here just in time!"

Stella walked into the dining room from the kitchen carrying steaming pots of black coffee, the smell of coffee filling the room. The radio was on and there was jazz music playing softly in the background. "We may have no choice but to arrange a marriage for Mary. She's too picky," Stella joked.

Santina's jaw dropped at the sight of her younger sister. "Stella!"

"What?" Stella knew exactly what shocked her sister but feigned ignorance. Standing behind Stella, Maria shook her head. She had given up a long time ago trying to convince her daughter to be less daring.

"Why are you wearing pants?" Santina asked.

Stella shrugged nonchalantly, her eyes twinkling as she laughed. "Oh, am I? I forgot that I put these on."

"You are going to get in trouble one of these days," Maria told her daughter. "Why must you be so reckless?"

"Because it's fun," Stella replied. "Mama, you and Santina worry too much." She walked over to Maria and kissed her. Crying came from the bedroom. Stella turned to Santina. "Do you mind taking care of Joseph? You may as well get some practice at changing diapers."

"Of course." Santina went into the back bedroom.

The smell of coffee and sweets made its way down into the basement, prompting the men to come upstairs just as Santina was walking back into the dining room. Everyone sat down and helped themselves to coffee, cake, and cookies. The members of the family typically around the table varied from one Friday to the next but the conversations were generally the same. The men discussed current events and politics while the women updated one another on what was going on with various family members.

Jack leaned forward, his voice rising above the din as he spoke to his father-in-law. "Did you see the governor just passed a bill requiring every automobile driver to have a license?" Alfio nodded. "What does Frank think about that?"

"He's actually in favor of it. My son says there are so many accidents on the road because there are unskilled drivers. He would feel a lot safer."

"But," Mario cut in, "I don't like seeing the government intrude so much in our lives."

True," Joe remarked. "On the other hand, if it's my brother's safety we're talking about, a little intrusion might be okay."

At the other end of the table, Rosie, her eyes bright with excitement, whispered to Maria, "Guess who got engaged last weekend?"

The room echoed with laughter and the gentle clink of coffee cups as the conversations flowed. As the evening wore on, Joe stood up, stretching. "Well, if we're done discussing politics and future marriages, how about we play some cards?" He reached into a pocket and pulled out a deck. Everyone agreed with murmurs of assent, and the table was cleared for a new activity. The card deck was shuffled, and the sound of cards being dealt joined the soft strains of jazz from the radio while thunder still echoed in the distance.

~ ~ ~

Two days later, Katie and Antonio, along with Santina and Mario, were at Maria and Alfio's house, seated at the table for Sunday dinner. The aroma of gravy filled the air and Santina felt her stomach rumble. She placed a hand over her stomach as Mario looked at her and smiled. "The baby is ready for dinner," he commented. As grace ended and forks hovered over plates, an urgent knock echoed through the house.

Alfio rose, a puzzled look on his face. Family members never knocked. They just walked in. No one else was expected that day. Everyone in the neighborhood ate dinner on Sunday afternoons and no one would be knocking at the door during dinner. Something must be wrong. Alfio tried to swallow his rising panic as he hurried to the door, his heart pounding in his chest. He opened the door to find Rosie's brother, Phillip there. Phillip looked at the ground, avoiding eye contact with Alfio.

"What's wrong? What happened?" Alfio demanded.

"Rosie had the baby. They are at the hospital." Phillip's voice was barely above a whisper, eyes still fixed on the ground.

"No," came Maria's voice from the dining room, a sharp, pained note piercing the air. She rushed from the dining room, her face blanching, her hands trembling. Standing behind Alfio, her voice wavered, "It's too early."

Phillip nodded, unable to respond.

"Where are they? What hospital?" Alfio asked.

"Harbor Hospital," came the whispered response.

Maria returned to the dining room, her steps heavy with foreboding. She paused in the doorway, her expression grave. "Rosie gave birth early," she announced, her voice breaking. "Your father and I are heading to the hospital. Please, stay here until we get back." Her request was met with a stunned silence, the family members exchanging worried glances. With a nod from Santina, the others reluctantly murmured their consent.

Maria's eyes were moist, betraying the fear she tried to conceal as she turned to leave with Alfio and Phillip, the door closing behind them with a soft click that echoed like a bang in the quiet room.

The following days were a blur, marked by hushed conversations and the clinking of Rosary beads in prayer. Three days later, the fragile hope that had been born with Joe and Rosie's premature daughter, named Mary in honor of Maria, was extinguished as the tiny girl slipped away.

A week later, the family gathered for Sunday dinner, but the usual warmth had been replaced by a somber atmosphere. The men, seeking solace or perhaps a moment to gather their thoughts, stood outside on the porch, the smoke from their cigarettes curling into the evening sky. Inside, Mamie and Rose busied themselves assisting Mary in the kitchen, a silent effort to maintain some semblance of normalcy. Mamie moved through the kitchen with a heavy heart, her movements mechanical as she assisted Mary and Rose. Each dish she prepared, each plate she set, was done with a quiet sorrow that had never truly left her since she had to give away her daughter, Zina. Rose, now Zina's adopted mother, tried to fill the silence with chatter, but the air remained thick with unspoken grief. Maria, her face etched with concern, had insisted Santina rest, leading her to the living room for a quiet conversation.

"I haven't gone to see Joe and Rosie yet," Santina confessed. "So often this week, I went to the door determined to go over there, and then changed my mind. I'm afraid for them to see me, seeing this…" She placed her hand on her stomach and then continued, "It would be a hurtful reminder of what they lost. I don't want to cause them more pain."

Maria, her voice gentle, responded, "Avoiding them is not the answer. Remember—I went through this myself. They need their family right now more than ever. Your love and concern are more important to them. Pregnant women will always be around. It is impossible to shield them from that pain. It will be there regardless." Her eyes misted as she recalled their time in Regalbuto, when she lost Giovannina at only six months old, the absence of Alfio and the older children making it all the more bitter. "Go to them," she urged, her voice a mixture of empathy and insistence. "They need you."

Santina nodded. "You're right. I should have gone to see them right away." The sounds of grandchildren playing could be heard from outside and Santina thought of Mamie, whose pain was visible in the way she looked at the children, especially at Zina, now growing up as Rose's daughter. The reminders of her loss were ever-present.

"You were trying to shield their feelings, to do what felt right in your heart," Maria reassured her, squeezing her hand.

"But I still feel like I've failed them," Santina admitted, her voice soft. "I'll visit tomorrow."

Maria smiled. "Joe knows your heart, Santina. He knows you care."

Just then, Mary's voice cut through the house. "Dinner is ready!" Everyone went into the dining room. The table was laden with dishes, steam curling up from plates of macaroni and gravy, the air thick with the scent of tomato and garlic. The family sat down and ate mostly in silence. Mario looked around the table at the downcast relatives. He waited for someone to break the ice and begin a conversation. Instead, everyone seemed intent on their meal. When it was apparent no one would talk, aside from some cursory remarks, he knew it fell to him to lift everyone's spirits and distract them from their sorrow.

After a stretch of silence, broken only by the clinking of cutlery, Mario cleared his throat. "The singer, Flora Perini, sang her last opera at the Met a few weeks ago. I wish we could have gone," Mario said.

Giacomo, grateful that someone started talking, jumped in to respond to Mario. "I didn't know you were a fan of opera."

"Oh, yes!" Mario said. "I became interested in opera because my great aunt was a famous opera singer."

Mary looked at her brother-in-law, one eyebrow arched. "You have a famous relative? An opera singer?"

"Yes. Adelina Patrizio. My youngest sister is named for her."

They all heard of Adelina Patrizio and were properly impressed. Mario continued, "Sadly she passed away the same year we came to America. It was such a shame because I'm sure she would have given us tickets to the Met to see her."

Mamie glanced over toward the kitchen where the children sat for dinner, Rose's daughter, Zina, joining the children she thought were her cousins. "Imagine going to the Met!" Mamie's eyes glistened with unshed tears as she spoke about the Met, her attempt to engage in the conversation a clear effort to push away her own sorrow.

As the conversation continued and they all spoke about opera, music, and possible famous relatives, the mood shifted just a bit. Santina looked at Mario and mouthed, "Thank you," to him. He smiled back at her.

~ ~ ~

A month later, the cycle of sorrow returned with a cruel familiarity. Santina's labor came too soon, and their daughter, Francesca, arrived in the world with a whimper rather than a cry. For two days, they watched over her, their hope a fragile thing, until Francesca's spirit gently departed. In their bedroom, where the air hung heavy with sorrow, Santina cradled their daughter as her body shook with sobs, tears streaming down her face. Mario, his face etched with grief, wrapped his arms around his wife, his head bowed against her shoulder. They remained there, motionless, as time seemed to pause.

The days that followed were a blur, marked by the silence of an empty nursery and the heavy footsteps of a father trying to move through his grief. Each day felt like wading through thick fog for Santina, her mind unable to focus on anything but the void left by Francesca.

On Sunday, Mario and Santina sat alone, both lost in their thoughts, when a knock roused them. Mario rose from the couch as Connie, Rosie, and Maria entered the apartment, each carrying a dish. "We brought Sunday dinner to you," Rosie announced. "We had to sneak it out before Papa and Joe devoured everything."

Santina managed a weak smile that didn't reach her eyes and quickly disappeared. She didn't feel like she could ever be happy again. Rosie put the dish she carried on the coffee table as Mario discreetly slipped into the kitchen. Rosie went to Santina, hugging her. Maria carried the dishes into the kitchen and returned to the living room. Connie and Rosie sat on either side of Santina, each with an arm draped around the grieving mother.

Maria went to her daughter and kissed her forehead. Questions raced through Santina's head as she searched for some meaning, some hidden purpose behind this tragedy. She looked up at her mother, her eyes glistening with tears, her voice barely above a whisper. "Mama, why did this happen?" She felt Rosie's arm tighten around her, pulling her closer.

"There is no answer." Maria brushed a stray strand of hair from Santina's forehead. "We need to get back because we left the men alone with the children." She paused and then added, " Before we do, why don't we say the Rosary together?"

The four women sat in the living room, Rosary beads clinking as they said the familiar prayers. The late afternoon light filtered through the curtains, casting a soft glow on the faces of the women as they prayed. From the kitchen, Mario could hear the murmured cadence and joined them, reciting the Rosary silently to himself. Santina felt a sense of peace come over her as the repeated words calmed her racing heart. She looked at these other women, all who lost a child. Focusing on them rather than herself, Santina prayed that they would all be healed from this pain, especially Rosie, whose loss was as new as her own. As the final prayer ended, the room fell silent again, but this time it was a silence filled with the unity of shared sorrow and hope. They lingered in the quiet for a moment before the women rose to leave. They embraced one another and the women left with promises to stop by during the week.

After the women left, Mario said, "Why don't we go into the kitchen and eat? Your mother brought us enough food to last for days."

"I'm not hungry," Santina replied. "Maybe in a little while." She picked up the book on the table next to her, opened it for a few seconds. The words seemed to float and she found herself rereading the same sentence over several times, unable to grasp their meaning. With a sigh, she closed the book and placed it back down on the table.

Mario saw that the bookmark seemed to make no progress in moving further along. Normally Santina would finish a book within a couple of days. "Isn't that the same book you've been reading for the past week?"

"Attempting to read," Santina corrected him. She sighed. "It's so hard to concentrate. I should just give it back to Katie."

"I'm sure she's in no hurry to have it returned. You should take all the time you need."

On Friday Mario suggested they go to Stella's house. "It will be good for you to be with your family," he urged. "It will be good for both of us."

Santina hesitated. "I don't know… I wouldn't be very good company."

"It is for times just like this that one needs to be with family," Mario insisted. "If the situation was reversed, you would be there for your sisters. You were there for Joe and Rosie."

"You're right. We should go."

When they arrived, most of the family was gathered outside, where the air was cooler and carried the scent of evening flowers. The men stood near the garage, puffing on cigarettes, their smoke mingling with the twilight, while the women conversed a short distance away. Stella was the first to greet Santina with a warm hug. "I'm so glad you decided to come! The fresh air will do you good!" she exclaimed, theatrically waving her hand through the cigarette smoke.

Mary and Katie joined them. "I'm glad to see you're not doing anything foolish like wearing pants," Mary chided Stella. "Mama told me all about that. She was horrified."

"She worries too much," Stella told her sister. "It's not like I was wearing them outside. Only in front of the family."

Katie glanced at Santina and tried to suppress a smile. "I wish I had been here that day," she whispered.

Mary put her hands on her hips. "I'm the only one home with Mama these days. I don't like to see her worry."

Stella studied Santina and her heart ached with each detail she noticed; the dark circles under her sister's eyes and how her dress hung on her. Stella's brow furrowed as she thought for a minute. Then she strode over to the men, her eyes fixed on Jack. "Darling, may I borrow your cigarette?"

Jack's eyebrows rose, a mix of confusion and apprehension playing across his face. "Why?"

She didn't answer, just extended her hand. He passed it over, and Stella took a deep drag, immediately breaking into a fit of coughing, tears springing to her eyes. Jack moved to steady her, but she waved him off, still coughing. Her sisters rushed over, their concern palpable.

"What is the matter with you? Why would you do something like that?" Mary asked, her voice laced with worry.

Stella, between coughs, didn't respond. Then, as her coughing subsided, a giggle escaped her, turning into full-blown laughter.

"Are you okay?" Katie exclaimed. "Why are you laughing?"

"You were so busy watching me, you didn't see the expressions on everyone else's faces," Stella managed to say. "They were pretty funny." Her laughter proved infectious. Gradually the concern etched on the others' faces softened into smiles, then erupted into shared laughter. As they headed back toward the house, that brief, silly moment served as a respite from their sorrow, lifting the heavy atmosphere for a fleeting moment.

CHAPTER FOURTEEN

Orazio

January 1925

Springing into a sitting position, his heart racing, Mario listened for whatever sound had woken him. Next to him, Santina was also sitting, clutching his arm. "What was that banging?" his wife asked.

The pounding came again. No longer in a deep sleep, they realized someone was banging on their apartment door. "Stay here," Mario told Santina. Draping a blanket around his shoulders, he went to the door. "Who is it?"

"Mario, please open the door," a woman's voice came from the other side. He opened the door to find his sister-in-law, Fanny with four of her children. He ushered them into the kitchen as Santina came out of the bedroom.

"What happened? Why are you in New York? Where is Diego?" Mario sputtered out questions.

In response, Fanny started crying. Santina went to her sister-in-law and hugged her. "Take your time. I will make some tea," Santina said. She picked up the kettle, filled it with water, and put it on the stove.

"Where is the little one?" Mario asked, referring to Diego's youngest daughter, Margaret.

"She is with Uncle Sam and Aunt Kathleen," Frances, who was twelve, replied.

"Why are you in New York?" Mario repeated the question.

"We took a train," nine-year-old Josephina said. "We came here all the way from Detroit and…"

"I'm hungry." Joseph interrupted his sister. He was a year younger than Josephina, the youngest of the four children who came to New York with their mother.

"We haven't eaten anything all day," Harry told his aunt and uncle. "We've been in a cab for hours driving around Brooklyn." Harry was a year younger than his sister, Frances.

Santina put bread, cheese, and fruit on the table. The children began eating before she had the plates out. While the children ate, Mario led Fanny into the living room where they could talk. "Where is my brother?" Mario asked.

"The police took Diego away," Fanny told him. "There was an accident."

"An accident? Here in New York? Why did the police take him?"

"It happened in October, back home."

Mario was confused. "There was an accident three months ago in Detroit but all of you are here in New York?"

"After the accident, Diego left Detroit so the police couldn't arrest him."

Mario wondered why Diego would be arrested because of an accident but remained silent. He waited for Fanny to continue as he attempted to piece together what she said. So far none of this was making any sense.

"Diego left for New York in October, right after the accident happened. We waited until we thought it was safe. Then I came with the children to join Diego. The police must have followed us from Detroit. When we got off the train, we saw several policemen meeting the officers who were on the train. We got into a cab but they followed us. We spent most of the day trying to evade them. Finally we saw they were gone and went to a boarding house, to Diego. But the police were still there. Soon as we arrived, they swooped in and arrested him and took him away." Fanny was crying again.

Santina walked into the living room and placed two cups of tea on the table in front of them. Mario took a sip of his tea, put the cup down and stood up. Turning to Fanny, he said, "Excuse me.

I'll be right back." Taking Santina's hand, he led her into the hallway.

"What's going on?" Santina asked.

"I'm not sure." Lowering his voice, Mario repeated what Fanny had told him about an accident, fleeing to New York, and the arrest.

"What sort of accident do they arrest you for?" Santina asked.

"I don't know. Nothing I can think of," Mario responded. "I think Fanny is leaving a lot out of the story." He looked toward the living room and then back at Santina. "I remember once when we were still in Italy, Diego thought someone was making advances toward Fanny. He wouldn't listen when I tried to say he was wrong. He beat the man up." He grimaced at the memory.

"They must be exhausted. Why don't we let them sleep and we can find out more in the morning."

Mario nodded and they returned to the living room. "Fanny, let's set you all up to sleep. We can discuss this in the morning. You take the couch and the children can sleep here on the floor," Santina said. The two women busied themselves with getting pillows and blankets. Santina helped Fanny get the children settled in. Then Mario and Santina went back to bed. Santina fell asleep quickly but Mario stared into the darkness wondering what happened to his brother.

The following morning, Mario sat at the kitchen table with Santina, both drinking coffee. Their sister-in-law, nieces, and nephews were still asleep. The husband and wife spoke in whispers.

"I have to leave for work, but I hope to be home early. I will call my brother-in-law. Victor has a friend who is a police officer. Maybe he can find out what's going on."

"That's a good idea," Santina replied. "I will call your sisters, Marietta and Jennie."

Late that afternoon, Mario returned home and they all went to Marietta's house. Marietta was expecting them for dinner and was in the kitchen preparing the food. Jennie, Mario's oldest sister, was also there with her husband, Peter. "Does Mama know?" Mario asked his sisters.

"No," Marietta said. "Adeline and Bart are keeping her upstairs in her apartment. She doesn't know you're here. We thought it would be best. It would be too confusing and distressing for her."

"Yes," Mario agreed. He left the women and children in the kitchen and went into the living room to talk to his brothers-in-law, Peter and Victor. Victor had a grim look on his face and Mario felt what little hope he clung to disappear. "Did you talk to your friend, that police officer? Was he able to find out what's going on?"

Victor looked uncomfortable and shifted in his seat. Glancing first at Peter and then at Mario, unable to meet their gaze, his eyes settled on a lamp. "From what the detectives were able to piece together, Diego and Fanny were fighting. Mostly Diego, from the sound of it. He started waving around a gun and fired off a shot into the ceiling. The landlady heard the yelling and the gunshot. She ran upstairs and tried to intervene. Diego ended up shooting both of them. Fanny was hurt. The landlady died."

The room fell silent. For several minutes no one moved or spoke. Mario stared at his brother-in-law. He shook his head as if trying to wake himself up from a bad dream. Looking around the room, he waited for the vision of his sister's living room to fade into his familiar bedroom. The surroundings didn't change and Mario was forced to acknowledge this was real and not just a nightmare.

Victor continued. "He left Detroit in October, right after it happened. On Saturday, Fanny left Margaret with Sam and took a train to New York with the four older children. I guess she thought after three months, the detectives had given up."

"Where is Diego now?" Peter asked.

"In the Tombs," Victor replied. When Peter and Mario both looked blankly at him, he explained, "A prison in downtown Manhattan. They are going to bring him back to Detroit to stand trial but he'll stay here in New York until he appears before a judge. The detectives from Detroit already have permission to bring him back."

"Does the rest of the family know?" Mario asked.

"Everyone but Mama," Victor replied. "She won't understand what's going on and even if she does, Jennie and Marietta think she won't believe it."

Mario went back into the kitchen. He walked over to Fanny, placed a hand on her shoulder and leaned in close to whisper, "Did my brother hurt you?" Expecting that she might be upset by his question, he was shocked when her reaction was anger.

"I told you it was an accident! That woman had no right to interfere in our business! If she had kept out of it, none of this would have happened!"

Mario took a step back from his sister-in-law. Marietta, Jennie, and Santina looked from Fanny to Mario surprised by the outburst. The children all stared down at the table, hoping no one would ask them anything. Josephina's hand trembled slightly, her gaze darting to her mother as if seeking reassurance that this was just another storm passing through. Marietta glanced around the table at the young faces, twisted in varying degrees of grief. She forced a smile and announced, "Let's sit down for dinner!"

Mario pushed the food around on his plate, his appetite gone after hearing the news. "How can this be? It's not possible," he thought to himself. "My brother always had a bit of a temper but he is not a murderer."

"Mario!" Jennie's voice cut into his thoughts.

"Huh?" He looked up. "I'm sorry. I didn't hear what you said."

"I think Fanny and the children should stay with us tonight. They can visit with Mama. It would make her happy to spend time with them."

Mario nodded. "Then they can get a train tomorrow and return to Detroit."

~ ~ ~

Mario and Santina hurried home after dinner, arms linked, as snow flurries swirled around them, painting the night with fleeting beauty that seemed to mock the sorrow in Mario's heart.

Mario was grappling with the revelation about his brother. "What could drive Diego to do such a thing?" His voice low, lost in the soft crunch of snow underfoot.

"It's all so incredibly sad," Santina replied softly, her breath forming misty clouds in the cold air. "Two families that will never be the same. So many people to pray for."

"Why did Fanny blame that poor woman and defend Diego?" Mario's confusion was palpable.

"I think it's easier for her to blame someone else," Santina explained, her arm tightening around his. "It's hard to accept that someone you love might be capable of such a thing."

"When you read about a murder in the newspaper, you feel angry. That's how I would expect to feel. I should be angry at my brother. I should think he is a terrible person. And maybe he is. But right now, I don't feel anger. I just feel sad."

"Sadness seems entirely appropriate," Santina responded. "We are sad that a life was lost, that a soul may be lost. We must pray for your brother, that he will repent and be saved. We must pray for healing for both families."

The conversation drifted to other topics as they neared home. "Are you feeling alright? You hardly ate anything at dinner." Mario's voice was full of concern.

"No one ate much. Everyone was too upset to eat."

"Yes, but even yesterday, before we knew about any of this, you barely ate anything," Mario noted with a hint of worry.

"I've just been a little nauseous."

"You should go see the doctor tomorrow."

"It's nothing. My stomach seems a little sensitive lately."

"This has been going on longer than just a couple of days? You must go to the doctor. I will take you there myself first thing in the morning," Mario insisted.

"That won't be necessary. I promise I will go. You shouldn't worry so much about me."

Mario looked at her with feigned indignation. "It is my job to take care of you. I could never worry about you too much." His face then took on a look of exaggerated terror. "If I neglect my job, your papa would send some bad men to break my legs. Maybe even my arms, as well."

Santina laughed. "I don't think you have anything to fear from Papa. At least not a fear of broken bones. If anything, he would withhold your favorite pastries when we go to visit."

Mario joined in the laughter. "Yes, that is true!"

The following evening, Mario came home from work and rushed to the kitchen where Santina was preparing dinner. She turned to look at him before he had a chance to say anything, a huge smile on her face. "Everything is good."

"What did the doctor say?"

"He couldn't say for certain but he's fairly sure I'm fine."

Mario frowned. "What do you mean he's not certain?"

"Well, it may be another month before he can be completely certain but nausea is perfectly normal."

He stared at his wife and her beautiful smile. Slowly, understanding seeped into him. He embraced her. "My Santuzza, you will be a wonderful mother!"

"And you will be a wonderful father if only you'd remember to take your coat off and hang it up when you first come home," Santina teased. "You've dripped melting snow all through the apartment."

As they ate dinner, Mario noticed a solemn look on his wife's face. "It won't be the same as when we lost Frances," he reassured her.

"We can't know that, but we will pray."

"Yes," Mario agreed. "Right after dinner, we will pray the Rosary together."

A few weeks later, they went to Alfio and Maria's house for Sunday dinner. Stella and Katie were there along with their husbands and children. Mary was in the living room with the children, keeping them out of the kitchen while the other women prepared dinner. When Santina joined her sisters in the kitchen, Katie elbowed Stella and whispered, "Something is up with Santina."

Stella said to Santina, "You have that smile on your face that says you have a grand secret that is trying to burst out of you."

"I don't know what you're talking about," Santina replied.

"You can't hide anything," Katie said. "You're just like Mama. Your face always gives you away."

Santina didn't reply but her smile grew even larger in spite of her attempts to look neutral.

Maria was busy at the stove, stirring the gravy. She glanced over her shoulder at her daughters before returning her attention to the pots bubbling away in front of her.

"Come on. You can tell your dear sisters your secret," Stella said, taking Santina's hand. "Lately you have looked so sad because of all that went on with Mario's brother and the murder. But now you are happy again. There is good news. You must tell us."

Finally relenting, Santina said, "I'm pregnant."

There were joy filled screeches and hugs as the women made a fuss over Santina. The men came in, curious about all the noise and the women shared the news with them. There were no shrieks from the men, although Mario was the recipient of handshakes and slaps on the back. Alfio went down to the cellar and came back with a bottle of wine to celebrate.

As Santina's belly grew over the months, Mario's fussing over his wife increased. By May, he would not allow her to carry anything, instead going grocery shopping with her each morning so he could carry everything home himself. When they entered June, he asked her to stop going to work at the sewing factory.

"I don't want you on your feet. You need to take it easy," he told his wife.

"It's too boring to just sit at home. Besides, we need the extra money," she protested.

"How about a compromise?" he bargained. "Mary can bring work here to you and you can sit at home and sew."

The arrangements were made. Each morning Mary dropped off material for the blouses. Maria would come over during the day to keep her daughter company while Santina sat, working on the blouses. When Maria left, she would bring the completed blouses home so Mary could bring them back to the factory the next morning. Each evening, after dinner, the expectant parents prayed the Rosary together.

The months passed in the gentle rhythm of anticipation and prayer. On a warm day in late August, their prayers were answered. Santina gave birth to a son, the soft cries of a new life echoing through the house.

They named him Orazio, after Mario's father, a name that carried with it the weight of legacy and the joy of new beginnings. As they looked upon their son, his tiny fingers wrapped around Santina's, their eyes shone with tears of joy. In that moment, Orazio was not just a child but a symbol of resilience, a new chapter for the family.

CHAPTER FIFTEEN

Alfio

October 1927

Two-year-old Orazio sat on the kitchen floor with a pot he dragged from a cabinet. Picking up a wooden spoon, he began banging it on the pot. Mary, who sat in Santina's living room with her sisters, made a face and put her hands over her ears. "Here," Stella handed a ball to her son, Joseph, "Go play with Orazio." The four-year-old boy ran into the kitchen and the banging stopped, replaced with giggling as the two cousins played.

"I am not marrying Giuseppe," Mary declared to her sisters. She flung the dress, with freshly attached buttons, onto a stack of finished sewing projects and folded her arms across her chest.

"I thought Papa and Zio Angelo already arranged it," Santina responded, reaching for one of the blouses from the pile of clothing in front of the women.

"I don't care. Neither of us wants to get married. It's absurd!" Mary snatched another dress and began furiously attaching buttons to it.

"I don't see that you have a choice. Once Papa decides something..." Santina shrugged and then struggled to her feet. Stella, who was cradling a sleeping one-year-old in one arm, put her free hand on Santina's back to steady her. Santina smiled. "I'm fine. You don't want to disturb Concetta." Looking down at her stomach, she added, "This baby better come soon. I don't think I

145

can possibly get any larger. I'll be right back." Slowly she waddled toward the bathroom. The two sisters remained silent until she returned and lowered herself back onto the couch.

"Santina is right," Stella told Mary. "You have to do as Papa says."

Mary scowled. "Giuseppe is our cousin. And he's dying. He doesn't want this. Why can't they just let him die in peace?" Mary returned to her sewing, her shoulders sagging slightly as she threaded the needle. She didn't look up, her gaze fixed on her work as if it could distract her from her thoughts.

"Papa's just worried about you. You're the only one left at home now. Maybe he thinks your prospects for marriage will be better as a widow than as a spinster," Santina said.

"How is twenty-seven a spinster?" Mary demanded. "You were married at that age and no one considered you a spinster." Mary stood and then stomped into the kitchen. The aroma of freshly brewed coffee grew stronger as Mary poured it into the small espresso cups.

Stella leaned over and whispered to Santina, "Must be her sparkling personality that Papa's worried about."

Fearful that Mary heard, Santina looked toward the kitchen, but the only sound was from the little boys. Mary returned holding a tray with three cups of coffee. They each took one and sipped in silence for a few minutes. Mary gave a small, defeated sigh and said, "If I have a daughter, I will never allow her to marry a man she doesn't love. Or a man who will try to boss her around and tell her what to do."

Looking down at her sleeping daughter, Stella nodded. "Yes. I agree with that plan."

Mary gathered up the empty coffee cups and walked toward the kitchen. Santina started to stand, but Mary held her hand out like a policeman stopping traffic. "I'll take care of cleaning up," Mary told her. "Stay in here where it's cooler." Her sister didn't argue.

"I can't believe tomorrow is the first day of October," Stella said. "It seems more like August. We should be sitting on towels at Coney Island right now." She looked at Santina's stomach and laughed. "Although you would never be able to get back up in your condition."

Santina smiled. "You and Mary would have to lift me."

Mary came back into the living room fanning herself with a dishtowel, beads of sweat making her face shine. The sun was setting, casting long shadows across the floor. Mary stared out the window, watching the light fade, feeling as if her own choices were slipping away with the day. Mary stood up, brushing her thoughts aside. "It's getting late. We should get home." She gathered up the sewing work. "I'll drop this off at the factory on my way home."

"Come on, Joseph," Stella called. "Say goodbye to your cousin and your aunts. It's time to go." Joseph came into the living room, Orazio following right behind him.

Mary and Stella hugged their sister and left the apartment, Joseph holding his aunt's hand and Stella carrying Concetta as they descended the stairs. Santina called down after them, "Goodbye! See you at Mama's on Sunday!"

The sisters parted ways with promises of Sunday's reunion. But life, with its relentless cycle, had other plans. Two days later, Santina and Mario walked down the steps from Church after Mass. Stopping in mid-step, Santina squeezed Mario's arm. Maria, who had accompanied them to Mass, noticed her daughter's grimace. "It's time?"

Santina just nodded until the pain passed and she was able to speak. "It started during Mass but I thought I had enough time to make it home."

Alfio, who was holding Orazio's hand, led the little boy to where Mary stood. "Watch him for a minute." Turning, he saw a fellow parishioner, Mr. Marchelli, heading toward his car. Stepping in front of Mr. Marchelli, Alfio took off his hat. "I am sorry to bother you but would it be an imposition for you to drive my wife and daughter back to her house? Santina is about to give birth."

"Papa, it's okay. I can walk home," Santina objected.

"No, no. You must not walk in your condition." Mr. Marchelli waved in protest and opened the car door. "I won't let you walk home in this heat. It would be my honor to help." Maria and Santina got in the car.

"I will bring the midwife," Mary called out after the car as it drove away.

~ ~ ~

Several hours later, the midwife left and Maria cradled a baby boy in her arms. Footsteps thundered up the stairs as Mario and Alfio burst into the apartment. Following closely behind came the newlyweds Adeline and her husband, Frank, the latter carrying little Orazio. Bringing up the rear was Adeline and Mario's mother, Francesca. The older woman climbed the steps as fast as her swollen legs would allow, gripping the handrails to assist in pulling herself up.

Mario rushed from the living room, passing through the kitchen to reach the bedroom where his wife lay. As he entered the bedroom, he could hear the excited chatter from the living room where his mother-in-law sat on the couch with her newest grandchild.

Alfio joined his wife on the couch, where she held the tiny infant. "Orazio, come meet your new baby brother," he called out. The toddler, hearing his name, made his way over, and Alfio hoisted him onto his lap.

Sitting on his grandfather's knee, Orazio stared at the tiny person his grandmother was holding. "Baby," he said, pointing.

Maria laughed. "Yes, this is your baby brother. His name is Alfio." The elder Alfio beamed upon learning the child was named after him. Softly, he sang to his namesake, a song from the past, from his days of driving a cart in Pedara.

Francesca slowly made her way over to the couch, her daughter and son-in-law on either side of her, each holding an arm. "Is it…" The older woman struggled to breathe, then tried again. "Is it a girl?"

"No, Mama," Adeline told her. "Mario and Santina have another son."

Francesca pouted. "No Francesca?"

"Not this time, Mama," Mario replied, walking into the room. "But don't worry. We are going to have many children. I'm sure the next one will be a little girl, named after you."

Pacified, Francesca held out her hands for the baby.

Footsteps on the stairs announced the arrival of more visitors. Mary and Giuseppe entered the apartment, each carrying several bags overflowing with groceries. Maria stood. "Let's put those in the kitchen before you go in to see your sister." Mary and Giuseppe followed her, heaving their sacks onto the kitchen table. "Santina is in the bedroom," Maria told her daughter as she unpacked the groceries. Then turning to Giuseppe, "Why don't you go sit in the living room."

Giuseppe retraced his steps and returned to the living room where he found a chair in a corner of the room, apart from the rest of the family. Francesca stared at the young man taking in his emaciated frame and pale complexion. His dark eyes were surrounded by even darker circles and his sweat-drenched hair was plastered to his head. Pointing to Giuseppe, she asked Mario, "Who is he?"

"Mama, may I introduce you to Mary's fiancé, Giuseppe Tordaro." Then to Giuseppe, "This is my mother, Francesca Patrizio." The young man nodded his head in greeting but remained silent. Steering his mother to a new topic before she commented further, Mario asked, "Why don't you go into the kitchen? I'm sure the women could use your advice."

"Oh, yes! Of course!" Francesca handed the baby to Mario, a smile on her face. Frank helped his mother-in-law to her feet and she walked into the kitchen.

Mario gently carried the baby back into the bedroom, placing him into a cradle next to his sleeping wife. Tiptoeing back out, he closed the bedroom door behind him. He walked through the kitchen, returning to the living room, then handed out cigars to all the men. As they puffed on them, Alfio turned to his son-in-law. "Do you still have that bottle of grappa?"

Frank looked on, his eyes widening. "Where did you manage to get grappa?"

Alfio put his index finger to his lips and winked. "We don't want the neighbors overhearing." He poured some into glasses for the men and handed them around. "Let us toast the new baby, Alfio! Salute!" He raised his glass. All the men followed suit, toasting the newest addition to their family and sipping the grappa.

Turning back to Frank, Alfio asked him, "Did you know your brother-in-law is quite the inventor? We are using his press for crushing our grapes. Each year we make wine and grappa. Thanks to Mario, our work is much easier."

Nodding, Mario added, "My patent for the fruit press was approved by the government two years ago. I was forced to invent it because Mama was getting upset about all those purple stains in the shape of footprints that we left all over the house." Frank looked at him, a puzzled expression on his face. "You know," Mario continued, "From stomping grapes." He stomped the floor several times to demonstrate.

The men laughed as they puffed their cigars and sipped their drinks, smoke swirling around the room. Clatter from the kitchen filled the air as the scent of garlic and tomato mingled with the aroma of cigar smoke. Francesca sat in a chair at the kitchen table watching Maria, Mary, and Adeline work. The women seemed to perform a choreographed dance as each moved about her task without getting in the way of the others. Adeline began putting the platters piled with food on the table. "Mary, go let the men know that dinner is ready," Maria instructed.

Mary stepped into the living room, waving in vain at the smoke that hung in the air like a veil. "Dinner is ready," she announced. She watched as the men headed toward the kitchen. She stared at their backs, remaining in the living room, her heart struggling with conflicting emotions. The joy for her sister and the new baby contrasted sharply with her own future, uncertain and unchosen. She felt the weight of her obligations, the warmth of familial love, and the chill of her own fears. Here they all were, moving forward with life, while hers felt like it was on hold, undecided. Tonight, the celebration was for a new beginning, but for Mary, it was a poignant reminder of the choices she had yet to make.

CHAPTER SIXTEEN

Francesca

May 1931

Wooden chair legs scraped the tile floor as Maria groaned and sat down. "Mama, why don't you go sit in the living room where it's more comfortable. We can take care of this," Katie told her.

"Your sisters shouldn't be on their feet too much," Maria protested, looking at Santina and Mary. "They need to rest."

Stella laughed. "You'd think you never had pregnant daughters before. How many grandchildren are you up to now?"

"Twenty..." Maria's voice trailed off for half a beat. Her instincts were to say 'twenty-three' as she thought about Frank's son. She stared at the wall as if able to see through it, to see Frank sitting in the living room. It seemed impossible that John's terrible motorcycle accident was already two years ago. Hoping that the brief pause went unnoticed by her daughters, she added, "Two! Imagine that! Twenty-two grandchildren!"

"Yes, and half of them are running around in your backyard right now." Stella raised the kitchen window a little higher and they could hear the children shouting outside. "Now go sit inside." She shooed her mother away.

"Only seven of them are outside," Maria responded as she allowed herself to be led into the living room by Stella. After the two were gone, Mary pursed her lips and Santina's eyes became glassy with tears.

Glancing around the kitchen at her sisters, Katie sighed. "She doesn't look good. She's gotten so thin and looks so tired." Standing by the stove, Katie turned the gas up higher under the pot of water in an attempt to get it to boil faster.

Mary agreed as she absently stirred the gravy. "But it's been two years since the doctor told us she was ill. For cancer that's a long time." She tried to sound hopeful but her furrowed brow and slumped shoulders betrayed her words.

Santina nodded. "I'm so grateful for every moment we get with her. Each day is a gift from God." She opened a drawer and fished out the cheese grater. Sitting back down, she began grating the Parmesan cheese into a bowl.

"And in a couple of months, she's getting two more grandchildren," Mary added, putting her hand on her stomach. Staring into space, Mary thought about how different her life was, just two short years ago. In 1929, she was already a year into being a widow. Within a few months of their marriage, Giuseppe was sent by the doctors to a sanatorium. He never returned home.

Nick was a boarder, renting the apartment upstairs from Papa and now they were married and expecting their first child. She remembered every detail of the first time she met him. The sky was bright blue and the air was filled with the smell of roses from the front garden. She was leaving the house as he entered the front gate. He smiled at her and said, "You must be Mary."

"Mary!" At the sound of her sister's voice, Mary jumped. Stella laughed. "You were a million miles away. I didn't mean to startle you but I had to yell. You didn't hear me the first two times. The macaroni is nearly done. Katie just went out to round up the kids."

The girls were the first ones to come inside. Right on their heels, the four boys burst into the room and ran for the children's table in the kitchen. Katie's son, Frankie sat on one side of the table next to Stella's son, Joseph. Santina's two boys, sat opposite their cousins.

"Oh, no! You all go straight to the bathroom and wash those filthy hands!" Mary told her nephews.

"My hands aren't dirty," Orazio replied as he held up his hands. Since starting kindergarten the year before, the family began calling the six-year-old Horace. Once in school, most of the children switched over to names that sounded more American.

"Horace, I can see a little dirt on those hands," Santina replied. "Just a little. And Alfio's hands are very dirty. Go take Alfio into the bathroom and make sure you both wash your hands." Obediently, Horace got up, took his brother by the hand, and walked to the bathroom. "Use soap!" Santina called after them.

"Yes, Mama."

"You two, also," Katie told her son and nephew.

"My hands aren't dirty," Joseph muttered as he and Frankie reluctantly rose from the table.

Once the children all returned, Mary started scooping macaroni into plates. Santina said, "You can say Grace and start eating. You don't have to wait for the adults." After making the sign of the cross, the children quickly said the prayer and started eating, while the women brought the remaining food into the dining room.

Once all the adults were seated around the dining room table, Alfio led them in saying Grace. For several moments after, the only sound was the clanking of cutlery against dishes as everyone helped themselves to sausage, meatballs, and braciole.

Nick leaned across his wife, Mary, to talk to Mario. "I hear you have a family wedding coming up."

"Yes," Mario replied in between forkfuls of macaroni. "Felicia is the sister of my brother-in-law, Peter. She lives with Jennie and Peter. That's how Diego met her."

"And Felicia isn't afraid to be married to a murderer?" Nick asked.

Mario's face twisted in anger and Santina put her hand over her husband's clenched fist. "Everyone is entitled to redemption," she told Nick and anyone else overhearing the conversation. "God does not say to one person, 'You are forgiven' and to another, 'What you have done I cannot forgive.' We all are able to go to confession, receive absolution, and change our lives for the better. Diego was punished for his crime in jail and now he is trying to start a new life."

"But isn't he divorced?" Nick pressed on.

Frank's head snapped up at the word 'divorced' and he glared at Nick. "Better to get a divorce than to lock your wife away to die in an insane asylum," he said through clenched teeth.

Everyone jumped as there was a loud bang on the table. They looked to the source and saw Alfio standing. "Enough! You are upsetting your mother."

Frank got up from the table, walked over to Maria, and kissed her on the head. "I'm sorry, Mama." Maria took his hand and squeezed it, a weak smile on her face. Then he returned to his seat and to his meal.

"Joseph says he wants to be a conductor and drive trains when he grows up," Stella said, filling the silent void.

"Yes," Jack laughed. "I was hoping he'd want to be a barber like me. Don't all young boys want to grow up to be like their Papa? Eight years old and he already has his mind set on an entirely different occupation. I even had to buy him an engineer's hat."

"Oh, Jack! He wants to be just like you," Stella reassured her husband, "Except for the part where he cuts hair."

"I wonder if either of my boys will grow up to be inventors." Mario turned to Santina. "What do you think?"

"Perhaps our boys will be inventors. Or maybe one of them will be a priest."

From the kitchen Frankie yelled, "Not me!"

Alfio didn't know what his cousin referred to but echoed, "Not me!"

The grownups laughed. Then Antonio called out to his son, "Maybe or maybe not. There are many years to decide."

Katie added, "Children, pray to know what God's will is for each of you. And stop eavesdropping on the grownups' conversation!"

"Have you invented anything new?" Jack asked Mario.

"A few things but only one was approved by the patent office. It's a shock absorber for cars. My brother-in-law was kind enough to discuss the matter with me and help me improve it."

"You did most of the work," Frank said.

"Don't be so modest. If I didn't have you answering all my questions, I never would have succeeded."

"Okay," Frank replied. "When you become a millionaire from this invention, I'll take ten percent."

Mario laughed and then stuck out his hand. "Deal!" Frank shook the outstretched hand.

"There's no backing out now," Jack said. "We all witnessed this agreement. Now you just have to quickly get to that first million. Just don't put any of your money into the bank or stock market. You'd be better off putting it all into your mattress." Suddenly the atmosphere around the table grew somber. "I'm sorry. I was just poking fun at Mario. I didn't mean to make light of a terrible situation."

"We know," Frank told his brother-in-law. "None of us took what you said seriously. It's just that we were suddenly pulled back into reality."

Santina smiled. "We are so blessed. There is food on the table. We all have a place to live. Most important, we have each other."

"And two new babies on the way," Maria added.

~ ~ ~

Wednesday, January 13, 1932

The gray, rainy day outside reflected the mood of the people crowded inside Alfio's house. Mud from the wet ground at the cemetery clung to the shoes piled by the door. Alfio sat in a chair in the living room, his eyes darting around the room searching for someone who he expected to be there but couldn't find. He knew Maria was gone but couldn't shake the feeling that she would suddenly walk in from one of the other rooms. Grace's widower, Angelo, walked over to his father-in-law.

"I am so sorry but Josephine and I have to leave. I was only able to get half a day off from work."

Alfio brushed off his concerns. "Don't worry about it. In these times, work is very important." Bending down, Angelo hugged his father-in-law and Alfio told him, "If anyone knows what I am going through, it is you. Thank you for being here for me today."

Mamie and Domenic sat on the couch, opposite Alfio, along with Rose and her husband, Giacomo. Domenic's arm was around Mamie who was crying. Rose bit her lip, trying to prevent herself from also crying.

Joe and Rosie stood in a corner of the living room, speaking in subdued tones with Frank and his girlfriend, Helen. "What a terrible way to meet the family," Rosie remarked to Helen. "I wish we all could have met under better circumstances."

"We have no control over these things. I'm glad at least Mama got to meet you." Frank put his arm around Helen and she smiled at him.

The dining room and kitchen tables were piled with so much food that it seemed an impossible task for both tables to hold everything without collapsing. It appeared that everyone who knew the family brought a baked dish or cake to Alfio. Connie sat at the dining room table next to her husband, Sal. Sal was talking to his brother, Jack, Stella's husband. "How are things going with the barber shop? Are you and Stella doing okay?"

"We're managing," Jack said.

Mario looked down at the table, his lips pressed together, hoping his brother-in-law wouldn't ask him the same question.

Nick reached across the table and picked up an apple. He looked over at Antonio. "Would you like one?" Antonio shook his head. Nick stared at the apple in his hand and then put it back in the bowl with the rest of the fruit. "Yeah, I don't have much of an appetite, either."

Connie got up from the dining room table and walked into the kitchen. Santina and Mary stood by the door leading to the basement. Stella sat at the kitchen table holding Santina's daughter, six-month-old Frances. Next to her, Katie sat with Mary's daughter, Mariuccia, who was born two weeks after Frances.

"I'm so glad Mama got to meet these two little girls," Connie said.

Santina nodded in agreement, not trusting herself to speak without crying. The women were all trying to put on a cheerful act in front of the babies. As the women sat in silence, they could hear the voices of their nieces and nephews rising up from the basement. Before the funeral Mass, the men set up tables downstairs. All of the grandchildren and their spouses chose to sit at the table in the basement, instead of crowding into Alfio's living room and dining room. Every once in a while, one of the men stomped up the stairs and into the kitchen to carry some food down to the others.

Daylight was long gone and the rain seemed to leave with it.

Families left Alfio, one at a time until only Santina and Mario remained with their three children. Little Alfio squeezed onto the chair next to his grandfather and the elder man put his arm around the little boy. "Let me hold the baby." Santina walked over to him and placed Frances in his lap. "Horace, what do you think of your little sister?"

"I'm glad Mama had a girl! I already have a brother. I wanted a little sister."

For the first time that day, Alfio smiled. Then he turned to Mario. "I know things aren't going well."

Mario looked at his wife, his eyes questioning. Santina shook her head.

"She didn't tell me," Alfio continued. "I can tell just by looking at you. I see how worried you look."

Embarrassed, not knowing how to reply, Mario stayed silent.

"Come live here with me. This house is too big for just one lonely old man."

"We are managing," Mario lied.

"Don't give me an answer now. Think about it. I wouldn't just be helping you. You would be helping me, as well. I need my daughter here to help me."

The couple assured Alfio they would think about his offer and they went out into the cold, dark night.

CHAPTER SEVENTEEN

Maria

Easter Sunday - 1937

A loud clang followed by curses in Italian issued from the kitchen. Mona hurried into the kitchen, her heart racing with concern, and went to her grandmother. "What's wrong, Nonna?"

"The stuffed mushrooms. They are no good!" Francesca glared at the mess on the floor. The pan containing the stuffed mushrooms landed right side up but the impact of hitting the ground sent many of the mushrooms airborne where they scattered about the kitchen.

Mona glanced at her mother. Jennie whispered so that her own mother couldn't hear, "She insisted on taking them out of the oven herself."

Mona nodded and turned back to her grandmother. "Nonna, it's okay. We have so much other food. And most of the mushrooms will be okay." She knelt on the floor to pick up the mushrooms, putting aside the ones that didn't seem too damaged.

Frances and Elizabeth wandered into the kitchen to investigate the commotion. At the sight of the two girls, Francesca was distracted from the mushrooms. She grasped the hand of her six-year-old namesake. "Come inside with me and tell me about school." Frances, uneasy about her grandmother's unpredictable behavior, looked at her mother, her eyes pleading to be rescued. Santina waved her off with a reassuring smile.

"You, too, Elizabeth." Francesca put her free arm around her other granddaughter and led both girls out of the kitchen and into the living room. Francesca sat on the couch and had each girl sit on either side of her. Once they were settled, she started rattling off questions in Italian to the two young girls.

All the adults spoke Italian and Elizabeth, who was nine, understood a little, but Frances didn't understand enough to make much sense of what her grandmother was saying. Every once in a while, Frances would nod as if paying attention but she was content to let her cousin do the talking. Through the open windows, she could hear her brothers outside with their cousins, yelling to one another. The boys were playing stickball in the street and there seemed to be some debate as to whether one of them was safe or out.

Smoke wafted in through the window as her father and uncles stood outside, puffing on cigarettes and talking. She couldn't quite make out what they were saying, but she could hear her father's voice speaking in animated tones and then heard her uncles laughing.

The front door opened, and their uncle, Peter, walked in with a woman Frances and Elizabeth didn't recognize. As they approached the group, Peter's steps slowed, his gaze lingering on his sister with a look of worry in his eyes. When he spoke to his mother-in-law, his voice carried a weight, "Mama, my sister, Felicia, is joining us for Easter dinner."

Francesca looked up, her eyes momentarily clouded with confusion before she recognized Felicia. Her face softened, but her voice was tinged with confusion as she asked, "Where is Diego?"

Seeing her grandmother was distracted, Frances took advantage of the diversion to jump off the couch and she fled outside.

Tears forming in her eyes, Felicia looked from her brother to her mother-in-law, not knowing what to say. Peter gently told Francesca, "Mama, Diego died nearly two years ago. Don't you remember?"

"Of course I remember," Francesca snapped. Abruptly getting to her feet, she muttered, "I better check on the lasagna," as she headed to the kitchen.

Peter looked at his sister. "It could have been worse. At least she doesn't know about the rest of the issues with Diego." Felicia's face grew red and she stared down at the floor. Putting his hand on Felicia's shoulder, he gave it a slight squeeze. "It will be okay," he reassured her. "I'm going back out with the men. Will you be alright?"

Felicia nodded. Glancing into the adjoining dining room, she saw Santina making her way around the table, placing silverware down. Looking back to her brother, she nodded again. "Yes, I'll be fine. I'll go help Santina. She shouldn't be on her feet." The siblings walked in opposite directions, Peter making his way to the front door and Felicia entering the dining room. "Let me do that," Felicia told Santina.

"I need to do something," Santina replied. "The others won't let me help with the cooking. Jennie, Adeline, and Marietta are treating me like an invalid." Santina was thinner now than with her previous pregnancy, accentuating the curve of her belly. In spite of spending fifteen minutes with the silverware, she had only prepared three place settings, stopping frequently to lean against a chair.

"Why don't you sit and fold the napkins? I will walk around the table and take care of the place settings," Felicia coaxed her. An involuntary sigh escaped Santina as she lowered herself into a chair. As Felicia walked around the table with the remaining silverware, she said, "I was so sorry to hear about your father's passing."

Santina's eyes filled with tears. It hardly seemed possible that both her parents were gone. Maria's death took place three years after the stock market crash. Mario's wages were cut and they could barely afford rent. Alfio offered to have Mario, Santina, and the children move in with him, but Mario's pride made him hold out for another year. Finally, in 1933, Santina was able to convince Mario to take her father's offer. Alfio's health was beginning to fail and Santina pressed that issue with her husband, that Alfio needed their help. It was an adjustment for Mario and the children but, for Santina, she was back in the house where she lived for seven years. She was home. "He's with Mama now."

Felicia continued, "It was good of you to move in with him to take care for him."

"I'm not sure who was taking care of who." Santina shook her head, trying to toss off the sad thoughts like a dog attempting to shake off water. She watched Felicia make her way around the table, shoulders slumped and with a frown on her face. "How have you been holding up? Jennie told me what happened."

Felicia's breath caught and she blinked back tears. "Yes," she whispered, her voice trembling. "I thought Diego's death was the worst thing to happen to me. I was wrong."

Her gaze dropped to the floor as she bit her lip. The realization that her marriage had been a lie, that her love had been nothing more than a sham, stung intensely. How could she have been so blind, so foolish?

"I'm sorry." Santina put her hand on Felicia's arm. "You couldn't have known. None of it was your fault. Diego was a very charming and a very convincing man. We all thought he was divorced from his first wife. None of us knew the truth."

"There were many things I didn't know about him. I'm not sure even he knew what was truth and what wasn't. He was so used to lying." Felicia looked up. "It's in the past, now."

Just then Jennie walked in from the kitchen. "Felicia, I'm glad you decided to come!" Jennie hugged her sister-in-law. "And I'm glad you're keeping an eye on this one." She motioned toward Santina. "Eight months pregnant and she thinks she can still do everything."

"I'm fine," Santina insisted.

"You are stubborn although nowhere near as stubborn as your husband," Jennie told her. "Even when we were children, he was so pigheaded."

Santina laughed. "He prefers to think of himself as strong-willed."

Jennie sat down and put her hand on top of Santina's. "Mario is so worried about you. He said the doctor advised you against having another child; that it was dangerous."

Santina smiled. "Every child is a gift from God. How do you say no to such a gift?"

"Of course. You are right." Jennie patted Santina's hand.

"I'm going to have Horace be the godfather. I know he's only twelve but he is so grown up."

"And so handsome," Jennie added. "Your children are all beautiful."

"Don't let Horace hear you calling him beautiful." Growing serious, Santina took her sister-in-law's hand in hers. "Jennie, I'd like you to be the godmother."

Jennie beamed with delight and hugged Santina. "What an

honor!"

~ ~ ~

Late Sunday afternoon, three weeks later, the family sat in the living room listening to The Shadow. The familiar organ music filled the living room followed by the narrator saying, "Who knows what evil lurks in the hearts of men? The Shadow knows!" The laugh that followed scared Frances a little and she retreated from where her brothers sat on the floor in front of the radio to sit next to Santina on the couch.

Once the story started, Santina whispered to Frances, "It's okay. Go sit with your brothers." Frances hopped off the couch and pushed her way in between the boys. Santina motioned to Mario to follow her as she rose from the couch and made her way into the kitchen.

"What's wrong?"

"Nothing is wrong but you need to go and get the midwife."

Mario smiled. "It's time?" Santina nodded and then put a hand on the wall and grimaced. "Come. Let me get you into the bedroom and then I'll go." The couple slowly made their way into the bedroom. After Mario helped his wife into the bed, he jogged back into the living room. "I'll be right back," he called out to the kids as he hurried out the door.

He arrived back home with the midwife as The Shadow was ending. Horace turned off the radio as Frances and Alfred got up from the floor. "What's going on?" he asked his father.

"The baby is coming," Mario told them as he walked past, leading the midwife through the living room and kitchen, into the bedroom.

Frances looked at her brothers. "I want a sister," she told them. "How long will it be before we can see the baby?"

Horace shrugged.

"Why do you want a sister?" Alfred asked. "I think another brother would be swell! Sisters aren't nearly as much fun."

Frances threw her doll at her brother in response. "Well, brothers…" Screams coming from the back of the house startled her into silence. A solemn mood dropped across the room.

The midwife came out of the bedroom, closing the door behind her and spoke quietly to Mario who was standing in the hallway just outside the door. "This is going to be a difficult birth. The baby is breech so there could be complications. You don't want the children here in the house. Is there somewhere you can send them?"

"Yes, they can go to my sister. She's just a short distance away."

"I think you should go with them. There is nothing you can do here."

Mario shook his head. "No. I will stay here." He put his hand into his pocket and pulled out a Rosary. "You are wrong. There is something I can do. I will pray."

"Maybe you're right. It would be best for you to be here so I can send you to fetch a doctor if there are complications." She stared at the Rosary swinging in Mario's hand. "Pray that I don't need to send you for a priest." The midwife returned to the bedroom and closed the door. Mario walked into the living room. Horace was looking down at the floor, pacing back and forth. Alfred sat in a chair near the window staring outside, chewing on his nails. Frances stood near Alfred, also staring out the window while she clutched her doll in her arms. Three heads snapped to look in Mario's direction when they heard his footsteps. Frances ran to her father. "Is Mama okay?"

"Yes, she will be fine. Mama and the baby will be fine but I want you to go to Aunt Marietta and Uncle Victor's house." Turning to his oldest son, Mario said, "Horace, take Alfred and Frances and stay there until I come to get you."

Horace opened his mouth to argue but seeing the look on his father's face, he pressed his lips together and nodded.

As the three siblings left the house, they could hear their mother's screams. Horace tried to reassure them, "Don't worry. That always happens when a woman is having a baby."

"Well I'm not going to have any babies!" Frances vowed as they hurried to their aunt's house two blocks away, anxious to get out of earshot of the house.

The siblings joined their cousins and sat around the radio, listening to The Magic Key of RCA. That evening's episode featured comedy and the children were able to briefly put aside their worry. Several hours later, one of their neighbors, Mrs. Sabello, knocked on the door to bring them back home.

"Is Mama okay?" Frances looked up at Mrs. Sabello as they made their way home in the dark.

"Yes, she is good and so is the baby," Mrs. Sabello assured them.

The children cautiously entered the house, the memory of Santina's screams still haunting them. Mario led them into the bedroom to see their mother and the new baby. Frances ran to the bed and climbed up to hug Santina who was propped up on pillows, cradling the baby. "Is it a girl?"

Santina smiled. "Yes, this is your new sister, Maria."

The boys stood on the side of the bed next to their mother and looked down at the little girl. Mario stood behind the boys, a hand on each of their shoulders. "Let's let Mama and Maria rest." He ushered them out of the room. Frances was the last to leave, her tiny arms wrapping around her mother in a long, loving hug before she climbed out of the bed.

They stood in the hallway. "It's late. Why don't you all go and get ready for bed?" They knew in spite of their father phrasing it as a request, it was a gentle command. The children shuffled off to their rooms, the soft click of their doors closing sounding like the end of a chapter.

Mario returned to his bedroom where Santina lay; her body still, her eyes reflecting a world of emotions as she held Maria close. He looked down at his daughter, her tiny chest rising and falling with each breath, a miracle wrapped in the soft blanket. The relief he felt was marred by a shadow of concern, his love for his wife and child deepening the lines on his forehead. He squeezed Santina's hand gently, trying to convey strength through his touch.

Santina's gaze drifted from Maria to the night table, where the old family Bible rested. Its leather was worn, the pages yellowed with time, a testament to the many years it had witnessed. Her mother had brought it over from Italy, a piece of her heritage, a silent guardian of their family's history. Her fingers brushed the edge of the book in a reverent gesture. It was as if she was silently acknowledging the journey she had just taken, and perhaps, the one she might not see through to the end.

CHAPTER EIGHTEEN

Family

May 1940

"Frances, hold the iron like this." Santina demonstrated, slowly moving the hot iron back and forth, as she pressed it against the trouser leg. Then she released the handle. "Let's see you try." Frances took the wooden handle and imitated the motions her mother just made. "Good!" For a few moments, Santina watched as Frances worked her way down toward the hem of the pants. "Okay, now see how the wrinkles aren't being ironed out anymore? That means the iron has cooled. Put it on the stove to heat it some more."

Frances went over to the stove and put the iron down. Long strands of dark curls clung to Frances's face, plastered there by sweat. She tried to focus on her mother's instructions but her eyes were drawn to the front of the house, the front door, outside, freedom. She didn't see the need to learn how to iron on a beautiful Saturday while her brothers were off on more exciting adventures.

Alfred was playing stickball with his friends and Horace was in the basement with Mario working on some new invention. Even little Maria was free to find her own adventure and here she was, stuck with a stupid iron.

The front door slammed and Alfred ran through the living room into the kitchen. He took a glass from the cupboard and filled it with water, which he then drained in a couple of gulps. He started to walk back toward the living room when he stopped and turned to watch his mother and sister. "What are you doing?"

Frances ignored her brother, took the iron off the stove, and went back to finish pressing the pants. "I'm showing your sister how to iron," Santina told her son.

A voice called from the living room. "Help, Mama! I'm stuck!"

Santina laughed. "What mischief have you gotten yourself into, Maria?" She left the kitchen and went to rescue the three-year-old who had climbed up onto a chair and was afraid to climb back down.

"I'm going back outside to play stickball. Too bad you have to work," Alfred teased Frances. A frown formed on his sister's face but she remained silent, continuing to work on the trousers. "It sure is a shame you can't play," he taunted.

"You better be quiet or I'm going to throw this iron at you," Frances warned her brother.

Alfred didn't heed the warning. "Ha ha ha! You're stuck inside ironing while we're playing."

Glaring at her brother, Frances said, "I mean it."

"Ha ha ha! You..." The iron hit Alfred in the chest, cutting him off mid sentence. He howled in pain.

Santina ran back into the kitchen where Alfred was holding his chest, tears in his eyes, and the iron on the floor at his feet. "Frances!" The nine-year-old looked down at the floor, unable to bear her mother's disappointment. Tears welled in her eyes, not from hurting her brother, but from the pain of knowing she had caused her mother sorrow.

"Lift your shirt," Santina told Alfred. He lifted it and she examined his chest. "You'll have a nice bruise there but it's good the iron was cool. There's no burn. Does it hurt to breathe?"

"No," Alfred replied.

"Good. I don't think anything is broken. Are you in a lot of pain?"

"It feels a little better. I want to go back outside."

"Frances, do you have something to say to your brother?"

"I'm sorry I threw the iron at you," she said in a low voice, still looking at the floor.

"I forgive you," Alfred replied. Then he turned to his mother.

"Can I go back outside?" Santina nodded and he ran off to rejoin his friends.

For a few moments, there was no movement in the kitchen. Then Santina walked over to Frances and put her hand under the girl's chin, gently raising her head so the two were looking into each other's eyes. "You can't hurt your brother. It was wrong to throw the iron at him."

"He was teasing me and he wouldn't stop. I warned him."

"Frances, I don't want you throwing things."

"Yes, Mama. I'm sorry."

"Finish ironing those pants and then you can go and play." Suddenly Frances was an expert at ironing and finished the pants quickly. She held them up for her mother to inspect. "Good job," Santina said. "Off you go while I get Maria to take a nap." Frances raced through the living room and outside, slamming the front door behind her.

Santina walked into the living room where Maria was playing with a doll. "Maria, your doll looks very tired. I think she needs a nap. Why don't you bring her into my bed? We will both lie down with her so she won't feel lonely."

"Okay, Mama!" Maria skipped into the bedroom and placed her doll in the middle of her parents' bed. She climbed up alongside the doll. "I will stay right here next to her."

"That's a good idea. I will stay on the other side. Why don't we both close our eyes so Dolly will see us and close her eyes, too," Santina suggested. Obediently the little girl closed her eyes. Within a few minutes, both mother and daughter were asleep. Ninety minutes later, the sound of giggles woke Santina up. She opened her eyes and saw Maria sitting on the bed, cradling her doll.

"Mama, you fell asleep. You're too big for naps!"

Santina smiled. "Sometimes even grownups take naps. Now why don't you come and help me get dinner ready?" Leading the child from the bedroom into the kitchen, Santina had Maria sit at the table. Santina, still weary despite her brief rest, sat down next to her daughter with a head of spinach and a bowl of water. "Tear off each leaf, rinse it in the water and place it on this towel," she instructed.

"Like this?" Maria ripped off a spinach leaf and vigorously

splashed it in the bowl of water, sending droplets across the table.

"Maybe a little more gently, like this." Maria watched her mother and then imitated her. "Good," Santina told her and then went to the icebox to remove a chicken. The door in the kitchen that led to the basement burst open. Horace and Mario came into the kitchen. Mario walked over to the counter where Santina stood and kissed her.

"Cara mia! My dear, go sit with Maria. Horace and I will prepare the chicken."

"I'm fine. I slept a little."

"No, I insist," Mario told her as he took her by the hand and led her to the kitchen table.

While Mario had his back turned to Horace, Horace looked at his mother with a grin and winked. Santina shook her head at her son and tried to look stern but a smile escaped her. Turning to Mario, Horace stated, "Cooking is woman's work!"

Indignant, Mario turned to look at his son. "What? My nonno was a chef! He was the greatest chef in all of Mazara del Vallo! No woman could cook as well as him except your mama."

Horace raised an eyebrow. "Was your grandfather really a chef or is this just one of your stories?"

Mario frowned. "Of course he was a chef!"

Suddenly Santina burst out laughing and Horace joined her. Mario looked from one to the other, realized his son was teasing him, and started laughing himself. Maria started laughing as well without having any idea what the laughter was about. That made the other three laugh even harder.

The four of them continued preparations for dinner while Mario told Santina about the newest invention he was working on with Horace. As it drew close to dinnertime, Mario stepped out onto the front porch. Putting his thumb and index finger between his lips, he whistled loudly. Suddenly, from opposite ends of the block, Alfred and Frances appeared, both running toward the house. As they entered the gate and bounded up the front steps to the porch, Mario said, "Both of you go wash up. Frances, set the table for your mother."

After dinner, the family sat in the living room. Mario sat on the couch with Santina beside him. Her head leaned back against the back of the couch and her eyes were closed. Horace, Alfred, and Frances sat on the floor in front of the radio. Maria stood by the couch, watching her mother. From the radio, came the familiar words, "From Hollywood, California, the Lux Radio Theatre presents Midnight!"

Maria climbed on the couch and touched her mother's cheek. "Mama, the show is starting. Are you sleeping?"

Santina opened her eyes and smiled. "No, sweetheart. I'm just resting my eyes."

"Shhhh!" Horace told the little girl. "We're trying to listen. Come sit here with me." Maria slid off the couch and ran over to where her siblings sat, plopping on the floor between Horace and Frances.

Silently the family listened to the show when suddenly Maria burst into tears. Frances looked down at her. "What's wrong?"

Immediately Maria stopped crying and asked, "Isn't this the sad part?"

Her brothers laughed. "They weren't saying anything sad," Alfred said. "You're just too little to understand."

Pouting, Maria said, "No, I'm not!"

Frances looked from Alfred to Maria, her brows furrowed. "How did you start crying and then just stop?" Maria lifted her hands and shrugged. Frances turned around to look at her parents. Santina's head rested on Mario's shoulder. Santina's eyes were closed again and Mario was looking down at Santina's hand which he held in his own. Turning back to her sister, Frances said softly, "Maria, cry." Immediately Maria started crying, tears rolling down her cheeks. "Okay, stop crying." The tears dried up and Maria smiled.

"That's a pretty neat trick!" Alfred said.

"Shhhh," Horace said. "Can't you be quiet for a few more minutes?"

The children listened to the rest of the show in silence. Frances started thinking about how her sister's newly discovered skill could prove useful. A mischievous smile spread across her face as she realized the possibilities. If she was in trouble, her sister could come to her rescue by crying on demand.

Mario looked at Santina, then whispered in Italian, "Come ti senti?," his eyes filled with concern.

She paused before answering quietly, "Non troppo male." Her slight grimace belied the reassurance in her words.

Frances overheard the conversation and memorized their words, her mind racing with curiosity. Her parents only spoke Italian when they didn't want their children to understand what they were saying, and she was determined to uncover their secrets. When her parents left the room, she whispered to Horace, "What does 'Come ti senti' mean?"

"How are you feeling," he answered.

"What about 'Non troppo male'?"

"Not too bad."

Frances filed this information away, her curiosity piqued by the allure of learning their secret language. As she settled back into the rhythm of the radio show, her mind returned to Maria's peculiar talent. A mischievous smile played on her lips once again; if she found herself in trouble, perhaps her sister's tears could serve as her escape. The days passed with this new knowledge at the back of her mind, waiting for the right moment to be put into action.

One afternoon, as the skies outside turned gray and the rain began to pelt the windows, Santina had taken to her bed for a rest. Mario quietly slipped into the bedroom to check on her. The children were in the living room listening to music on the radio. The girls sang along with enthusiasm, while Alfred's attention was divided between the music and the weather outside. "I was supposed to meet the guys to play stickball after dinner," he complained, clearly irritated by the downpour.

"You'd be playing in the mud today," Horace remarked, looking up from the book he was reading.

A song called "I've Got a Lovely Bunch of Coconuts" came on. Little Maria sang enthusiastically, sometimes substituting words when she didn't know the exact lyrics. An idea popped into Frances's head and she ran into the kitchen, coming back with two oranges. Handing them to Maria, she said, "Put these down your blouse while you sing."

Obeying her older sister, Maria slid the oranges into her blouse. Alfred turned from the window to watch and Horace put his book down. With the oranges in place, Maria continued singing, "I've got a lovely bunch of coconuts. There they are all standing in a row. Big ones, small ones, some as big as your head."

Horace, Alfred, and Frances roared with laughter.

Suddenly Mario burst into the room yelling, "What are you doing turning my baby into a putana!" Stomping across the room, he snapped the radio shut.

Frances knew they were all about to be in trouble. She whispered to Maria, "Cry," thinking Maria's crying would give their father pause. How could he continue to yell at his children if his anger made his baby upset? Once Mario saw the baby crying, he would no doubt stop scolding them.

On cue, tears squeezed out Maria's eyes as she cried. Mario turned to look at the little girl. Instead of the tears rescuing them from his wrath, he grew angrier. "You upset the baby! The three of you should be ashamed of yourselves!"

"But I didn't do anything," Alfred protested. "Frances…"

Mario interrupted him. "I don't care who was responsible. You all were laughing and encouraging her. It was a terrible thing to do. I don't ever want to see this behavior in my house again!" As silence descended on the room, the only sounds were the gentle patter of the retreating rain. Mario's words echoed, a stark reminder of the boundaries within their home.

Alfred, picking up the oranges from the floor, tossed one back and forth between his hands, a thoughtful look on his face. He wondered if stickball in the mud would have been the better choice today.

Returning to the bedroom, Mario sat beside Santina, who stirred from her nap. Seeing her husband's troubled face, she reached out to touch his face. "What's wrong?" she asked softly.

Mario shook his head, not trusting words yet. He looked at Santina, her pallor reminding him of his fear for her health. His outburst wasn't just about the children's play; it was the culmination of his anxieties. His heart ached with the thought of losing his precious wife, of their children growing up without her gentle guidance.

He spoke softly, almost to himself, "I want them to stay innocent, to keep them safe from anything that might harm them." He glanced at Santina, who gave him a weak but understanding smile. "And with you... I just want to protect you all."

Santina took his hand. "They'll learn from us, Mario. Even from our mistakes. I'm here. Together we'll face whatever comes."

Mario nodded and held Santina close as the gentle patter of rain outside morphed abruptly into a relentless downpour.

CHAPTER NINETEEN

Loss

August 1942

Santina's kidney disease progressed and she could no longer care for her baby on her own. Instead, her sisters would take turns watching Maria. The older sisters couldn't commit to caring for Maria more than once a week and the younger sisters had their own families to care for, so each weekday Maria stayed with a different aunt. Every morning Alfred would drop her off. Every evening after work, instead of going home, Horace would pick her up.

Just once, Horace thought to himself, it would be nice to go straight home. The sleeves of his white shirt were rolled up and he held his suit jacket flung over his right shoulder but felt just as hot as when he was wearing it. He walked up the three steps and pressed the doorbell. When there was no immediate response to the doorbell, he held his finger on the button. The door swung open. "Give me a chance to walk to the door," Connie scolded. Behind her, Maria came running and wrapped her arms around her brother's legs. The smell of fish cooking floated out the door and Horace felt his stomach rumble.

"Sorry, Aunt Connie. It's been a long day and I just want to get home." Turning to his sister, he asked, "Where's your doll?"

Releasing her hold, Maria took a step back and turned to look at her aunt. "You left it in the living room," Connie told her. The little girl ran into the house and returned, holding her doll. They said goodbye to their aunt and headed home with five-year-old Maria clasping her older brother's hand.

"I don't like staying at Aunt Connie's house. There's no one to play with." Maria pouted. "Why can't I stay home with Mama?"

"You know why," came the reply.

"Because Mama needs to rest a lot?"

"Yes," Horace agreed. "It will be better next month. You'll start school and make lots of friends."

"I wish Aunt Stella were still here. Frances said she was so much fun. Who will I be staying with tomorrow? Aunt Mary or Aunt Katie?"

Horace agreed with the observation about Aunt Stella. They all missed their aunt and wished she were still alive, but he didn't address the comment. "You won't be staying with anyone. Tomorrow's Saturday. Everyone will be home."

"Hooray!" The little girl began to skip.

~ ~ ~

October 1942

"You need to prepare," the doctor told Mario.

"Prepare for what?"

"Santina's kidneys are failing," he replied. "I don't think there is much time."

Mario suddenly felt like he was suffocating. His heart started racing and for a moment, the idea occurred to him that maybe he was having a heart attack and would die before Santina. "That would be preferable to living without her!" he thought to himself. Then he immediately felt a rush of guilt and shame at the thought. How could he be so selfish and deprive his children of both a mother and a father?

Every moment of that afternoon was etched into Mario's mind: the crisp air, smelling like rain was coming despite the deep blue, cloudless sky; the loud chirping of a flock of black starlings that descended onto the grass in front of the house, and the words of the doctor.

It was ten p.m. and Santina was fast asleep beside him. Mario tossed and turned, unable to fall asleep in spite of his exhaustion. The doctor's words kept replaying in his head over and over again like a skipping record. "There's not much time. There's not much time." It wasn't fair! Santina was twelve years younger than him. She was not supposed to die first.

Half an hour later, feeling as though he'd go mad if he stayed in bed any longer, he quietly got up, grabbed his shirt and pants, and left the room. Slipping into the bathroom, he changed out of his pajamas and into his clothes. Leaving his pajamas on the bathroom floor, he stepped into the hallway. He tiptoed past the girls' bedroom and paused. Opening the door, he saw they were sleeping. He did the same as he passed the boys' bedroom.

Mario let himself out of the house and wandered down to 18th Avenue where he found himself standing in front of a bar. He decided to go in and sat down on a stool near the end of the bar in a dark, empty corner. The bartender looked at him, eyebrows raised, waiting for Mario to say what he wanted to order. It was very rare for Mario to be in a bar and he was never there alone. He paused to think before muttering, "Whiskey, a double." The bartender placed a glass of whiskey in front of him. He immediately drank the contents, coughing as he set the glass down.

"Another?" the bartender asked.

Mario nodded and another glass appeared in front of him. He drank the second more slowly. As he drank, he started feeling the effects of the first serving. His muscles felt a bit rubbery. His head felt slightly dizzy. The tension dissipated. By the time he finished the second drink, the room seemed to move. He pulled some bills from his pocket and left them on the bar.

Carefully he slid down from the stool. His legs were wobbly and his head started to spin. Struggling to retain his balance, he made his way back home, occasionally stumbling and finding he needed to lean against the nearest wall. Carefully he made his way up the front steps to his house, leaning his head against the front door until a wave of nausea passed. That was the last thing he remembered before waking up in the morning beside his wife.

~ ~ ~

November 1942

Mary closed the door behind her as she entered her sister's house. It was the day after Thanksgiving. Mario sat on the couch, his head resting in his hands. He didn't move when Mary came in. He seemed oblivious to anything that was going on around him. "Nick is outside with the car," Mary told him. He sat motionless, staring at the floor. His glasses were thrown onto the coffee table in front of him as if to further aid in blurring reality. Tears streamed down his face but he didn't bother to wipe them away. When Mary put her hand on his shoulder, he continued to remain frozen, his face twisted in grief.

Looking into the kitchen, Mary saw the four children sitting at the table. Horace frowned. Alfred seemed to be fighting back tears. Frances and Maria both were crying. She felt anger rise up in her at the sight of her nieces and nephews. Why was their family going through this nightmare again? Four years ago she saw Stella's children go through this horror when Stella died from complications due to childbirth. Tina was nearly the same age as Frances at the time and Joe had been the same age as Alfred.

Mary shook her head, trying to expel the negative thoughts from her mind and continued to the bedroom where her sister was in bed. She sat down on the bed next to her sister and took her hand. Taking a deep breath, Mary forced herself to sound matter-of-fact, as if she were talking about the weather. "Mario has to get you to the hospital."

Santina nodded. "Send the children in. First the boys, then the girls."

Mary left the room and Santina's sons reluctantly went into the bedroom. Horace, who was seventeen, suspected why they were being summoned but tried to pretend that he was mistaken. Maybe there was some sort of miracle and his mom was going to say she was better. He knew it was absurd but it was better to think the impossible than the unbearable.

Alfred, fifteen, looked down at the floor as he walked, afraid that if he looked at his mother, he'd start crying. He wished he could be stronger, like his brother. If he was just a little older, maybe he could be brave like Horace.

"Uncle Nick is waiting for me and Papa outside," Santina said. "We need to go to the hospital."

Horace nodded. Alfred bit the inside of his cheek to keep from crying.

Her voice breaking, Santina told them, "Look after each other and take care of your sisters." She paused, unable to go on for a minute, then added, "And Papa. Take care of him, too."

Both boys nodded. Tears welled up in Alfred's eyes regardless of how hard he bit down. Santina opened her arms and they both went to the bed, one on each side, to hug her and be hugged by her. Alfred couldn't hold the tears back and started sobbing while Santina held both boys close. Horace was determined not to cry and felt his head start aching with the effort to keep his emotions inside. After a while, the boys stood up. Each felt their mother's weak squeeze as she held their hands. A thousand thoughts went through Santina's head. There were so many things she wanted to tell them but she didn't have the energy to verbalize her thoughts.

"Should we send the girls in?" Horace asked once he composed himself.

"Yes."

He bent down to kiss his mother and then left, Alfred did the same and followed, closing the bedroom door behind him. Whispering came from the hallway. Then the door slowly opened and Frances and Maria tiptoed into the room.

Santina smiled. "You don't have to worry about disturbing me." Both girls ran to the bed and Maria climbed up to sit next to her mother. Frances walked around to the other side of the bed. Santina patted the empty space beside her and Frances gingerly sat down, trying to make the bed move as little as possible.

"Papa is going to take me to the hospital." The girls remained silent. Eleven-year-old Frances looked across at Maria and wished she could be as innocent as her five-year-old sister. Maria didn't know that people only went to the hospital to die. Tears began rolling down Frances's face. Santina put an arm around each girl. Looking into her older daughter's eyes, she took a deep breath. "Frances, take care of my baby."

The sorrow Frances felt was briefly replaced by anger. She buried her face on her mother's chest so Santina wouldn't see her scowl. "Who's going to take care of me?" she thought. Santina's arm tightened around her as her tears soaked her mother's house dress. Squeezing her eyes shut, Frances could hear Maria crying and she felt her anger dissipate. At least she understood the gravity of the situation. Poor little Maria didn't realize she was saying goodbye to her mother and was only crying because she saw her older sister in tears.

The girls stayed in their mother's embrace until Frances raised her head, worrying that perhaps her mother had died already. Santina felt the movement and opened her eyes, smiling through her own tears. "I'm sorry," she whispered to her daughters. Santina attempted to hug each girl tightly but had no strength left. Her thoughts drifted back to the days of her youth. The fever had come and gone, but it had whispered promises of future weakness. She'd always known, deep down, that the illness had never truly left her, like a shadow waiting for the right moment to show its true form. Now, as her body betrayed her, she felt the echo of that childhood ailment, the rheumatic touch that had sneaked into her heart and kidneys, waiting for life to push it forward.

She inhaled, summoning enough strength to speak. "I love you both so much," she managed in a normal tone. Then, dropping in volume, she said, "Go to your brothers."

The girls hugged and kissed their mother. Then Frances took Maria by the hand and led her out of the bedroom, returning to the kitchen where they joined their brothers.

Sixteen days later, Mario sat in a chair by Santina's side, holding her left hand in both of his. Tears streamed down his face. Santina's eyes were closed. The hospital bed seemed to swallow her up, enveloping her in white. Her face was almost as white as the pillows beneath her head. He looked out the window at the sky, just beginning to darken. The smell of disinfectant burned his nose as he inhaled but he welcomed the physical sensation of discomfort. It took his mind briefly off the mental anguish he suffered as he sat vigil by his wife's side.

Mario felt Santina's hand tighten around his. "It will be alright," she whispered.

"No," he pleaded. "You cannot leave me. I can't do this alone."

For a while there was no reply. Then came a whispered

response. "You can. You need to be strong and you need to trust in God." Santina paused, gathering her breath and strength to continue speaking. "Fear not. Trust." She was silent. Then her face lit up and the illness seemed to leave her. She opened her eyes and looked into Mario's, seeming to look through them, deep within his soul. "I love you. I will always be with you, interceding for you." For the last time, she closed her eyes.

Mario sat there, still grasping Santina's hand, willing life back into her. The room was silent except for his sobs as his body shook with each breath, his mind replaying scenes from moments they had shared, desperate for one more.

The night after Santina passed was spent in quiet, with the children asleep in their rooms, their father sitting in the dark, staring at nothing, Santina's last words echoing in his mind. By morning, life had moved on, but for the family, time had stopped. The funeral arrangements were made in a blur of activity and sorrow. Santina's children sat outside on the front porch in spite of the cold. Aunts and uncles came to the house, hugging them, attempting to comfort their nieces and nephews, and trying to get them inside. All the spoken words seemed to scatter into the wind. "Your mama is in heaven now. I'm so sorry. At least she's at peace. Come inside, it's freezing out here. Have something to eat." All those phrases bounced off the four siblings like gibberish, neither pulling them out of their inconsolable sorrow nor convincing them to come in out of the cold.

As it neared time for the Mass, their mother's youngest sister stomped out of the house and onto the porch. Her heart ached watching the children but she decided it was best to deal sternly with them. "We have to leave for the Church soon. Come inside to say goodbye," Mary ordered them.

The four children, bound by their shared loss, moved as one toward their mother's final resting place. Yet, each step was laden with different shades of grief. Horace, murmuring to his siblings, "Let's get this over with," led the way with a determination that belied his inner turmoil. His stomach churned, each step feeling like an eternity. Frances and Alfred, their faces streaked with tears, followed, their sobs echoing softly in the room.

Maria remained where she was, her small figure frozen, her

eyes, wide and unblinking, fixed on the casket. She understood that her mother was gone, yet the finality of it seemed unthinkable to her young mind. Suddenly Maria felt someone push her from behind. "Go kiss your mama goodbye!" The girl let out a scream, spotted Mario across the room, and ran into her father's arms. He held the little girl while she sobbed until she calmed down. Holding tightly to his baby, Mario silently prayed. "Santina, I know you are in heaven now, one of the saints. Please watch over all of us. Help us. Help me," he pleaded.

At the sound of Church bells, the adults gathered up their coats and prepared to leave for Mass. The children left the house. As they stepped into the brisk morning air, Frances clutched Alfred's hand, their fingers interlocking in silent solidarity. Their father directed them to a limo waiting in front of the house, trying to get them seated before the men carried the coffin out of the house and loaded it into the hearse. A lone sparrow perched in a leafless branch sang from a nearby tree, its melody both a lament and a reminder that life, in all its complexities, continued around them.

CHAPTER TWENTY

Aftermath

January 1943

The two girls hid behind some bookshelves in the library, eating the lunch their father had sent them to school with. Whenever they heard footsteps, Frances would take Maria by the hand and lead her around to hide behind a different stack of books so they wouldn't be seen by anyone. Last week they spent their days in the park but it was raining today. "I don't like it here," Maria whispered loudly.

Panic swept through Frances as she shook her head and put her finger to her lips. Her head snapped from side to side as she assessed the room, looking to see if anyone heard her sister. Everything seemed quiet and some of the tension left her.

"I wish we could go outside," Maria whispered again but in quieter tones.

Frances bent to whisper in her sister's ear. "It's raining out. Eat your lunch. When the rain stops, we can go outside." Nodding, Maria took another bite of her sandwich. Realizing the need to keep her sister occupied, Frances reached up and removed a couple of books from the bookshelf. She leafed through them until she found one with a lot of pictures. Handing it to Maria, she whispered, "Look at this book while we wait for the rain to stop." The little girl turned the pages while she finished her sandwich. Another book sat on Frances's lap and she looked through it, trying to keep her mind off her concern about getting caught.

Engrossed in the books, the girls were suddenly jolted back to reality. "What are you doing here? Why aren't you in school?" A stern looking woman towered over them. Frances quickly calculated that they wouldn't be able to slip past the woman because she was large and blocked the entire aisle. Peering at them over her glasses, the woman seemed to sense the older girl was considering bolting and she grabbed Frances by the arm. Frances tried to shake loose but the woman was too strong.

"Come with me!" Resigned to the fact that there was no escape this time, Frances took Maria's hand and the two girls were marched toward an office. As they passed the front desk, the large woman called out to a thin, white haired woman behind the desk, "Margie, call the truant officer!"

Looking at the older woman, Frances thought, "Why couldn't this Margie woman be the one to find us? We could have easily run past her. And she's so old, she wouldn't have caught us." Her shoulders drooped in resignation as they were led away.

"Harriet, shouldn't we try calling their parents first?" Margie called after them.

"No! I've seen these two here before. They were able to slip away last time but I'm not letting them get away again." Harriet directed them into the office and shut the door. Locking the door, she dropped the key into her pocket. She pulled a chair up and sat down outside the door waiting for the truant officer to arrive.

"I hope Charlie gets here soon," Harriet told Margie. "I don't want this responsibility. It's not my job to watch over children." Charlie arrived ten minutes later and Harriet jumped up from her seat to unlock the door. She stepped aside to let the truant officer into the room and then returned to the front desk.

Charlie found the girls sitting on the ground, leaning against a wall. Frances scowled with her arms folded across her chest. Maria's cheeks were tear stained but she was no longer crying. When the truant officer saw the girls he sighed.

"Frances, I explained to you last time that you can't keep skipping school."

"I'm not going to school," Frances told him. "I'm the only one there without a mother," she thought to herself. "How can I go to school with all the others talking about their mothers?"

"It's not fair to keep Maria out of school."

"Well I don't want to be alone," Frances said.

"I want my sister!" Maria moved closer to Frances and wrapped her arms around her older sister.

Charlie sighed again. "Come on, girls. You know I have to bring you back to school." Both girls rose and followed the truant officer out of the library and into his car. They drove to the school in silence.

After entering the school building, they stepped into the principal's office. The secretary looked up. "Hi, Charlie. Miss Gibbins is in a meeting. If you don't mind bringing Maria to her classroom, I'll walk Frances to her." Frances scowled as she was led away while Charlie took Maria by the hand and brought her to the first grade classroom.

~ ~ ~

That evening the four children sat around the kitchen table for dinner with their father. "How was school today?" Mario asked the girls.

Frances shot Maria a warning look before replying. "It was okay."

"We did counting and reading," Maria added.

A knock at the door interrupted their conversation. Mario told Alfred, "Go answer the door. I'll be right there." Turning to Frances, he said, "Please clear off the table."

"Can I help, too?" Maria asked.

"Yes. Do whatever Frances tells you." He left the kitchen and walked into the living room. Charlie, the truant officer, was standing there with another man dressed in a suit. Stepping forward, Charlie shook Mario's hand but did not meet his gaze. "What's wrong?" Mario asked. "Did the girls skip school again? Who is this man with you?"

Taking a step back, still staring at the floor, Charlie said, "I'm so sorry. There was nothing I could do."

The other man moved forward. "I take it you know Charlie Russo very well." Mario stared at the stranger, waiting for him to get to the point. "I am Mr. Russo's superior, Mr. O'Malley. According to Mr. Russo's reports, the girls have skipped school well over a dozen times. And those are only the times they were caught. We have come to take the girls."

Horace and Alfred were standing in the hallway listening and now Horace walked into the room and stood beside his father. "You aren't taking them anywhere," Horace said.

"It's the law. You had multiple warnings about what would happen if they continued to play hooky."

"I walk them to school every morning. I watch them enter the building," Mario said.

"Well they are obviously not remaining in the building. I'm sure Mr. Russo explained what would happen if this behavior continued. The state must intervene." Mr. O'Malley's steel blue eyes gave no hint of the kindness exhibited by Charlie.

"Give us time to make some other arrangements," Mario pleaded.

"You've had enough time."

Horace was about to say something but Mario held his hand up to his son and shook his head, then said, "Give us until the end of the month. Just ten days."

"Ten days won't..." Mr. O'Malley started saying when Charlie cut him off.

"A few more days won't make a difference to the city," Charlie said. "Let him try to make other arrangements."

O'Malley glared at Charlie for several seconds. Then he nodded curtly and said to Mario, "You have one week." He started walking toward the front door, yelling over his shoulder, "If nothing is done by this time next week, make sure you have their suitcases packed. I will bring police officers with me and we will remove them by force if necessary." The front door slammed.

"I'm so sorry," Charlie told them as he hurried after his boss.

Frances came running into the room from the kitchen, Maria following. She flung her arms around her father and Maria did the same. "Papa, don't let them take me away!"

Mario didn't respond. He stood for a few minutes hugging his daughters while his sons watched. Then he released the girls. "I'm going out. I'll be back soon." Grabbing his hat, he went outside, softly closing the door behind him.

He walked two blocks to his sister Marietta's house. Victor was standing outside when he saw Mario approaching, crossing 71st Street. He hurried into the house where Marietta was drying the dinner plates. "Your brother is coming."

His wife glanced at him and then looked back down at the plate in her hand. "Are the children with him?"

"He's alone," Victor said. "You know what he's going to ask. We cannot take in the girls. You wouldn't have any more luck making sure they attend school than Mario. Santina's sisters tried and it was useless." Their conversation was cut short with a knock on the door.

Marietta dried the last dish and put it away while Victor went to answer the door. Walking into the living room, she sat down on the couch next to her brother. Victor sat in a chair across from them. With no preamble, Mario said, "They came to take the girls away."

Marietta gasped and put her hand to her mouth. "Where did they take them?" Victor asked.

"They didn't take them. We have a week to make arrangements."

"Have you spoken to Santina's sisters?" Marietta asked.

"Yes. One of them was willing to take Maria but not Frances." Mario looked up at Marietta and said through clenched teeth, "I will not allow my girls to be separated." He looked down at his hands, clasped in his lap. In a quieter tone, he said, "They all said the same thing. Put them in St. Joseph's."

Marietta put a hand over her brother's hands. "I don't think you have any choice," she said softly. "They will be together and the nuns will take good care of them."

In spite of his efforts to appear in control, Mario started crying. His sister and brother-in-law looked at each other, at the floor, anywhere but at Mario until he was able to calm down. Then, with his voice barely audible, he said, "I will call St. Joseph's in the morning." His sister hugged him and he left, slowly dragging himself back home.

There were tearful goodbyes the morning Mario begrudgingly took the girls to St. Joseph's Orphan Asylum for Girls on Willoughby Street in Brooklyn. The three stood by the gate as they waited for the nuns to come for the girls. Frances and Maria each held a small suitcase, and Maria clutched her doll tightly. "It won't be for long," Mario tried to assure them as they watched the nuns approach. "Be good and obey the nuns. Do not be afraid. God is with you. I will try to find a way to bring you both home."

As the nuns ushered the girls through the gate, Mario turned abruptly to leave so they would not see his tears. His footsteps echoed hollowly on the pavement as he walked away from St. Joseph's, the weight of his decision pressing down on him like the gray sky overhead. He paused at the corner, the familiar streets of Brooklyn now felt foreign without the laughter of his daughters.

The memory of that last family meeting drifted back to him. They had gathered around the kitchen table, the very heart of their home, now a place of hard decisions.

As the family sat at the kitchen table, the air was thick with a palpable sorrow. Mario, with lines of worry etched deeply into his face, spoke softly, "The girls need stability, a place where they can feel safe and cared for."

Horace studied the faces of his aunts and uncles, each reflecting a mix of sympathy and helplessness. "It's not a matter of not wanting to," Mary began, her voice gentle yet strained, "but my household is already stretched thin. Between my own children and the demands of daily life, there's barely room for more."

Mamie, another of Santina's sisters, nodded in agreement, her eyes downcast. "It's the same for me. My health isn't what it used to be. We simply can't manage the extra care Frances and Maria would need."

The room was silent for a moment, each person wrestling with their own limitations. Mario's eyes glistened with unshed tears as he looked at Horace. Horace's gaze swept around the table, glaring at all of these relatives who refused to step in and rescue his sisters. Mario read the anger in his son's eyes and tried to reassure his son, reassure himself. "It's not about abandoning them; it's about giving them a chance to thrive, to have what we might not be able to provide right now."

Mario continued his trek home, brushing away a tear, praying his daughters would forgive him.

~ ~ ~

Frances looked at the sidewalk, her jaw set hard. Her body was rigid, almost as if she was bracing herself against an invisible force. She shifted her weight from one foot to the other. Maria wrapped her free arm around her sister, her little hand grasping Frances's coat. Two of the Sisters of Charity, dressed in black habits with black bonnets, stood with them just inside the gate.

"Good morning! I am Sister Irene and this is Sister Margaret." Sister Irene's voice was almost apologetic, a look of sympathy on her face. "Girls, please come with us."

They heard the metal gate click shut behind them as they followed the nuns toward the imposing four-story brick building. "We're locked in here," Frances thought. "But Papa promised he'd find a way to bring us home. Maybe we won't be here long."

They entered the building and Sister Margaret turned to the girls. "Frances, you will go with Sister Irene. You will be staying in a different dormitory, with the older girls. I will take Maria to her dormitory with the younger children."

Maria's lip began to quiver. It never occurred to her that she would be separated from her sister. She squeezed her doll tightly against her body as she allowed herself to be led away. After they passed through a door and it closed behind them, Sister Margaret stopped and turned to face Maria. "You can't take the doll with you. It's not fair to the other children who don't have a doll. I'm sorry but you must leave it behind."

As her last link to her old life was ripped away from her, Maria started crying. She entered the dormitory where the two rows of beds were blurred by tears. Sister Margaret took Maria to a neatly made bed near the center of the room. The other girls were already getting ready for the day, some brushing their hair, others folding their nightclothes.

Sister Margaret pointed to a small locker at the foot of the bed. "You can keep your personal items here, Maria. Classes will start soon, so make sure you're ready." Her voice was kind but firm, the tone of someone who had guided many children through these initial days of adjustment.

As Maria unpacked her few belongings, she caught sight of a

girl about her age watching her from across the room. The girl gave her a shy smile and then returned to her own morning routine. Maria swiped at the tears still streaming from her eyes and wondered how any of the girls in the orphanage were able to smile.

~ ~ ~

The months passed by and that September, Frances and Maria sat in the living room with their father, aunts, and uncles. Frances kept looking at the clock while Maria chatted away. "We went to the beach in the summer. It was in a place called Wading River. It took so long to get there but it was so much fun. And on Friday, Father Browne came to visit. I like when he comes to the Home. He sings such funny songs, doesn't he, Frances?"

"Yes."

"Some of the nuns are a little grumpy but I love Sister Ursula. She is so nice."

"Sister Ursula is very kind," Frances agreed. "But I think my favorite is Sister Jane."

Maria giggled. "She's funny. Just like Father Browne."

Mario felt a sense of relief listening to the girls talk. "They are safe," he told himself. "Maybe not happy, but safe."

Peter stood up. "It's almost five. We need to leave if we're going to make it back on time." Frances pouted and remained sitting. "Already?" Maria asked.

"I'm afraid so," Mario told them. The girls got up and hugged their father goodbye. They left with their Uncle Peter and Aunt Jennie who were driving them back to the orphanage. Santina's sister, Katie, and brother, Joseph, with his wife Rosie, remained in the living room while Mario stepped out onto the front porch to see his girls off.

"We need to get going," Joe told Mario once the girls were safely off.

"I'm glad you were able to come visit for a while with your goddaughter," Mario told them.

"It was wonderful to see Frances! It is good they are able to come home for the weekends once a month," Rosie said.

They said their goodbyes and the couple departed, leaving

Mario alone with Katie. "I think coming home makes it harder to return," Mario said. "Especially for Frances. Maria seems to be adapting much better."

"She is younger. Maria probably finds the familiar routine comforting. It was difficult for her, being shuffled off to one aunt or the other every day while Santina was so sick. She has some stability now."

"I miss them so much. I hate when they leave. But maybe it is good that they aren't here to see the state Alfred is in. My boy hasn't been the same since he lost his mother. None of us are the same, but he is such a sensitive boy. His mind is so fragile." Looking at Katie, he added, "You know, better than anyone, what we are all going through."

"Yes. Antonio was taken from us much too soon. Just like poor Santina."

"How do you deal with being alone? With your husband gone?"

Katie shrugged. "It's life. We all just do our best."

For a few moments, they sat in silence, sipping wine. A thought started forming in Mario's mind and his eyes opened wide. "What a perfect solution," he thought. "We are both alone. Why should we remain alone? If we get married, then the girls can come home for good. They would have a family again. Everything would be normal." He stared at Katie, wondering what she would think of his idea.

Katie stood and picked up their empty wine glasses. "I'll wash these and then I must go."

"Wait a minute. I wanted to talk to you about something. We're both alone. Why don't we get married? It would be better for us both. We would be company for each other. You could move in here, back into your childhood home. No more rent."

"And the girls could come home," Katie added.

Mario nodded. "Yes, that would be a consideration, as well."

Katie smiled. "Yes, a consideration." She stood back up again and headed to the kitchen with the dirty glasses.

"So what do you think?" Mario called after her.

"Let me think about it."

Later that evening, Katie sat at her kitchen table talking with her daughter. "Uncle Mario asked me to marry him."

Frieda looked at her mother, eyes open wide. "You turned him down, didn't you?"

"I'm thinking about it. I've been so lonely since your father died. Mario is lonely. And he misses his daughters. The poor man looks so miserable and sad. Men aren't good with being alone."

"No," Frieda said.

"It would be a great help, financially," Katie added.

"No!"

Katie looked at her daughter, surprised at her insistence that she should not marry Mario. "Why? It seems it would benefit everyone."

"Mama, you're fifty-one years old. You can't take care of a six-year-old. You can't start being a mother all over again when you're a grandmother. And what about Frances? You know she'll run off again. And then you'd be responsible for her. No, Mama. You can't marry him."

Katie slumped in the chair, her eyes fixed on the floor. "He'll be devastated if I tell him I can't marry him. I feel so bad for him, for the girls."

"Mama, you know I'm right," Frieda persisted. "You are a wonderful, kind woman and I know you want to do the right thing but this is not the right thing. You need to be here for your grandchildren. Not running after a child and a runaway."

Continuing to stare at the floor, Katie nodded. The room was silent. She looked up at Frieda, her daughter's resolve clear in her eyes.

"You're right," Katie said softly, the weight of the decision settling over her. "I'm not ready to start over, not at my age, not after everything. But what will happen to Mario and the girls?"

Frieda reached across the table, taking her mother's hand. "We'll keep visiting them, help where we can. Perhaps one day, when the war ends, things will change. But for now, we must trust that they're where they need to be."

The decision hung in the air, a bittersweet resolution. Katie thought of Mario, his lonely figure on the porch, watching his daughters drive away.

Later that evening, Mario stood alone in his quiet house, the echo of children's laughter now just a memory in these walls. He poured himself a glass of wine and stared out the window at the setting sun. He had hoped for a reunion, a return to normalcy, but in his heart he knew their lives would never be the same.

The girls would remain at St. Joseph's for now, perhaps for years. They were safe there, cared for, even if not in his arms. Mario looked out over the street where his life once played out in the simple joys of family. Now, a darkness had crept in, blanketing their lives.

CHAPTER TWENTY-ONE

Dorothy

August 1943

Horace and his friend, Louie, walked along the wooden boardwalk in Coney Island. Louie noticed two young women in front of them. He elbowed Horace in the ribs. "What's the matter with you? Did the noise from the Thunderbolt scare you?" Horace teased. They were just passing Steeplechase Park as the Thunderbolt rollercoaster rushed by, filling the air with screams.

"Don't you see those swell girls there?" Louie nodded toward the girls.

"I'm not blind," came the response from Horace.

As the girls continued along the boardwalk, the boys followed behind them. To their right was the beach and bodies seemed to fill every spot of sand on that hot August day. Beach umbrellas dotted the landscape and the volume of noise from the beachgoers overshadowed the sound of crashing waves.

The girls turned left, toward another huge rollercoaster, the Cyclone. Turning as well, Horace caught the eye of one of the girls and took the opportunity to talk to her. "Are you going on the Cyclone?"

Just then the rollercoaster rushed by with a gust of wind and a loud rumble, shaking the wooden planks beneath their feet. The girl waited for the cars to roll past before replying. "I don't like heights."

"Me, either. I'm Pat. Well Horace to my family, but everyone else calls me Pat, short for Patrizio." He shrugged. "And this is Louie."

"I'm Dorothy and this is my friend, Trina."

Horace turned to look at the Cyclone. "I heard one time this fat lady went on the rollercoaster. Then she got stuck in the car and they couldn't get her out. They didn't know what to do. The operators didn't want to stop the ride and wait for the fire department to get there to help because they'd lose money from all the people they would need to turn away." He turned to look at the girls, a serious look on his face. "The woman just kept going around on it. After forty-five minutes, the fire department finally arrived. They used a giant crowbar and some engine grease and were able to get her out of the car."

The girls stared at Horace, horrified at the idea of the woman enduring that. "Don't listen to him," Louie told them. "He's always making up stories."

"That's not true," Horace protested. "How about when I went to give blood on Tuesday and the nurse took out this giant needle?"

"Why would she need a bigger than normal needle?" Louie asked.

"Because I have bigger veins than normal. It left quite a big mark." Horace showed them the large black and blue on his arm.

Louie decided to change the subject. "We were just on our way to Nathan's to see if there are any hot dogs left."

"With the rationing, I'm sure they're all out," Trina said. "Look how crowded the beach is."

"You never know," Horace said. "Maybe everyone is thinking the same thing and no one has bothered going over to find out. Do you want to come with us?"

Dorothy smiled up at the handsome young man, then looked to her friend who nodded and the four headed toward Nathan's.

As their evening progressed, filled with laughter and the warmth of budding friendships, the shadow of national duty loomed over them. Before their courtship could fully blossom, Horace found himself called upon to serve his country. Their time together became precious, each moment tinged with the knowledge that it might be their last for a while. The war was calling, and whether by choice or by obligation, Horace's path was set to stray from the simple joys of local gatherings and into the uncertainties of naval service.

~ ~ ~

December 1943

Crumpling a piece of paper, Horace tossed it into a trash can across the room. John watched the wad of paper arc through the air and land in the garbage. He looked at Horace who was frowning. "Bad news from home?" John asked.

"It's just a letter from my father," Horace replied. "Nothing new at home. I'm heading out for a walk." He walked west, toward Narragansett Bay. The sun was sinking into the horizon, turning the sky pink. Stopping near the edge of the bay, he looked across at Conanicut Island. The air was cold but Horace didn't notice.

"I wonder what it would be like," he thought, "To live on an island instead of a city. If where we grew up was different, would our lives be different now? Would Mama still be alive? Would the girls be home and would Alfred be well?" He started looking for flat rocks to skip on the water. "I don't know what Papa expects me to do about Alfred when I'm hundreds of miles away. It's not my fault Alfred won't listen to him." Darkness started creeping in and he turned around to head back to the barracks.

A month later, Horace was called to the lieutenant's office. Puzzled as to why he was summoned but not overly concerned, he knocked on the door and entered when commanded. Lieutenant Anderson was sitting at his desk, hidden behind stacks of papers. Horace saluted the officer, standing at attention. The lieutenant saluted back and then said, "At ease. Take a seat." He pointed to a chair and Horace sat down.

Anderson was frowning at a piece of paper in his hand which he seemed to be reading. He looked up at Horace and then back at the paper. Putting it down, he pushed it across the desk toward Horace. "Your request for a hardship discharge has been granted. You're being sent home. Dismissed."

Horace gave a terse nod and rose from his seat. He saluted and left the room. As he was walking away, he heard his friend Jake call out to him. "Hey, Pat, did you get a promotion?"

"No, they're reserving that for you."

Jake walked over to him. "Seriously, was it good news or bad news?"

"I guess most would consider it good news," Horace said. "Although I'm not sure being sent home to help take care of your brother who had a nervous breakdown is exactly good."

"Things at home got that bad?" Jake's eyes widened slightly.

"My dad's been writing to me every day saying he doesn't know what to do with Alfred. That my brother can't hold a job. He's up all hours of the night either pacing or he doesn't leave his room for days. Between the girls being sent away and all the crazy stuff going on with my brother, Dad's at the end of his rope. He can't cope by himself."

"That's a tough situation."

"I leave Friday," Horace said as the two headed back toward the barracks.

Several days later, Horace stood on the front porch of his house, suitcase in hand. He stared at the closed door, a feeling of dread washing over him as he wondered what he would be facing on the other side of that door. Would his brother be stable or not, would his father assume some of the responsibility or would it all fall to him? Would Dorothy still be waiting for him?

The floorboards of the front porch creaked beneath his feet. As he looked around, the memories of Alfred, his younger brother, and the night that broke him, flooded back. That night the streets of Brooklyn were under the tense hush of wartime curfew. Alfred, always the more sensitive of the brothers, had been restless since their mother became so ill, the silence at home amplifying his inner turmoil. He ventured out, seeking solace in the familiar paths now dimmed by blackout regulations. Alfred was caught breaking curfew, his youthful face illuminated by the moonlight. He spent the night in jail.

The next day, when he was released, Alfred was different. The light in his eyes had dimmed, and he spoke little of what had transpired. His family, wrapped in their own grief, didn't press him for details, assuming the stress of curfew and the war had been too much.

Horace shook his head, dispelling the memory. Steeling himself, he reached for the doorknob, ready to face his father and brother.

~ ~ ~

August 1944

Upon Horace's return, there were several obstacles to overcome: visits with mental health specialists for his brother, finding employment, and reuniting with Dorothy. The biggest challenge he faced was placing his brother in a mental institution. After being forced to place his daughters in an orphanage, his father found it unbearable and it fell on Horace's shoulders to make the decision. Once all the difficulties were overcome, it was time to introduce his girlfriend to the family.

Dorothy followed Horace into his aunt's house and into the dining room. Halfway through their first date, Horace knew this was the girl he wanted to marry and he wanted to introduce her to his family. Mario sat at the table next to his brother-in-law, Nick. Sitting with Mario and Nick were two young men who seemed about the same age as Horace and a younger boy. Mario rose with a warm smile on his face. He took Dorothy's hands in his. "You must be Dorothy. I'm so glad you could join us for dinner. This is Horace's Uncle Nick. He is married to my wife's sister, Mary."

Mario spoke in broken English and Dorothy struggled to understand every word but caught the word 'kitchen'. She could hear female voices talking in the kitchen and assumed that's where the women of the family were. Just then a woman walked out of the kitchen and into the dining room carrying a cutting board piled with freshly sliced Italian bread. Behind her were two girls. Mary nodded to Horace and Dorothy as she put the bread on the table and then wiped her hands on the apron she wore.

"Hello, Horace," Mary greeted her nephew. "Have you introduced your girl to everyone?" Without waiting for a reply, Mary continued. "I am Mary Benvolio, Horace's aunt. This is my husband, Nick Benvolio. Those are his sons, Arthur and Eugene." She indicated the two older boys. "And these are Alfred, Vera, and my youngest daughter, Mariuccia."

"It's a pleasure to meet you, Mrs. Benvolio," Dorothy said. She looked around the room at Horace's cousins. "So nice to meet you all. Horace and I brought a cake for dessert."

"Come. Bring it into the kitchen," Mary told Dorothy. Horace turned to hand Dorothy a package and she followed his aunt and the girls into the kitchen. Mary pointed to the kitchen table, indicating that was where Dorothy should put the cake. A large pot of macaroni was boiling on the stove and the girls were carefully scooping meatballs and sausage out of another pot onto a platter.

"We save our meat rations for Sunday dinner," Mary explained. She handed Dorothy a chunk of Parmesan cheese along with a grater. "Put that on the dining room table." Turning to the younger girls, she said, "That's good. Go with Dorothy and bring the meat into the dining room."

Dorothy and the girls carried out their orders and Mary soon followed them with a huge bowl brimming with macaroni. After everyone was served, Mary announced, "We will say grace." The family all made the sign of the cross as Nick led the traditional grace.

For a few moments there was silence as everyone began eating. Mary was the first to break the silence. "What a shame the girls couldn't be here this week to meet you but they were just home last week. St. Joseph's has strict rules and the girls can't be home every week."

Furrows appeared on Dorothy's brow as her right eyebrow rose slightly. Mary could see the confusion on the young woman's face. "Didn't Horace tell you about his sisters and brother? I guess the two of you haven't been dating long enough for him to explain the family situation."

Horace looked down at the table and Mario cleared his throat. "Alfred had some..." He broke off, struggling to find the right words. "He's ill. He's in Brooklyn Hospital."

Mary looked from her brother-in-law to her nephew and then interjected, hoping to soften the starkness of Mario's words, "He had what the doctors call a nervous breakdown. It's been hard on everyone. But we're hoping he will be back with us soon." She paused and then, deciding the matter was closed, changed the subject. "Have the two of you seen Going My Way yet?"

Dorothy nodded, still taking in the information about Horace's siblings.

Mary continued. "What did you think of the movie?" Dorothy looked over at Horace. "I was asking you, not Horace," Mary told her. "You can answer for yourself."

"I enjoyed it," Dorothy replied. "Bing Crosby was very good and he's a wonderful singer."

The older woman nodded in approval.

Dorothy looked at Horace. He was still staring down at the table, his fork motionless, his knuckles white as he gripped the utensil. His discomfort was palpable, his usual easygoing demeanor replaced by a tense stillness that caused an ache within her. "Is there any word about when Alfred will be released?" she asked gently.

"They were pretty vague when I was there last week. They mentioned something about after they're done with their treatments." He seemed to shudder slightly while saying the last sentence.

"Mary!" Mario said his sister-in-law's name louder than he intended. Then he lowered his voice. "My son's mental state should not be a topic of conversation during dinner, especially when we have company."

"The poor boy." Mary shook her head sadly. Looking across the table at Mario, she said, "I'm just worried about him."

Nick jumped in with a different subject in an attempt to defuse the situation. "Isn't the gravy good? I had quite a large crop of tomatoes this year."

"It's delicious," Dorothy said. She was glad the conversation turned to food. Glancing over at Horace, she could see he was less tense than a few minutes ago. He looked at her and smiled.

"Uncle Nick's biggest issue is the squirrels. He's at war with them over the tomatoes."

"Yes," Nick agreed. "You have to be on guard all the time or those nasty animals will eat your entire crop."

"Maybe after the war, you can get a bazooka," Horace said.

"Then the squirrels would be so scared, they wouldn't even touch a tomato if it rolled under the fence and landed at their feet."

Nick smiled at the thought. "Don't get any ideas!" Mary told him. Mario and Horace laughed and the men proceeded to discuss anti-squirrel battle tactics, each trying to outdo the other with outlandish methods.

~ ~ ~

June 1947

Mario beamed as he looked around the dining room table. The girls were home for the weekend. They all attended Mass together that morning, and now Horace, Dorothy, and Frances were in the kitchen preparing dinner. Alfred seemed to be doing better after his last hospitalization. Ten-year-old Maria sat next to her father, her chair drawn up as close to him as possible.

As they waited for everything to be ready, Maria asked Mario, "Why do you go to Mass every day?"

"What happened this morning?" Mario asked her.

"You were sneezing a lot." Maria looked up at her father and then giggled. "And you said a bunch of bad words."

"Yes! That is why I have to go to Mass every day—because of the bad words," Mario told her. "Every morning I have a fit of sneezing and say bad words so then I must go to Mass to beg forgiveness."

The rest of the family came into the dining room carrying bowls of macaroni and meatballs. "Sister Ursula wants me to stay in St. Joseph's until I graduate high school," Frances said as they sat down for dinner.

"That sounds like a good idea." Mario looked at his daughter, nodding his approval.

"No," Frances replied. "I don't want to stay in St. Joseph's any longer than I have to. I can leave when I'm sixteen. That will be next year. Maria and I will both be able to come home then. I want to get a job. Sofia left as soon as she turned sixteen and found a great job and now she's earning thirty-five dollars a week."

Maria, torn between wanting to be home with her family and

leaving the security of St. Joseph's, decided to change the topic. She turned to her oldest brother. "When are you getting married?"

Horace and Dorothy looked at each other. "Well," Horace said, "We were just talking about that. I think by next year we'll have saved up enough money so we plan on getting married in June 1948."

"Will you live here with us?" Maria asked.

"There's not enough room," Horace replied.

"Of course there is," Mario said.

"How? There are only three bedrooms. You have one, Alfred will be in one, and the girls will be home and be in the third."

"We'll turn the living room into a bedroom. It will be the biggest bedroom in the house! Think of how much you will save if you're not paying rent." Mario leaned back in his chair, satisfied that he made a compelling case for having all of his children living with him. "I need Horace here to help with Alfred," Mario thought to himself, "In case there's another episode. Horace is the only one who can control him."

"Let us think about it," Horace said.

"Of course. You both talk it over. And we will plan a wonderful wedding. We have so much to look forward to."

CHAPTER TWENTY-TWO

Frankie

October 1947

It was a beautiful fall day and Frances walked with her friend, Sadie, along Thirteenth Avenue. The sky was a vibrant blue and the air was crisp. As they approached the butcher shop, they saw three guys loitering in front of the store, all puffing on cigarettes.

"That guy is really keen!" Frances exclaimed.

"Who? Which one?" Sadie peered through her glasses, trying to identify the young men. As they neared, she was able to make out their faces. "I know them. They're friends with my brother. The one holding the paper sack is Tony, the one standing in the street, leaning against the car is Pete, and the one with his foot on the fire hydrant is Frankie."

"Frankie," Frances repeated softly.

Smiling, Sadie put a hand on her friend's arm. "I'll introduce you." They walked up to the group. "Hi!"

"Hi, yourself," the one identified as Tony responded. "Where's Johnny?"

"He's working today."

Tony made a face, threw his cigarette on the ground and crushed it beneath his heel.

Sadie turned to Frankie, "Frankie, this is my friend, Frances."

Frankie's brown eyes lit up as he smiled down at her. Removing his foot from the hydrant without taking his eyes off her, he took a step closer to the girls. "Nice to meet you."

The group of young adults talked for a while and then the girls returned to their original mission of buying meat from the butcher shop. Frankie watched the door of the store. When Sadie and Frances came back out, he walked over to them. "Frances, can I have your number?"

Frances took a pencil out of her purse and searched in vain for a piece of paper. "Tear off a piece of the butcher paper," Sadie suggested.

"Great idea!" Carefully, Frances tore off a small piece of brown paper and wrote her phone number down. She couldn't stop smiling as she handed the scrap to Frankie who carefully folded the paper and put it in his pocket. The girls said their goodbyes and continued walking on 13th Avenue toward 70th Street.

Once they were out of earshot of the boys, Frances said, "Gee, Frankie has such dreamy eyes."

"He does," Sadie agreed. "He's the best of the bunch, the nicest of those three."

"I think he's the cat's meow. I hope he calls soon."

Her wish was granted when Frankie called that very night to ask her out for the following evening. They went to the movies. Frankie walked Frances back to her house from the movies and they stood outside the house on the front porch. He was smiling down at her and took her hand. Her heart started beating a little faster. Hoping he would kiss her goodnight but unwilling to encourage such behavior she said, "My mama is watching from the window."

"I don't think she can see us in the dark but don't worry. I'll be on my best behavior." He leaned in and kissed her, then gently squeezed her hand. "I'll see you tomorrow at Church." Frankie waited until Frances went into the house and closed the door before he walked out the gate and started walking home.

Frances smiled as she pushed the door closed. Turning, she walked into the kitchen to find her father waiting for her and the smile slid from her face. "I'm home on time, aren't I?" she asked.

"Yes, yes." He looked down at his watch and then back at her. "Barely." He didn't rise from his chair and Frances remained standing, looking longingly past her father to the hallway that led to her bedroom. After a few minutes, her father spoke again. "Do you like this boy?"

"Yes."

"Why don't you invite him over for coffee tomorrow afternoon? I would like to meet him." Frances nodded in reply. Mario pushed his chair back and stood. "Good night." He walked out of the kitchen and down the hall to his bedroom, quietly shutting the door.

Frances sighed. "Well at least I have Dorothy," she thought. It won't be just Papa and my brothers questioning him like the Spanish Inquisition."

The following day, Frankie lingered by the corner of 14th Avenue and 70th Street, checking his watch. He wanted to arrive at Frances's home exactly at four o'clock. "If I arrive too early, I'll look too eager and if I arrive late, it's rude and disrespectful," he told himself. "It has to be exactly at four, like we discussed after Mass." Every ten seconds, he peeked at his watch until it was half a minute before four. He walked down to the house, ringing the bell right on time. He could hear running and saw a young girl peeking out a window to the left of the door and then disappear. The door was opened by an older man wearing glasses.

"Hello, I am Frank Antonino," he said to the man, assuming this was the father and held out his hand. "Everyone calls me Frankie."

Mario took the outstretched hand and shook it. "Welcome," Mario told the young man. "I am Mario Patrizio, Frances's father. Come join us in the dining room." Mario walked down the hallway with Frankie following behind him. Once in the dining room, Mario sat at the head of the table and waved his hand toward an empty chair in between two men. "Please have a seat."

Frankie sat down in the seat indicated, nodding at each of them. "These are my sons, Alfred and Horace. And this," he smiled and put his left arm around the young girl Frankie had seen looking out the window, "Is my baby, Maria."

Frances and Dorothy came into the dining room carrying coffee and cookies. Looking over to see her brothers on either side of Frankie leaving no room for herself, Frances glanced at Dorothy and rolled her eyes. Dorothy gave a barely perceptible shrug, hoping Mario didn't notice the exchange. The women joined the others at the table.

Frances began pouring coffee and passing the cups around while Dorothy passed around the cookies. Frankie looked at the empty seat next to Alfred. "Where is Frances's mother?" he wondered.

The conversation bounced between the weather and the upcoming presidential election between Truman and Dewey. Mario let his sons and Frankie do most of the talking while he sat back listening, trying to gain some insight into the type of man Frankie was. When the conversation started to wane, Mario said, "Frances has not had an easy life. I had to be both a mother and a father to my girls."

Frankie's mouth dropped open as he struggled to comprehend the comment. His eyes narrowed and he stared at Frances as Mario continued. "It was not easy for any of us losing my Santina but it was especially hard on the girls." Frances looked across the table with a slight smile that looked more like a grimace and quickly looked away from Frankie.

Dorothy could see Frances was embarrassed by something but didn't understand what had just transpired. She decided to intervene with a diversion. "Why don't we play cards?" she suggested.

"Yes!" Maria said. "Can we Papa? Please?" Mario nodded and Maria jumped up to get a deck of cards.

As Mario began shuffling the cards, he said, "Rummy or poker?"

"Rummy!" Maria said.

Mario dealt out the cards. As they began playing, Mario asked, "Are you looking to have a good time with Frances?"

"Yes," Frankie replied.

Mario threw the cards he held face down onto the table. "No one has a good time with my daughter!"

Frankie's eyes widened and his face flushed as he understood that the question Mario asked him was different from the way he interpreted it. Alfred snickered and Horace's lips quivered as he fought to hold back a laugh. "No, no!" Frankie responded. "I didn't mean it like that. I was just talking about going to the movies or getting a soda at the diner. I would never do anything to disrespect Frances or you." He glanced nervously at Alfred and Horace, who were clearly enjoying his discomfort, then turned back to Mario. "I'm sorry if I gave you the wrong impression. I just want to spend time with her, that's all."

Mario slowly stretched his hands across the table and began to pick up his cards and the family went back to the game.

As daylight started dimming, Frankie said his goodbyes to the family and Frances walked him to the front door. "Why did you tell me your mother was watching us?" Frankie asked Frances.

"I'm sorry." Frances looked down. "I just didn't..." She looked up at him without finishing.

"You don't have to worry," he told her. "I meant what I said to your father."

"You're not mad at me?"

"Well I was," he said. "At first. I felt like an idiot. And it didn't help matters when he asked if I wanted to have a good time with you. But I'm not angry anymore." He bent down to kiss her. "See you tomorrow?"

Frances smiled up at him. "Yes." She stood on the front porch watching him walk down the street, the sound of his feet crunching on the leaves underfoot. When he turned the corner and disappeared from view, she went into the house. As the door closed behind her, Frances leaned against it, a smile playing on her face.

~ ~ ~

Spring 1948

Dorothy and Horace talked over Mario's offer and decided to move into the family home after their wedding. Mario's proposal to convert the living room into a bedroom was met with enthusiasm, and the men of the family dedicated their Saturdays to this project. Working for several hours each Saturday, Horace, Alfred, and Frankie transformed the space and their laughter filled the house as they worked. Mario supervised more than helped with the physical work as his sons, seeing him tire more easily these days, insisted he rest.

Maria, trying to sound like the cool teenagers she watched from afar, piped up, "Daddy-o, the men will take care of this. You need to rest," her voice carrying the playful tone she thought made her sound grown-up.

Mario tried to wave off their concern with a chuckle, "I'm just getting old, that's all," but his eyes betrayed a flicker of worry when he thought no one was looking.

Each evening as dusk neared, the family gathered around the table for dinner. The men engaged in lively discussions about current events and sports, their voices filling the room with energy. Meanwhile, the women talked excitedly about the upcoming wedding, their plans taking shape with each passing week.

Amidst all this, eleven-year-old Maria sat quietly, her eyes shining with happiness. Having spent many years away at St. Joseph's, she found comfort in being home again, surrounded by the people she loved. Though she occasionally offered a suggestion for the wedding plans, she was content to listen, soaking in the warmth of the conversations around her. It was as if her mother, in her wisdom, had orchestrated this meeting of souls, bringing together the people who would soon become her new family.

One afternoon in May, the men sat outside on the porch talking and smoking. The conversion of the living room into a bedroom was finally done and they were glad for the leisure time. The women sat in the dining room playing cards.

"I went with my mother this morning to pick up the wedding dress," Dorothy told Frances.

"I can't wait to see it!" Frances replied.

"I have my dress, too," Maria added.

Dorothy smiled at the young girl. "You will look beautiful." Dorothy turned to Frances. "When are you and Frankie getting married?"

"What makes you think we're getting married?" Frances asked. "One never knows what the future might bring."

Dorothy laughed. "Please! I've seen the way you both look at each other."

Frances smiled. "We decided it would be best to wait until he turns twenty-one. Frankie is worried about being drafted and feels he'll be safe if they don't come for him by then."

Maria clapped. "Another wedding! I can't wait!"

A few weeks later, Horace and Dorothy were married. The day passed in a blur of photographs, food, and laughter. The house was filled with joyful chatter well into the night as a new chapter in their lives began. As the leaves turned and the air grew crisp signaling the approach of winter, the family settled into their new routines. Maria was sure this was the start of a new beginning for her family. A time filled with joy and happiness.

That joy was destroyed the following January when Mario passed away suddenly due to a heart attack. The little family was plunged into turmoil. Horace was thrown into the position as head of the household, having to handle arrangements for his father, comfort his devastated sisters, and tend to his brother's fragile mental health. He was thankful for Frankie's presence as Frances relied on her boyfriend's strength to help her through the ordeal.

Maria was devastated by the loss of her beloved father and was inconsolable. Her thin frame grew thinner still as she ate sparingly, her hunger driven out by sorrow. The adults exchanged glances of concern when nothing they said seemed to help.

One Saturday afternoon, she sat in the kitchen, looking blankly at the empty seat where her father used to sit. She heard a sharp whistle outside that she recognized as Frankie. When she remained there, unmoving, she heard it again. Sighing, she left the table and walked through the house, opening the door and stepping out onto the front porch. Frankie sat there, a small dog in his lap, Frances sitting next to him. For the first time in weeks, Maria smiled.

"His name is Princie," Frankie told her. "He needs a new home because his owner died. Do you think you can care for him?"

Rushing over, Maria threw her arms around the small dog, burying her face in his soft fur. As she knelt there, the dog licked her cheek and for a moment, the world seemed less dark. Holding the dog, she felt a peace wash over her that she hadn't felt in a long time. Frankie and Frances smiled at one another over her head.

~ ~ ~

1951

The years that followed saw the slow healing of their wounds. In preparation for their upcoming wedding, Father Browne prepared Frankie to be confirmed. With finances tight, Frankie's family decided to invest in a new suit for his brother's graduation rather than fund Frankie's Confirmation, which was necessary before the wedding. With Father Browne's assistance, Frankie made his Confirmation. That was followed by his twenty-first birthday, a milestone that brought with it the promise of permanence for him and Frances.

The family spoke about living arrangements and it was decided that Dorothy and Horace would live in the attic apartment after the wedding, and Frankie and Frances would live on the first floor with Alfred and Maria. The middle floor was rented so the family would have an additional source of income. Each evening after work, Horace prepared their house for the wedding.

They married in June, the same day as the anniversary of Mario and Santina's wedding. They had a typical Italian football wedding, a day filled with love and the hope of future happiness. Father Browne officiated at the ceremony and Frances's cousin, Mariuccia, was her maid of honor. The newlyweds moved into the Patrizio home and began their new life together.

Just three months into their married life, an official letter arrived that would upend their world: Frankie was drafted. The news hit Frances like a tornado, ripping apart her world. Overwhelmed with despair, she retreated to their bedroom, where she remained for weeks, too heartbroken to face the world or go to work. The family, still healing from past losses, now faced a new kind of uncertainty, as Frankie prepared for his duty in the military.

CHAPTER TWENTY-THREE

Al

New Utrecht High School, January 1953

There she was, sitting across the library during what was called Study Class. The moment Al saw her, he was mesmerized and knew she was special. She had a beautiful smile, was very thin, and her dark hair and brown eyes sparkled. He just had to find out who she was and get to meet her. He whispered to his friend, Jimmy, "Do you know who that girl is?"

"Yes, she's in one of my classes," Jimmy told him. "Her name is Maria Patrizio. Everyone calls her Marie. She's a sophomore. Her mother and father died and she lives with her sister."

"I don't ever remember seeing her around McKinley," Al said referring to the junior high school he previously attended.

"I think she went to Shallow, the school over on 65th Street."

Al got up and pretended to browse through some books. Slipping a copy of the Bible off a shelf, he worked up the courage to approach her and nonchalantly sat across from her at the table without glancing at her. Marie gave him a quick look and turned her attention back to the book that was open on the table in front of her.

Eventually, he introduced himself and made sure she could see the Bible he was holding. "Hi, I'm Al. I'm studying to be a priest."

Marie seemed very shy and instead of laughing at his made-up opening line, took it rather seriously. She raised an eyebrow slightly, studying Al for a moment. After carefully considering his comment, she smiled. "I'm Marie. I hope your studies are going well."

Her radiant smile reflected a pure, innocent personality, and his heart started racing. He just had to get to know this Marie Patrizio. "Slow down," he told himself. "Don't come on too strong, go very slowly, wait a few days, and then ask her to go out."

Later in the week, the Study Class was not held in the library but in the school auditorium. Al wanted to ask her for a date but there was no opportunity to get near her because of the number of students spread out in such a large room. He decided he would attempt to leave exactly when she did when the period ended, timing his exit to position himself near her. His plan worked flawlessly and he was right next to her as she was exiting the auditorium. His words came out easily, "Marie, would you like to go out with me this coming weekend?"

Her answer was spontaneous, her eyes briefly scanning his frame before she spoke. "I don't go out with boys."

As Al watched her walk away, he felt as though his heart shattered and hundreds of questions went through his head. "What went wrong? Does her sister forbid her to date? Am I ugly, too short, too clumsy? Do I smell? Is my hair combed?" He was stunned and confused but still very much attracted to her. He was not going to give up this easily; there would be other opportunities, and she would say yes.

From that day onward, Marie avoided him like the plague. She would take off from school on the days they were scheduled to have Study Class together and even cut classes to avoid him. He attempted to ask her out again and was again flatly turned down. The girl of his dreams wanted nothing to do with him and he had no idea why.

It was a hot August evening in 1953 and Al had just completed a day's work at the A&P Supermarket. It was 8:00 p.m. and God was about to spring a major surprise, which would rewrite his future. As he walked out the supermarket door, there she was directly in front of him walking past with another girl. Marie Patrizio herself, live and in person. Thump, thump, thump went his heart. Could this really be true?

She greeted him with a friendly hello and then added, "This is my friend, Eleanor." They started walking together along Thirteenth Avenue toward Al's house, which was four blocks away. "We were at the St. Bernadette's bazaar and we're on our way home."

"How was the bazaar? I had to work all day so I'm going there tomorrow." Al tried to keep his voice casual, even as he remembered her earlier rejection.

Marie's gaze softened slightly as she answered, "Hot," She smiled. "But fun."

Eleanor continued the conversation. "We tried the ring toss but didn't do well with that. When you go, make sure you go to Mrs. Fornaio's table. She has the best coconut custard pies."

Al swallowed hard as a memory came back to him. When he was in grammar school, he was playing stickball in back of the schoolyard. One of his friends accidentally threw a ball over the schoolyard fence. Al went with the friend to retrieve the ball, which landed in someone's yard. As they walked up the alleyway, they noticed a pie cooling off on a window ledge. It looked really good so they decided to take it and eat it. It was a golden brown coconut custard pie, cooked to perfection. Although it was quite delicious, the guilt he felt over enjoying someone else's labor still left quite a bitter taste even after all those years.

As they traveled along 13th Avenue, an older woman walked out of the grocery store and stumbled, her groceries spilling all over the sidewalk. Al immediately stopped and gathered up the woman's belongings, racing after a couple of oranges that were rolling away.

Marie watched as Al returned the oranges to the woman and made sure she was okay before walking back toward the girls. Before Al could catch up to them, Eleanor whispered to Marie, "I don't understand why you don't want to go out with him. He's very cute."

"He's not my type," Marie replied softly, glancing over her shoulder to make sure Al wasn't in earshot. "I like guys who are tall and thin."

Eleanor laughed. "He seems very sweet. I think you should give him a chance."

Marie's eyes softened as she looked at him and he sensed there was a shift in the air. Before he knew it, Al found himself standing in front of his house with the girls. Figuring he had nothing to lose, Al asked her for her phone number and to his great surprise, she wrote it down for him. They said goodnight and went their separate ways. Later that week, he called Marie and she agreed to go out on a date with him.

Thursday evening, August 27, 1953, at exactly 7:30 in the evening, Al picked Marie up at her house. They walked from her house to the RKO Dyker Theater to see Mighty Joe Young. They almost immediately started going steady.

Twelve days after their first date, Marie started her junior year of high school. Al should have graduated the prior June but didn't have enough credits due to cutting classes. Still a senior, he would graduate that January.

In the fifties, boys did not look kindly upon peers who 'dated steady.' This is not to say that they were upset in any way; however, if you ventured into the steady girlfriend relationship, you were inviting a heap of verbal abuse upon yourself. Nicky Moose, Johnnie Sap, Neon, Mousy, Eddie the Maniac, and Jerry the Lawyer would eat Fat Al alive if they found out he was going 'steady.' Fortunately, most of the guys went to Fort Hamilton High School, so he was fairly safe.

Al confidently walked down the corridors of New Utrecht High School, hand-in-hand with his dream girl. Suddenly, out of the corner of his eye, he caught sight of a familiar face walking directly toward him. "Oh no!" he thought. "Jerry the Lawyer!" He quickly dropped Marie's hand and sidestepped about two paces to her left before Jerry had a chance to spot him. Then he proceeded to enter into friendly chitchat with The Lawyer, completely ignoring the girl of his dreams as if she didn't exist.

Marie's cheeks flushed a deep red and she bit her lip. As Al continued his discussion with Jerry, her eyes narrowed, and her jaw clenched, her fists balling up at her sides. She turned sharply on her heel, the sound of her shoes clip-clopping down the hallway, and disappeared from sight.

Looking up too late, all Al saw was her back as she turned a corner. He immediately regretted his behavior. Running down the hallway in the hopes of catching up to her, he skidded to a stop where he last saw her. She was gone. Hanging his head, he slowly trudged toward his next class wondering if Marie would break up with him.

After Al's last class, he pushed open the doors and exited the school. As he walked toward 16th Avenue, his friends called after him but he was preoccupied with regret over his earlier actions. As he approached the corner, he saw Marie standing and talking with her friend, Sally. Cautiously he approached the girls. Sally glared at him as he neared.

"Aren't you embarrassed to be seen with me?" Marie asked him.

"I'm sorry," he told her. "I'm not embarrassed by you at all. It's you who should be embarrassed by me. I was stupid. Please forgive me." He stared at the pavement, afraid to meet Marie's gaze.

Marie was silent for a few minutes as she looked at Al. "He does seem truly sorry," she thought to herself. "And it was brave of him to apologize in front of Sally." She looked at Sally, whose expression had softened. "Okay," Marie said.

Al's head snapped up, his blue eyes wide with shock. He expected to be rebuked but instead, he was forgiven. Smiling sheepishly, he took her hand and walked her home.

~ ~ ~

By the fall, Al had become a regular visitor at the house on 70th Street, where he not only courted Marie but also formed a fast friendship with her sister, Frances and her brother-in-law Frankie, recently returned from the army. During this time, Al also bonded with Marie's family: her sister-in-law, Dorothy and brother Horace, who had welcomed their son Richard the previous year, and Alfred. Al's certainty that Marie was the one he wanted to spend his life with grew stronger as he watched her interact with her family and her nephew.

One evening, with Alfred watching from the couch, Al and Marie played with one-year-old Richard, their laughter masking the voices coming from the kitchen. Alfred was sitting closer to the kitchen and could hear the low chatter. Furtively he glanced toward the kitchen and then back toward Marie and Al.

The two couples in the kitchen stood close, their bodies

forming a semi-circle, speaking in low, urgent whispers. Frances pressed her hands against her mouth, her eyes wide and glistening with tears that threatened to spill, her posture stiff with shock and anger. Her whispered voice a higher pitch than normal, "How could she do this to us? We built our lives here..."

Dorothy's arms were folded tightly across her chest. Her face was pale, her lips drawn into a thin, worried line. She kept glancing toward the doorway, her concern for Marie palpable. "We can't let her hear this," she murmured.

Frankie's fists were clenched by his side, his jaw set in anger. His voice, though low, carried the weight of his frustration. "There has to be something we can do about this," he insisted, his eyes darting between his wife and brother-in-law.

Horace had his arm around his wife in a protective embrace, yet his expression was one of fury. He spoke with a controlled anger, "Remember when Papa was working for Mr. Truffat? He borrowed money, I think for one of the patents on another invention. He paid it back, every cent. But after he died, Mr. Truffat's ex-wife claimed the money was never repaid. There's nothing we can do. We have no proof that Papa paid back the debt. It's her word against ours and she has money to afford a lawyer. We don't. We need to vacate the house by February."

Dorothy nodded, her face filled with a mixture of sympathy and frustration. "She's notorious for her lawsuits, preying on those who can't fight back."

"That penny pinching, check bouncing pig and his witch of a wife!" Frances hissed. "I wish Papa never worked for them. I wish we never got talked into working for them. None of this would be happening if we never knew them." She glanced toward the doorway where the sounds floated toward them of Richard and Marie giggling. "We can't let her know. Not until after the holidays."

They all nodded, then the men returned to the living room while Frances and Dorothy put up coffee and set cookies on a plate. Frances looked around the room as she worked, picturing her mother still there, preparing meals, brewing coffee. She felt a burning rage toward the woman who was turning them out from their home, from their parent's house. Biting her lip, she scolded herself. "Stop dwelling on it. We have one last Christmas to spend here. We have to pretend to be happy for Marie and the baby."

As the air grew crisper and festive decorations appeared around town, everyone's spirits were lifted and they were able to forget their troubles. For Al, the season only deepened his feelings, making every moment with her feel like a scene from a holiday movie. Two days prior to Christmas, Al realized it was appropriate to send a Christmas card to your girlfriend. He walked over to Blind Benny's candy store and carefully browsed through the cards. With the prior incident that September still fresh in his mind, he wanted to make sure he did everything right. After much contemplation, he found just the right selection: a card with red candles on the cover that included the word 'Greetings'. On the inside of the card, all it said was 'Season's Greetings'. It was simple and he was certain Marie would be pleased with his selection. He stuck his fingers deep into his pocket, dug down, and found the dime, and filled with the spirit of Christmas, joyfully handed it over to Blind Benny.

The next dilemma was what to write inside the card. "Dear Marie, Hello Marie, Merry Christmas Marie." Which one should he use? Finally he settled on simply writing 'Marie' followed by a colon. Just one detail remained and he would be all finished with this card writing torture. "How do I sign this? Love?" In his whole life, he had never signed 'love' to anything. After much deliberation, he proceeded to write the word 'love,' however, using every bit of what Al thought to be his superior wisdom and intelligence, he wrote the word so tiny it was barely visible. He signed his name "Al" in such large letters that the 'love' word would never be noticed at all. It was a complete masterpiece of a Christmas card that would never, ever be forgotten or cease to be a topic of conversation even decades later.

That last Christmas in their familial home was a tapestry of bittersweet emotions. The air was thick with an unspoken sorrow, each family member carrying the weight of knowing this would be their final holiday in the house where memories were etched into every corner. The thought of having to break Marie's heart with the news of their impending departure loomed like a dark cloud over their festivities. Yet, amidst the shadows of loss, there shimmered rays of joy. The new love blossoming between Al and Marie offered a beacon of hope, and the wonderful news that Frankie and Frances were expecting a child painted smiles on faces heavy with grief, bringing a promise of new beginnings and family growth to counterbalance the end of an era.

CHAPTER TWENTY-FOUR

New Beginnings

Frances and Horace had underestimated Marie's strength and resilience. When they broke the news to her about the house, she was upset but accepted the news.

Frankie and Frances sat at the kitchen table with Marie and Al, overwhelmed with the task of emptying the rooms and finding a place to live. They heard the front door open and Horace and Dorothy joined them, Richard running ahead of them. The newcomers sat down in silence, the air thick with cigarette smoke. Horace studied his sisters. "I spoke to Aunt Connie. She said the three of you can move in with her."

Frances made a face. Frankie put his hand over hers. "I know it's not an ideal situation but it will work out."

Looking down, Frances nodded. "Maybe just until after the baby is born," she agreed. "And Marie won't have to change schools with West Street being so close by."

Marie looked around at the dishes and glassware stacked on the countertop. "What are we going to do with all of these? We can't bring them to Aunt Connie's."

Horace rose and went to a cupboard, removing two bottles of wine. He carried those and several glasses over to the table. "You can't bring this, either. Might as well finish it."

As they started drinking, an idea started forming shape in Horace's mind. "Why don't we just bury the dishes in the backyard. Then we won't have to haul them off anywhere."

His siblings contemplated the idea. The more wine they drank, the better his plan sounded. Horace and Frankie got up, disappearing into the basement and coming back with shovels. The three men marched outside and started digging while the women began carrying out the plates and glasses.

Once the hole was deep enough, they started placing the plates and glassware into the hole. At first they placed them gently into the dirt but eventually, they started throwing plates, the action acting as a release of tension. Now laughing, they all began tossing plates and glassware, the sound of breaking glass filling the air. The last items to go into the ground were the empty bottles of wine and their glasses.

The men covered everything back up and they returned to the kitchen. Horace was staring at the floor as he spoke. "I have something else to tell you. Dorothy and I are moving to Chicago."

"No!" Marie cried out as she reached for Richard and picked him up, hugging him tightly. "You can't take my baby away!" The room fell silent, the weight of their circumstances pressing down on everyone. Al stepped closer, wrapping his arms around both Marie and Richard. "It's going to be okay," he whispered, his voice a promise in the quiet room. "I will be here for you."

The weeks that followed were a blur of adjustments. After several months of cramped living at Aunt Connie's house, the family managed to find a small apartment for Frankie and Frances just before little Joseph was born, offering a slice of normalcy amidst the upheaval. With the new baby, the family's focus shifted to the future, embracing the joy of new life. Al and Marie found their love growing stronger, each moment together a precious escape from the chaos.

As spring blossomed into summer, the heat of Brooklyn seemed to bring with it a new rhythm of life. Al and Marie often found solace in the small park near the apartment, where they would sit and talk about their dreams, and plan for a future that felt increasingly tangible. The loss of the family home lingered like a shadow, but the warmth of the season and the joy of Joseph's first smiles began to heal the wounds.

By the summer of 1954, with the sun setting later and the nights filled with the sounds of the neighborhood, Al and Marie found themselves at a crossroads. Sitting at the kitchen table in the modest apartment, the moonlight casting gentle shadows across their faces, they faced the next big chapter of their lives. Frankie and Frances had put their infant, Joseph to bed and retired early. The apartment was quiet. Al, with his voice steady but with an edge of excitement, broke the silence. "So when are we getting married?"

Marie's gaze dropped to her hands, fingers twisting around each other. "Frankie was drafted right after he married Frances," she said, her voice barely above a whisper. "I've never seen her so... broken. Not even when Papa passed." Her eyes, now glossy with unshed tears, met Al's. "The thought of that happening to us terrifies me."

Al's face softened, his own concerns reflected in the slight furrow of his brow. He reached across the table, his hand covering hers, warm and reassuring. "You're right," he murmured, his voice thoughtful. After a pause, he continued, "If you're okay with waiting, I could enlist now. We could get married after I'm out of the army."

Marie's breath hitched, her eyes wide with a fear she couldn't voice. The room seemed to close in, the walls whispering of the losses she had endured—her parents, their home, her nephew.

"It will be okay. I have a plan. Marie's soft brown eyes met Al's gaze with a hopeful look. Al smiled. "The trouble is everyone wants to do the interesting jobs so they're not placed in infantry but those get filled up really fast and once those options are taken, well—you end up in infantry anyway. What I'm going to do is ask around and see what everyone is putting down. Then I'm going to put in for the least popular jobs."

True to his word, Al put down for the least attractive jobs including pallbearer and water purification. He received his orders to report to Fort Dix in December for basic training and to be trained in water purification. To the annoyance of his mother and aunt, he spent his last day with Marie and her family. Al sat next to Marie on the couch in the small apartment she shared with Frances, Frankie, and Joseph. Five-month-old Joseph sat on Al's lap, laughing as Al made faces. As the day drew to a close, Frances picked up her little boy to put him to bed. Frankie followed her into the bedroom so Al and Marie could say their goodbyes alone.

"I'll write every day," Al promised. "The time will go fast."

"Not fast enough." Marie looked down at the floor. Gently Al brushed back her hair and she looked up to meet his eyes.

"We have our entire lives in front of us. This is just a drop in the ocean."

Marie forced a smile to her face. "You're right."

"I need to get home. There will be hell to pay that I spent all day here."

Making a face, Marie said, "Yes, I know."

"Don't worry. They just need to get to know you better. And Papa already loves you."

Laughing, Marie said, "Yes, but he loves everyone." In a more serious tone she said, "He is such a kind, gentle man."

"He is," Al agreed. "I don't take after him."

Marie laughed again and Al smiled. "I really need to go. I love you." He kissed her and she watched him walk out of the apartment and down the stairs.

~ ~ ~

1955

The days Al was away seemed to drag endlessly. Late one October afternoon, Marie sat at the table, Al's latest letter in front of her, a pen poised in her hand, hovering over a blank page. She looked out the window, at the last of the leaves blowing wildly as they seemed determined to cling to the tree against the autumn wind. The room was quiet, save for the occasional coo from Joseph, just over a year old, playing on the floor.

Sighing softly, her pen finally touched paper. "I miss school," she wrote, her heart heavy with the admission. "I was so close to finishing, but with everything... I had to help out."

Her eyes drifted around the small apartment, shared with Frances, Frankie, and little Joseph. "There's no room for dreams when there are bills to pay," she thought. She remembered the day she decided to leave school, the resentment she felt, not for the lack of a diploma, but for the necessity that forced her hand.

Shaking off thoughts of self-pity, she began writing about the good news, telling Al how Horace and Dorothy had recently moved back to Brooklyn. She was thrilled to have her brother back, to be reunited with her nephew.

Frances walked into the room and looked at the clock. "Frankie will be home from work soon. I need to get dinner started. Would you keep an eye on Joseph?" Marie nodded and continued staring at the stationery in front of her, now half filled with her neat script. Frances opened the ice box and stared inside. There was one egg, a stick of butter, and half a container of milk. For several minutes she continued to stare as if that action would make more food appear inside. Sighing, she closed the door. Walking over to the cupboard, she took the last box of shell macaroni. "We have no meat," she called over to Marie.

"I know. I wasn't able to buy more. I don't get paid until Friday." She folded up the finished letter and put it into an envelope. Then she got up and started setting the table for dinner. While the shells cooked, Marie opened the cupboard looking for tomato sauce. Finding none, she turned to Frances. "What will we put on the macaroni? We can't make gravy."

"I don't know. Use whatever you can find."

The only item in the house containing tomatoes was ketchup. Marie held up the bottle and looked at Frances. "Do you think this will work?"

"Let's try it."

Frankie arrived home and the three sat down for dinner. Marie cautiously speared a shell onto a fork and lifted it to her lips. "Pretend it's gravy," she told herself. She put it in her mouth and grimaced, swallowing quickly and then grabbed a glass of water to wash the taste out of her mouth. She looked at her brother-in-law in amazement as he shoveled the food into his mouth without a word. Marie was never able to eat shell macaroni after that.

~ ~ ~

After two years in the army, Al finally arrived home in November of 1956. Three months later, on February 16, just two days after Valentine's Day, they stood before the altar at St. Rosalia's Church, the same place where Marie's parents had married years before. Marie wore the borrowed wedding dress with grace.

The ceremony was intimate, but filled with the warmth of family and friends. Marie's brother, Horace, walked her down the aisle, his arm a comforting presence in place of their late father. The vows exchanged in that sacred space echoed with the promise of a shared future, the echo of past love stories whispering through the stone walls.

The reception, though modest, was a joyous affair. Laughter mingled with the clinking of glasses, and for a moment, everyone could forget the hardships, basking in the simple happiness of the union.

After the reception, Al and Marie returned to Frankie and Frances's apartment. The room buzzed with the energy of family; Horace and Dorothy's son, Richard, scampered around with his cousin, Joseph. As Marie changed out of her borrowed dress, Al held little Barbara, Frances and Frankie's daughter.

The newlyweds said their farewells and departed for their honeymoon in the Poconos. As the door closed behind them, Frances, overwhelmed by a mix of joy and sorrow, looked at Frankie and suddenly started crying. Frankie struggled to fight back his own tears.

"What's wrong?" Horace asked, his voice filled with concern.

"It feels like we just lost our daughter," Frankie said, his own emotions threatening to spill over.

Horace laughed, but then grew serious. "This was a day filled with joy. They looked so happy." He reached out and took Dorothy's hand.

Dorothy smiled, the memory of her own wedding day vivid in her mind. "The day I married Horace was one of the happiest days of my life."

Smiling through her tears, Frances reached out for Frankie's hand. "Yes," she said. "I felt that way when I married Frankie."

Nodding, Dorothy said, "And now Marie and Al can share in that same experience."

Alfred picked up a bottle of cognac and poured everyone a small glass. They each lifted their glass up. "Salute!" they all exclaimed in unison.

Frances's gaze drifted across the room to where a photograph of her mother, Santina, hung on the wall. The image captured Santina in her youth, perhaps around twenty, mirroring Marie's current age. In the photo, Santina's right hand rested on the back of an ornate wooden chair, her lips forming a subtle smile. Frances felt her mother's presence, as if Santina was there with them, her smile a beacon of hope and love for the future.

Acknowledgments

When I took on this project, I had the support and encouragement of so many people—family and friends alike. If it weren't for them, I don't think I could have crossed the finish line. Listing everyone would fill a book of its own, but I must highlight a few who were instrumental:

My deepest gratitude goes to my family: my husband, Frank; my son, Stephen; my daughter, Theresa; my son-in-law, Brett; and the three greatest joys in my life, my grandsons, William, Matthew, and Joseph.

I want to thank my alpha and beta readers: my sister, Janet; my cousins, Cindy and Rick; Annemarie Berube, and Nancie Laird Young. Their positive feedback and suggestions are what kept me going. Special thanks to my Aunt Dorothy, who filled in some gaps.

Thank you to my brother, Paul, who patiently listened to my vision for the front cover and brought it to life.

I also extend my appreciation to my cousins, Stella and Toni, for their input and clarification on details about their grandmother and great-grandmother, respectively.

I am deeply grateful to everyone who has been part of this journey—those named here and the many others who cheered me on in ways big and small. This book is as much a testament to your support as it is to my efforts. Thank you all for helping me bring this story to life.